Eric Wilder

City of Spirits

Gondwana Press

Edmond, Oklahoma

Other books by Eric Wilder

Ghost of a Chance
Murder Etouffee
Name of the Game
A Gathering of Diamonds
Over the Rainbow
Big Easy
Just East of Eden
Lily's Little Cajun Cookbook
Morning Mist of Blood
Prairie Sunset – of Love and Magic

Gondwana Press LLC
1800 Canyon Park Cir., Ste 401
Edmond, OK 73013
gondwanapress@gmail.com

For information on books by Eric Wilder
www.ericwilder.com
www.gondwanapress.com

Front Cover by Higgins & Ross
Photography/Design

ISBN: 978-0-9791165-5-1

Acknowledgments

I would like to thank James Higgins and Joan Ross for their evocative front cover, and Oklahoma County Deputy Sheriff Gary Kinney for sharing his knowledge of police work.

For Marilyn

City of Spirits

A novel by
Eric Wilder

Chapter One

Thunder rattled the roof on Ron Bernard's house. Awakened with a start, he watched the lightning show with sleepy eyes as rain and gusting wind whistled through an open window, whipping his wife's flowered curtains. When his fading dream had vanished into darkness, he got out of bed and shut the window with a thud.

Grabbing a pack of cigarettes, he started to light one up but thought better of it. Relaxing against the bedpost, he jumped when his wife touched his arm.

"Damn it, Angelica! You scared me half to death," he said.

"It ain't Katrina, just a little storm out over the Gulf. Come back to sleep."

He stroked his young wife's hair, muted brown amid lightning flashing through the window, and then kissed her forehead.

"I'm okay. Go back to sleep. I need some coffee."

"You mean coffee and a smoke?"

"Just coffee," he said.

She didn't see him hide the cigarettes behind his back as he grabbed his robe from the four-poster bed and walked down the hall to the kitchen. Coffee in the pot on the stove was cold. It didn't matter as he filled his mug, lacing it with vodka from a flask he kept in the robe.

The alarm in his head wouldn't stop ringing. When nicotine and coffee laced with vodka failed to calm him, he took one of the pills Doc Brown had given him for the problem. The phone rang, startling him again, and he answered quickly so as not to arouse Angelica. He immediately recognized the throaty voice of U.S. Marshal Terrance Blake.

"What's up?"

"Trouble for me, money for you," Blake said. "We got goods heading your way. Meet us in twenty minutes at the chopper pad."

Blake's voice faded and was gone before Bernard had a chance to respond. It didn't matter. Now there was a job to do, and no need waking Angelica to tell her about it. He'd leave a note beside the bed and call her from the boat in the morning. His deceased wife, married to a sea captain for twenty years, would have understood. His new bride might not.

He grabbed his Navy pea coat before heading out the door, into a driving rain peppering the hood of his old Army truck. His hands were finally steady when he turned the ignition and slammed the clunky gearshift into gear. Reaching the chopper pad, he didn't have long to wait.

Gulf wind continued lashing trees as a moving light appeared through thick cloud cover and strobelike flashes of lightning. Rain was mostly gone when the Government helicopter landed near the dock in a flurry of flying debris.

Hours of darkness remained as five men exited the chopper, one a prisoner dressed in a bright orange jumpsuit. He was handcuffed, with belly chain and leg irons attached, armed guards in camouflage fatigues and bullet-proof vests surrounding him. Blake climbed into the cab of Bernard's truck as guards and prisoner scurried into its canvas-covered truck bed.

"Last time you had this many guards, we were transporting ten prisoners. I thought all your transports were dangerous."

Blake's gap-toothed smile revealed a mouth filled with gold and silver, his own eyes dark as Bernard's.

"Yeah, well you don't drive a railroad spike with a tack hammer."

"He's that dangerous?"

"If you look up the word in the dictionary you'll see his picture beside it."

"What'd he do?"

"Kills people," was Blake's terse answer.

Down a muddy road from the chopper pad, they reached the little town's boat harbor. High seas crashed over the breakwater rocking boats docked at the marina. Bernard's boat, the Clancy Jane, lay moored at the end of the pier. He watched as guards jumped from the back of the truck and escorted the prisoner toward it.

"Take him below," Blake ordered. Turning to Bernard, he said, "Now get us up the river to New Orleans."

The haunting cry of a bayou loon sounded from across the bay as Blake left Bernard standing on the dock. He followed them aboard, going to the driver's cabin where he cranked the boat's massive diesels and started checking gauges.

The storm had moved back into the Gulf, occasional flashes lighting up the southern sky as Bernard piloted the old crew boat through the maze of marshes, swamps, and river passes. The wake of the sleek boat rippled the bank, cluttered with flood debris, turtles, and an occasional gator plunging into brown water.

Bernard loved the Clancy Jane, still the fastest crew boat plying the Gulf of Mexico, and worth every penny he'd saved so long to buy. Only Angelica knew how much.

They reached the Mississippi River before dawn. Near Southwest Pass, the narrowest part of the river passage to New Orleans, hazy sunlight poked up through an early morning mist. Pelicans, rising upward in an explosion of beating wings, took flight in the wake of the passing craft. Bernard didn't notice.

"What's the hurry?" he finally asked. "New Orleans isn't going anyplace."

Blake didn't take his eyes off the pinks and reds blemishing disappearing darkness.

"Keep your foot in it. We got important people waiting with bated breath for our cargo."

"If we crash this baby, they'll still be waiting tomorrow."

"I'm expecting you to get us there in one piece."

The boat's hull bounced as the three guards wrestled the prisoner on deck, giving Bernard a close look at him for the first time. Their eyes locked momentarily.

The large man with short-cropped hair stared up at him, his strange, gray eyes looking as menacing as the scorpion tattoo on his forearm. While two men watched, their rifles ready, the third guard attached the prisoner's belly chain to a metal restraint.

"Jesus! That's one big dude. Why are they bringing him on deck?"

"It's way too rough down there, and this tub doesn't have seat belts."

Ignoring the slight to his boat, Bernard asked "Who'd you say he is?"

"I didn't, but he's Jacque Leguerre, former mob assassin. If he got the chance, he'd take us all out and never bat an eye."

"Why's he so important?"

"He's set to testify against his former bosses and has a price on his head."

"You could have just choppered him to New Orleans."

"We thought about it. Local crime seems to know our every move, and you don't have to say 'dirty cop' when you're talking about the N.O.P.D. Only a handful of people knows we're bringing him up the river. No one else will know until we have him locked up in New Orleans."

The wake of a passing boat caused the Clancy Jane's bow to rise out of the water again, driving one of the guards to his knees.

"You can't keep me locked to this thing," the prisoner said. "If this tub sinks, I won't have a chance."

One of the guards, a big man with a crooked nose, responded harshly.

"Shut your mouth. You got no say in what's happening here."

"At least put the keys where I can get to them if I need to."

The bent-nosed guard rattled the keys attached to his belt. "You'd like that, wouldn't you? Forget about it. You're not going anyplace."

Blake monitored the conversation with his headset as Captain Bernard watched with interest.

"What's all the commotion down there?"

"Our prisoner's whining about a little choppy water," Blake said.

"Your men need to put on their life jackets if they're going to stay on deck. They wouldn't last thirty seconds in the river with its currents and undertows."

Blake nodded and spoke into his microphone. "Jones, you and your men get your life jackets on."

"What about the prisoner?" the man asked.

"What about him?"

"We'll have to take his cuffs off to get the jacket on him."

"Then forget it," Blake said.

Captain Bernard glanced at him. "You know you're breaking the law."

"I am the law."

The boat bounced again as it hit another wake, water splashing over the bank into a reed pond, sending a flock of ducks skyward.

"Then at least unhook him."

Blake mumbled something to himself, grabbing the railing for support as the boat topped another large wave.

"Detach the prisoner from the restraint. Stay ready. Just don't kill him."

Bernard watched as Blake's men reacted to his orders. He wanted to call Angelica. The river much too choppy, he couldn't take a chance on removing his hands from the wheel. Blake wouldn't understand anyway.

Swirling fog had formed a sheer curtain over the river as the Clancy Jane and another boat entered Southwest Pass simultaneously from different directions. Before either captain could react, it was already too late.

The boats collided, the impact knocking Blake and Bernard off their feet, banging them against the rear wall of the cabin. Both mortally damaged boats began to sink immediately, two of the guards on deck washed overboard and quickly sucked under.

Thrown to the deck by the impact, Jacque Leguerre grabbed the metal restraint as water rushed over the bow. The guard with the keys somehow managed to hold onto the railing, until the current finally dislodged him. As he swirled across the deck, struggling to keep his head above water, Leguerre snagged him, wrapping his leg irons around his neck and pulling him toward him.

Grasping the flailing man, Leguerre dived into the river before suction of the sinking boat could pull them under. Racing to find the keys on the guard's belt, he unhooked the life vest that had precariously kept them both afloat. Ignoring the guard's cries, he ripped his arms and hands off the vest, and then pushed him away.

As undercurrents sucked the struggling man's head below the river's swirling surface, Leguerre detached his cuffs, belly chain, and leg irons. Free of his shackles, he held on to the life vest, stroking toward the nearest bank, praying the river's deadly currents wouldn't drag him under as it had the others.

Finding her husband's note, Angelica called his phone to assure him his recurring nightmare had no real meaning. His recorded message, answered on the first ring, was the last time she heard his voice.

Chapter Two

Mardi Gras rocked the French Quarter, excited tourists and locals alike being driven into collective frenzy as passing floats, populated by colorful characters in masks and costumes, tossed beads, trinkets, and doubloons to the agitated crowd. Reluctant N.O.P.D. Lieutenant Anthony Nicosia was among them.

Tony didn't look like a cop. At that moment, he didn't feel much like one either. His baggy green shorts, black Reeboks, white socks, and plaid windbreaker, did little to change anyone's first impression of him. Along with his thinning hair, sallow complexion, and plump shape, he looked like a middle-aged couch potato, more interested in soap operas than crime.

Tony's muscles ached from the extra pounds he carried, due to his failed diet plans, and continuing lack of exercise. His promise to return to the gym when Mardi Gras had ended failed to relieve his aching joints. It didn't matter. Sore knees or not, the world's biggest block party was in full swing, and he was on duty.

The approaching Muses parade had the crowd already worked into a state of mass hysteria. Consecutive days of policing parades and parties had frayed Tony's nerves and shortened his temper. His extra twenty pounds of flab pounded his sore knees and tired feet like a jackhammer. His shoulder holster chafed a tender spot on his chest, and he felt like screaming. It didn't matter because no one would have heard.

Anxious onlookers surrounding him had already raised the noise level to an ear-splitting roar when his younger, ruddy-faced, red-headed partner, Sergeant Tommy Blackburn, tapped his shoulder, breaking his rapt spell.

"You okay, Tony? You look like warmed over shit."

"Yeah, and Fat Tuesday still a week away."

"I'd feel sorry for you, except me and every other man on the force are in the same boat. Hey and Mardi Gras is just once a year."

"Same for Christmas. Instead of Santa Claus, we're stuck with more gangs and bigger guns."

"You right about that. I don't remember ever having so many gang bangers on the street."

"Katrina."

"Maybe we should have moved to Houston with everyone else."

Tony bent down and rubbed his legs. "I might just yet, if my knees don't quit aching."

"You just getting old and fat," Tommy said with a smirk.

The engine of one of the tractors pulling the floats backfired, causing both men to jerk, and then touch the shoulder holsters hidden beneath their windbreakers. Tony frowned and shook his head.

"I can still kick your young ass. It's these back-to-back fourteen hour shifts that are wearing me out. Hell, it'd be tough if I was still twenty-one."

"And you're not. You looked at yourself in the mirror lately? Too many cold Dixies and Lillian's red beans and rice. It might help if you tried pushing away from the table every once in a while."

Tony felt a sudden pang of hunger at the mention of his wife's cooking. "Great advice for next Carnival, assuming I survive this one."

"We'll make it. Flannery heard the Chief has convinced the Governor to send a squad of State

Troopers to help us out. He says they'll be here tomorrow."

"I'll believe it when I see it. If you ask me, we'd do more good in uniform than going undercover, dressed up like a bunch of over-aged, college dorks."

"Can't upset the tourists. They all think this is Never Never Land."

"Yeah, until Captain Hook sticks a sharp one up their ass."

The piquant smell of boiled crawfish reminded Tony of his growling stomach. Though Tommy was also dressed in civilian clothes, he looked more like a recently retired defensive end than a middle-aged beer drinker like his older partner.

A young woman in a red and blue Ole Miss sweatshirt made eye contact with Tony. Grinning drunkenly, she approached him and exposed her breasts, then hugged his neck, caking crimson lipstick on his face. Her jealous boyfriend grabbed her arm, pulling her into the crowd. It didn't stop her from blowing Tony a kiss.

"You may be old and fat, but you ain't lost your effect on women. I think that college girl had her sights on you. Maybe you oughta get yourself some of that."

"Shut up Tommy! I'm married you know, and we're on duty. Besides, that big jock that dragged her away looked like he could bench-press me."

As the parade's first float rumbled off St. Charles Avenue and headed up Canal, the already rowdy crowd grew even noisier. Feeding the chaos, masked and costumed Musers began raining colorful beads and souvenir doubloons off the gaudily decorated floats. Canal Street revelers parted in a wave as the first float rumbled past.

With conversation suddenly becoming impossible, Tony and Tommy endured the crowd, but not for long. Gunfire erupted, a hail of bullets zooming over their heads as a shooter unloaded a semi-automatic pistol into the crowd, miraculously doing little damage.

Tony dropped to his knee, quickly drawing his

revolver. Tommy was faster. Slapping his badge on his purple and gold L.S.U. windbreaker, he started after the shooter, bulling his way through the crowd. When Tony tried to stand, his leg collapsed beneath his weight. Clutching his left knee, he could only grimace as unwitting revelers closed around him.

Floats continued passing on the street, people chaotic as beads and trinkets rained down on them. Above, gray February clouds further darkened the already gloomy day as the mass of excited parade watchers engulfed him. When the third float had passed on Canal, he shielded his face and head. The mob, intent on retrieving beads and doubloons, didn't notice the crouching cop.

Unaware of his partner's pain, Tommy bulled his way through animated spectators, bowling over revelers in his wake. The going was slow, the man he pursued having the same problem. The shooter's pistol empty, he swung it ineffectively at the crowd of people crushing around him. Most of them, their attention focused on flying beads and trinkets, didn't even notice. Blood flew from the mouth of a woman, dropping to her knees when he nailed her with the barrel of the gun.

Tommy gained on the shooter. When he saw the woman on the ground, he kept going, close enough to the man to see gang tattoos on his neck and arms. Redoubling his efforts he fought to within six feet of the shooter, his stare focused on the man's dark pigtail.

When he finally saw an opportunity, he dived forward, grabbed a pair of legs he prayed were the right ones and rolled the person to the ground, knocking down half a dozen unsuspecting revelers along with them. A woman screamed, kicking as she tried to get away from the fight.

When Tommy transferred his grip to the man's tee shirt, the Chicano gang member backhanded him and then ripped the shirt down the front. Tearing it off, he bounded to his feet in a single fluid motion. Ignoring his busted lip and skinned knees, Tommy didn't bother yelling for him to stop, charging after him instead.

Standing six-four and weighing two hundred twenty pounds, Tommy was an imposing man. Ten years out of high school, he still held the State shot-put record. When his hand snagged the strap of a digital camera, he quickly palmed it, aimed and slammed it into the fleeing man's back. The shooter dropped in pain. All the time Tommy needed to overtake him, rolling him through the crowd and knocking down screaming people. He wasn't prepared for what happened next.

The gang banger retrieved a long knife from his baggy pants. Opening it with a flip of his wrist, he stabbed it directly into Tommy's mid-section. Yanking the blade free, he went for the throat, trying to stop the larger man's attack. Tommy grabbed a strong wrist and held on, though his own strength was ebbing as blood gushed from his exposed wound.

The crowd drew away in fear, unwittingly forming an almost impenetrable barrier around the two combatants. Though mesmerized by the struggle, no one stepped forward to help the severely injured police sergeant fighting for his life.

The gang banger's blade slashed a deep gash across Tommy's cheek. He continued to resist, even though he could no longer feel the intense pain that had set his stomach afire. Neither could he feel his arms or legs, his mind becoming progressively numbed. What he did see was his mother's face, and his grandmother's. They were both crying.

✦

After surviving the weight of the crowd, Tony pushed himself off the ground, dragging his sore leg through the melee, following the fleeing man and his partner.

"Police," he yelled as he waved his badge. "Get the hell out of my way."

The beignet he'd eaten that morning sat in his stomach like a broken sandbag as he dragged his gimpy leg through the crowd, internal warning sirens screaming above the din surrounding him. Sensing something was terribly wrong, he plunged ahead, adrenaline coursing through his body overcoming the pain in his knee.

He kept moving, knocking protesting people out of his way when he reached the ring where his partner was gasping his last breaths. Seeing the two men on the ground, he knew his instincts had proved correct.

Tommy was down, his eyes closed, pluming blood painting a growing stop sign on his tee shirt. Tony had learned the chokehold maneuver in police academy. It was no longer taught and no longer used, at least officially. It didn't matter. The situation was dire. It was either the choke hold or else a bullet through the man's brain.

If he could have used his service revolver before the gang banger's knife slashed Tommy's throat, there would have been nothing to decide. As it was, he only had enough time to dive for the man's neck, grab it, and squeeze.

Chapter Three

I'd taken a sabbatical from the Catholic Church for most of the past few years. Today was different. My ex-wife Mimsy had died of breast cancer after a year-long fight.

I called her once during her ordeal and it puzzled me that her new husband so readily allowed me to talk to her. When she answered, her voice seemed hoarse and faint, likely from the pain killers she was taking, and she didn't seem to know who I was.

"Mimsy, it's Wyatt. I called to see how you're doing." I didn't truly mean it when I said, "Is there anything I can do for you?" The last thing I wanted was to see the beautiful woman I'd married ravished by cancer, her long, dark hair ruined, face sallow, figure gaunt, and hope waning from once beautiful eyes.

"Fine, I'm fine," she said. "Thanks so much for calling. Please don't hang up."

I could only imagine what I'd done or said to cause her to think I would hang up on her. Maybe it had something to do with the unmistakable neediness so evident in her voice that it seemed to emanate from the receiver. We'd had a five minute conversation interspersed with long pauses, as if she were trying to catch her breath. Finally, her husband took the phone from her.

"Thank you so much for calling," was his

unexpected response. "You don't know how much we appreciate your concern. Mimsy's extremely tired. Please call again. It helps her spirits when someone calls."

Her new husband, Rafael Romanov, was a strange man I'd met once before. His words were almost a plea. I could hear his grief and realized he loved her far better than I'd ever had.

I had no answer for his desperation, the only response I could think of at the moment inane.

"Try to hang in there."

Mims and I had met in college. I was on the rebound; she was the new girl in town. I was seeking a good time; she wanted a house full of babies. Ultimately, neither of us got what we wanted. Our marriage ended seven years, almost to the day, after it had begun. Too many harsh words and broken dishes had left us less than friends, and we soon lost touch. It didn't seem to matter because my life went further downhill from there.

My badge for years, alcoholic excess and uncontrolled anger, rapidly grew worse. When the sleazy client I'd shoved against a wall filed a bar complaint on me, I quickly learned he had far-reaching connections. After being disbarred, I spent the next six months in a drunken haze, managing to insult, incite, and piss off almost every friend I had. Everyone except Bertram Picou, that is.

Bertram owned an eclectic bar on Chartres Street. Finding me at a local soup kitchen, he'd given me a room upstairs and a constant ration of shit until I'd finally given up the bottle. He and Lady, his trusty collie, stayed with me through my abusive ranting, emotional tirades, and suicidal jags.

Whenever I begged for whiskey, Bertram gave me lemonade. Before long, lemonade became my crutch. That was a while back. Now, it was a quiet February night, a cold breeze blowing up from the Gulf of Mexico, as I stood alone outside St. Validius Cathedral, buying time before going in to view Mimsy's body, seeing her husband Rafael and all her grieving relatives who still thought of me as part of the family. It was the same church where I'd been an altar boy and where Mimsy and I'd been married.

Unable to move, I stared at the moon as powerful tsunami memories crashed against my brain, flooding it with guilt and my own terrible grief I dared not acknowledge. When someone unexpectedly tapped my shoulder, shattering my musings, I wheeled around, staring into Father Alphonso's gray eyes.

"Wyatt Thomas, I thought you must be dead."

My old parish priest was at least four inches taller than my own height of six feet. His slate-gray hair was whiter than I remembered and the wrinkles in his face slightly deeper. His voice hadn't changed, resonating deep from within his barrel chest, his words accented by native Italian even though he hadn't left New Orleans in fifty years.

"You're looking good, Father Alphonso."

My words sounded hollow, even as they raced from my mouth. Father Alphonso smiled, either not noticing or else just overlooking my lack of communication skills.

"Thank God, you've come back to the Church. I prayed you would return."

"I'm not here for myself. Mimsy divorced me years ago. Even so, I felt I needed to pay my last respects in person."

"Of course, you're here for Mimsy's vigil. I'm sorry it was her death that brought you back. At least you've finally returned."

I thought seriously about pretending I hadn't heard. Hell, she didn't even make thirty-five.

"God needed her in another capacity," he said.

"I guess. They say only the good die young. If so, then I'll live to be a hundred. I wasn't lying when I said I almost didn't come tonight."

"Nonsense," he said, grasping my shoulder. "I'm here for you. We'll go in together."

Father Alphonso was convincing, and he wasn't

taking no for an answer. He pushed me ahead of him, through the dense cypress doorway of St. Validius, not giving me the opportunity to bolt and run.

When the hallway of the old church opened up to me, I took a deep, almost instinctive breath of antiquity and dimming memories. The distinct odor of the church caused poignant images to confront my senses, even more than my thoughts and distaste at peering into Mimsy's open casket.

"Are you okay?" he asked.

"I was an hour ago."

Father Alphonso grasped my hand and squeezed, then kissed me on the forehead, like a father reassuring his son there wasn't a monster under the bed. It had the same effect on me as I headed down the darkened hallway with strengthened resolve.

We soon reached the entrance to the anteroom. When we opened the door and entered, I saw Mimsy's mother Betty. Sight of her caused my newly found strength to drift from my body soon as it had arrived. Too late! Seeing me, she grasped me in her fleshy arms and held on tightly, her tears dampening my collar.

"Oh, Wyatt, I don't think I can handle this."

It was all I could take. My own tears, dammed inside for so long, welled up and flooded down my face. Soon, sobbing uncontrollably, I was in a group hug with half the family.

The first person I saw when we all finally got control of our senses was Rafael Romanov, Mimsy's grieving husband. With the exception of Father Alphonso, he was the only person in the room without tear-streaked cheeks. Still in a daze, I gravitated toward him.

Though I'd met him once before, this was like seeing him for the first time. Like Father Alphonso, his eyes were also a strange shade of gray, causing me to do a double-take when I noticed them. His nose and fingers were long and his hands expressive. Though taller than me, he was just as slender, his curly hair dark as his eyes.

"Thanks for coming. It would have meant a lot to Mimsy. And Wyatt, it means a lot to me."

"It feels so strange. This is a place for her family. Not ex-husbands."

"She was closer to you than any of them." Before I could reply, he added, "Please, forget what I just said."

The smell of whiskey on his breath told me he'd had more than just a mind steadying drink or two. He maintained his grip on my hand, almost as if he were holding on to a buoy in a storm. Still, he seemed sensible and spoke in a confidant manner. He released my hand, just as Father Alphonso appeared through the multitude of grieving friends and relatives.

"Wyatt, come with me," he said, frowning and ignoring Rafael.

It was then I noticed Rafael was standing alone amid the crowded room. A circle of space surrounded him, separating him from the rest of the family who all seemed to have their backs to him.

"I'm visiting with Rafael."

"Please," Father Alphonso said.

"No problem," Rafael said. "We'll talk later."

The old priest led me back into the hallway. "What's so urgent, Padre?"

Father Alphonso put his hand on my shoulder and drew me closer, as if he were about to reveal some conspiratorial information.

"You know Rafael was a priest. Well, he is no longer with the Church. He was defrocked. Although he technically will always be a priest, he can no longer hear confessions or perform duties incumbent to the Church."

"I didn't know. What did he do?"

Father Alphonso paused before answering. "His mother is a witch. She casts spells and prays to the Devil. He is her son."

I waited for further explanation but got none. Though it sounded like a joke, Father Alphonso wasn't laughing.

"You're kidding. You don't believe in that malarkey,

do you?"

"Real evil exists. It's not a joke and certainly not malarkey."

"Didn't the Church know this before they ordained him into the priesthood?"

"We are men and women of God, not seers into the future."

My next questions brought an even graver expression to Father Alphonso's face. "Even if Raphael's mother is a witch, what did he do? Should he have to suffer for her sins?"

"He deceived the Church. He had no right to invade the priesthood. Wyatt, he is a gypsy."

"You mean like a spy for the Devil?"

Father Alphonso stepped back and stared at me. "You think you know more about good and evil than does the Church?"

My mouth opened, but words were slow in coming. When they did, it was only to say, "Father, I'm sorry."

We reentered the church's dimly lit nave where vigils for the faithful were held in St. Validius' diocese. Mimsy's casket, surrounded by wreaths of wilting flowers, sat at the far end of the room. Candles burned on both ends of the coffin. I could see it was open.

Mimsy's friends and relatives clustered around it, some kneeling in prayer. Mimsy's father and mother were at the head of the casket, Betty's tears still flowing profusely. I made my way through the mourners, knelt before the ornate chest and said a little prayer, continuing to kneel, staring at the floor, dreading the inevitable glance into the coffin. When I finally got off my knees, Betty hugged me again, sobs of grief wracking her body.

"God damn it, Wyatt! God damn breast cancer took her beautiful hair, and that awful wig makes her look like some Vegas showgirl. I don't even have a lock of hair to remember her by."

Wrestling from Betty's grasp, I bent over and kissed Mimsy's forehead, feeling a knot tighten in my gut. Looking away, I fished in my pocket for the brooch

Mimsy had given me so many years before, opening it to reveal a locket of her hair. Showing it to Betty, I pressed it into her hands.

"Forgive me for not giving it to you before now. I'd almost forgotten I had it."

Saddened and deeply troubled by my glimpse into the coffin, I finally managed to pull away from Betty and her husband Mike. After paying my condolences to the rest of the clan, I hurried out the door and down the darkened hallway to the parking lot outside. Father Alphonso intercepted me as I went out the door, grabbing me by the arm.

"Wyatt, you need to confess. Let's do it now."

"Not now, Padre. I'm not ready, and I may never be."

"God and Satan are wrestling for your soul. Don't let Satan win."

"Seeing Mimsy in that box shook me to the essence of my being. I can't deal with anything else tonight."

The priest squeezed my hand. "Her death reflects your own humanity. You have serious issues you need to resolve. Please, let me help."

"I can't. I'm too upset right now," I said, pulling away and hurrying across the parking lot. "I'll talk with you later."

"Wyatt, don't wait too long," he said, calling to me as I walked away.

Except for cars of the mourners, the lot was deserted. I started walking toward St. Charles Avenue hoping I wouldn't have long to wait for a streetcar. Headlights from a car coming up from behind startled me. It screeched to a halt, and a familiar voice called out my name.

"Wyatt, can I give you a ride? I promise not to cast an evil spell on you."

It was Rafael, smiling from the open window of a silver Cadillac Aviator that flashed in the moonlight. A tugboat on the river blew its whistle.

"A spell, or maybe even a shot of Novocain, would be appreciated about now. I'm sorry. You must be in much more pain than me."

If you took my pain away right now, I'd disappear.

We both needed to change the subject, so I opened the door and climbed into the plush, leather, passenger seat beside him. The vehicle smelled brand new.

"Nice car."

"Thanks. You must be wondering how a defrocked priest can afford such an expensive S.U.V."

"Actually, I was wondering how anyone can afford such an expensive S.U.V."

We both laughed as Rafael turned up Napoleon Avenue. "Where to?" he asked.

"Picou's bar on Chartres. I have a room upstairs. It's in the Quarter," I said.

"I was living in the Quarter when I met Mimsy. She helped me land a job as a rent-a-priest."

"A what?"

Rafael laughed again. "I work on one of the cruise ships that sail out of New Orleans. Many passengers are comforted to cruise with a Catholic priest. The company I work for pays me extremely well."

"But you're—"

"Not a priest? In fact, I am. Once a priest, always a priest. As the ship's chaplain, I perform marriages and conduct services. The passengers don't know I'm defrocked, and the cruise line doesn't care."

"Hey, it's no business of mine. I'm just glad you were there for Mimsy when she needed you."

Rafael's smile disappeared at the mention of Mimsy. "I'm still in shock. I never thought the cancer would take her, even when she was in constant pain and on oxygen twenty-four hours a day."

"Why was she so glad to hear from me when I called? Our marriage didn't exactly end on friendly terms."

"Toward the end, everyone, family and friends, seemed to abandon us. Days would pass with the phone never ringing. Maybe it was the aura of impending death. Sometimes I would call a friend of hers, or someone in her family. When they answered the phone, I'd give it to Mimsy and tell her they had called her. I don't feel guilty about doing it because it always perked her up. Occasionally, an old friend, or an ex-husband would call unexpectedly. It was then I knew there is a God up there."

"I wish I did," I said.

"Oh, there's a God, and Devil, all right. Sometimes it's hard to tell the difference."

I had little time to contemplate his cryptic words as we neared the lights of the French Quarter. Mardi Gras was in full swing the surrounding venues crowded with noisy revelers. Most of the streets were cordoned off by the police, allowing only foot traffic into the Quarter. Rafael stopped the Cadillac on Canal Street, near the intersection with Rue Chartres.

"Sorry I can't get you any closer."

"Thanks for bringing me this far. There's a parking lot down the street. Sure you won't join me at Bertram's? I have many more questions to ask you."

"Not tonight, my friend," he said. "A half-empty bottle of Wild Turkey awaits me."

Before I could walk away, he lowered his window and spoke to me. "Wyatt, my mother has a shop near Royal and Toulouse. It's called Madeline's Magic Potions. You obviously have lots of questions. Please go see her. She'll have answers for you."

Chapter Four

Except for a particularly ripe apple he'd salvaged from a neighborhood trashcan, Jacque Leguerre hadn't eaten in two days. Still dressed in a conspicuously orange uniform, he couldn't just go into a local eatery and order an oyster po'boy, even if he'd had money. Concealed from view of the passing people by darkness and well-placed shrubbery, he had plans to change all that.

Mardi Gras madness gripped the city, loud music and sounds of drunken revelry emanating from the nearby French Quarter. Another time and he might have been there celebrating with them. Now, he had only one thing on his mind—to find a suitable target and relieve him of his clothes and money. Since Jacque was six-ten, weighing in at nearly two hundred sixty pounds, he knew it would not be easy finding someone as large as he was.

Jacque was in the right place at the right time. Many tourists were in town for Mardi Gras, not to mention the passengers of the two cruise liners docked nearby. His stomach growled as he watched the endless stream of visitors walking past on the sidewalk paralleling the Mississippi River. Soon, a suitable candidate passed close enough that he could almost reach out and touch him—an unusually large man, strolling alone.

"Hey," Jacque said. "Over here."

The man stopped and glanced around, trying to see who was calling to him.

"You're not gonna believe this. Hurry or you'll miss it."

The man walked the several steps toward the shrubbery, stopping when lights from the sidewalk disappeared and shadows began engulfing him. He didn't need to go any further because an equally large man reached out and grabbed his arm, yanking him into the shrubbery, strangling him before he could issue a sound.

Like most of Jacque's victims, the man died easily. Jacque glanced at his disbelieving eyes, not bothering to close them as he searched the body for a wallet and identification. He found what he sought in the inside pocket of his dark sports coat. The passport told him everything else he needed to know.

A Norwegian citizen from the city of Stavanger, the person named Harald Gjertsen was on a cruise aboard the Scandinavian Queen. The ship was docked within sight at the Julia Street Terminal. Gjertsen's wallet contained a hundred kroner, and only twenty dollars in American currency; enough to buy a po'boy and not much else.

There was also a magnetic cabin key and cruise ship I.D. card bearing Gjertsen's photo. Along with the key, Jacque found some colorful Mardi Gras beads and a silver doubloon emblazoned with the name of the Carnival krewe that had tossed it. Harald Gjertsen had watched the parade, and had even managed to grab some souvenirs tossed from the floats.

The photo proved no problem as Jacque and the dead man looked enough alike to be brothers. Both had short-cropped hair; both measured six feet, ten inches. Only their eye colors were different, Gjertsen's Nordic blue, Jacque's a rare shade of gray. He realized his job would be easy and began removing the man's clothes, slowly, so as not to tear or soil them.

Another three hours needed to pass before rigor

mortis would have made his job difficult. By then, he would be ensconced in the man's cabin aboard the Scandinavian Queen. Gjertsen's body would still be submerged in the murky depths of the Mississippi River, strong currents propelling it toward the Gulf of Mexico.

Once he had the Norwegian stripped to his boxer shorts he dragged him through the shrubbery to a secluded spot by the river. His progress was cloaked by shadows, away from streetlights and tourist traffic. He waded knee-deep into the river until he felt the first strong undertow. Lowering the body into the water, he watched as it drifted away, finally disappearing beneath the surface.

Satisfied the dead man would never be seen again, he slipped out of his prisoner's uniform, rolled it into a ball and let it drift away, along with Gjertsen's body. After a quick glance around to see if anyone had observed his nefarious deed, he slipped back into the shadows, returning to the place where he'd left the Norwegian's clothes, passport, and money.

Jacque was dressed in the dead man's clothes when a commotion at a nearby row of trashcans caused him to react. He reached the cans in time to see a little dog, backed against the wall by a huge rat, its fangs barred. The object of their disagreement was a half-eaten hamburger someone had tossed there.

The little dog was barely more than a puppy, probably recently weaned. Still, it was hungry and not willing to give up the sandwich to the equally hungry rat. Jacque launched a tin can at the rodent. The rat ducked the can, snatched the burger, and then scurried away. Jacque grabbed the dog.

"What's your name, little girl?"

Still hungry, though happy for the rescue, the dog wagged her tail and then licked Jacque's nose. She had the triangular head and pointed ears of a German shepherd, though Jacque could tell by her smaller size, and russet and black color she was a combination of different breeds; a mongrel, just like himself, he thought.

"I don't know what you're doing out here alone, but you better come with me before one of those humongous rats eats you for dinner. Don't worry. I'll find us something to eat."

One day, she would be a large dog. Now, she easily fit into the inside pocket of the Norwegian's sports jacket. After giving her a quick head rub, Jacque started off toward beckoning lights along the bank of the river.

The Julia Street Cruise Terminal Complex was located within the same building as the Riverwalk Mall, a world class shopping center with everything from a food court to Victoria's Secret, Gap, and Limited. Most cruise line passengers shopped there until time to return to ship. Jacque stopped long enough to buy two Lucky Dogs from a street vendor, eating one of them on a bench facing the river as he listened to passing boat whistles, and hum of countless tourists plying the riverfront sidewalk. The little dog gobbled down the other.

Tourists were on their way to the Aquarium of the Americas, riverboat casinos, or the ongoing Mardi Gras celebration in the nearby French Quarter. Jacque had other things on his mind.

Fearing pickpockets, the Norseman had probably left most of his money in his cabin on the cruise ship. Knowing the twenty bucks was already almost gone, Jacque intended to find out. His first hurdle would be getting past the ship's security guards at the terminal complex. He found the lobby crowded with passengers coming and going. If the guards became suspicious of him, then he planned to disappear into the crowd. He needn't have worried.

The security guard was texting a message on his phone to his girlfriend. When Jacque showed him the photo I.D., he smiled and beckoned him through the gate after little more than a cursory glance. Jacque found a "you are here" map as he entered the ship, squeezing past several passengers on their way to dinner. The little dog squirmed inside his jacket.

When he located the cabin and inserted the plastic card into the entry slot, the door unlocked with a satisfying click. Since there were no other passengers in the hallway, he slipped inside the cabin unnoticed. The door to the bathroom was ajar and he heard someone softly humming to herself.

A woman, brushing her long hair, stood in front of the bathroom mirror when she heard Jacque moving behind her. He could see her pretty face in the mirror when she glanced up.

"*Er at du*, Harald?"

When she turned around, Jacque could see she'd been crying. He also saw the angry bruise on her face and her swollen eye. When she realized he wasn't her husband, a nervous hand went to her mouth. She had no time to react before he grabbed her, muffling her scream with the palm of his hand.

Lieutenant Anthony Nicosia stood by Sergeant Tommy Blackburn's hospital bed, gently holding his injured partner's hand. The sterile room buzzed and flashed with electronic devices monitoring Tommy's bodily functions. His blood pressure and pulse rate readings had finally stabilized. He was no longer receiving blood. Still, after more than six hours, he had yet to regain consciousness.

When the nurse entered through the curtained door, she tapped Tony's shoulder. She had frizzy hair the color of a russet apple peel, and spoke to him in a high-pitched, Chalmette-flavored accent that he'd heard all his life.

"I know you're concerned, Lieutenant, but Sergeant Blackburn needs his rest. You can come back tomorrow. Now, you gotta go."

"I'm afraid to leave. He may not be here tomorrow."

"He's a tough one, him. He'll still be here."

"But the Doctor said—"

Nurse Randall's frizzy hair bounced when she shook her head and frowned. "Me and the other nurses work here all day, every day, bathing the patients, bandaging their wounds, and changing their bed pans. Doctors have lots of patients and come by maybe once a day, for five minutes or so. Now who you think knows more about what's going on around here?"

Duly chastised Tony could only lower his head and smile. Like police officers E.R. nurses were also on the front lines. He could feel the tension in her voice.

"I know how tough my partner is. Still, he wouldn't be alive right now if it wasn't for you, the doctors, and other nurses."

Apparently used to high praise, Nurse Randall's expression didn't change as she fluffed the pillow beneath Tommy's head.

"You the one that saved him, sweet talker. Don't matter, though. You still gotta go. And Lieutenant, there's someone waiting outside for you."

Tony backed out of the eerily silent, Critical Care Unit, bumping into Chief Wexler, head man of the Eighth District, the police department serving the French Quarter and Superdome. Wexler folded the Times Picayune he was reading and placed it on the coffee table. He wasn't smiling.

"You okay? You look like hell."

"So I'm told," Tony said, still wearing the same green shorts, sans plaid windbreaker that had been so soaked in Tommy's blood that he'd discarded it in a nearby dumpster on his way to the hospital. His white tee shirt said Tulane University.

"I'm so sorry about Tommy. The Doctor isn't optimistic about his recovery."

"Yeah, well I got it from a good source he'll be just fine."

Wexler averted his gaze, glancing at the floor. The Chief had come to New Orleans via Covington, a nearby town. Slight of build and soft-spoken, he had a wispy brown, disappearing hairline.

"I know you're beat, but we got a problem and I need you."

"We're already working around the clock, my

people about to drop. What we need is some outside help here."

Wexler raised a placating hand, ignoring or disregarding Tony's thinly disguised criticism.

"I called in some chits. We got help coming from as far away as Baton Rouge, maybe even the State Police. That's not the problem I'm talking about."

"What then?" Tony asked.

"An unexpected situation. A cargo container ship and an offshore supply vessel collided seven miles south of Pilottown in Southwest Pass. It's the main channel to the mouth of the Mississippi. Both boats sank and are blocking the pass. Forty cargo ships are stuck in port or on their way here, prevented from either entering or leaving the river. Cruise ships are also affected. Julia Street Wharf is scrambling to find alternatives. Some passengers are being bused to other facilities while the rest are being sequestered on the ship."

The Julia Street Wharf, Tony knew, was the point of embarkation for many cruise ship lines in the Crescent City. He and his wife Lillian had once taken a cruise to Cozumel, and the Lieutenant was familiar with the busy wharf. He could only imagine what the result of its total shutdown would have on the City.

"That's all we need. Bigger crowds to deal with." he said.

"That's not all we got to worry about. A body floated up behind the Golden Bough Casino. It's too close to our tourist traffic, this time of year. It could give our impression of positive recovery a black eye."

"Murder?"

"Looks like it. A large male. Late thirties. He had no clothes or I.D. No record of anyone fitting his description being reported missing."

"Hell, with several thousand extra tourists in town, he could be from France for all we know."

"Don't remind me," Wexler said. "That's why it's so urgent to get a handle on the situation quickly. I'm relieving you of Carnival duty and putting you in charge of the investigation."

"But what about Tommy?"

"I'm assigning you a new partner until Tommy recovers. He's waiting to meet you." Chief Wexler opened the waiting room door and signaled to someone. "This is Marlon Bando. He's your new partner. Get to know each other and I'll check back in a few days." Wexler started for the door, stopping before he reached it. "And Tony, there's one more thing. Feds are crawling all over town."

"For what reason?"

"Don't know, and I can't get anyone to tell me. See what you can find out."

"It's late, and I'm beat, Chief."

"Take the rest of the night off," Wexler said. "The trail is already cold. You can get up to speed tomorrow."

"Thanks," Tony said.

Wexler ignored the sarcasm and quickly disappeared down the hallway as Tony assessed his new partner. Bando was tall. Unlike Tommy, he was slender instead of strapping. From his thinning brown hair and loose skin beneath his chin, he appeared less physically inclined than Tommy.

"Marlon Bando, huh?"

"Mom's little joke. She loved Brando in *On the Waterfront*."

Tony tried not to smile. His new partner seemed the antithesis of Marlon Brando, slight of build, soft spoken and quite ordinary looking.

"I could use a beer at Carlucci's. Want to join me?"

"Sure."

"Good," Tony said. "I'll buy you a couple."

"Thanks, but I don't drink."

Tony studied his new partner's expression a moment and saw no change. "Little problem you need to tell me about?"

Marlon shook his head. "I just never took it up."

"You never got drunk in high school or college?"

"I was on the debating team. My friends were all

pretty sedate."

Tony broke his disbelieving stare. "Fine, you want to meet me at Carlucci's?"

"Can I ride with you? My Fairlane's in the shop."

"You drive a Ford Fairlane? They don't make them anymore, do they?"

"Bought her used in college. It's the only car I've ever owned. The old doll has almost 400,000 miles on her."

"Don't make them like they used to," Tony said, too tired to smile. "You're not exactly the impulsive type, are you?"

"Not exactly."

"Forget about Carlucci's. "I'm dog tired. I'll give you a ride home and then pick you up first thing tomorrow morning."

Marlon didn't show it if he were disappointed. Tony drove him down St. Claude Avenue to his washboard apartment in what was left of Arabi, a little suburb of New Orleans decimated by Hurricane Katrina.

"Thanks, Lieutenant," Marlon said.

"Just Tony. I'm your partner now."

"Thanks, Tony. There's an all-night convenience store up the street. They have beer there in case you still want one. Just be careful the attendant doesn't shoot you. Everyone's still jumpy around here."

Tony took Marlon's advice and stopped at the convenience store. The place was no more than a lone beacon of light in an area still devastated by the storm. The attendant's eyes danced a nervous tango as he watched Tony walk to the refrigerated display. After paying for the Dixie tallboy without comment, Tony chugged it in the parking lot before reaching the patrol car.

Lillian, his wife, was asleep when he got home, though she'd left a pot of gumbo simmering on the stove for him. Grabbing Tabasco sauce and another cold Dixie from the refrigerator, he sat at the kitchen table. When he finished his bowl of gumbo, he glanced longingly at the stock pot before deciding one bowlful was enough. Lillian didn't stir when he joined her in bed, and he fell asleep almost immediately.

Chapter Five

Tony awoke to the aroma of strong New Orleans coffee wafting down the hallway to his bedroom. It was still dark outside. Though not yet six, he felt almost rested for the first time in a month. The feeling waned when he remembered Tommy.

His wife Lillian wasn't smiling when she brought him a cup of his second favorite beverage. Only four years younger than him, she'd been mistaken for his daughter more than once. Dim lighting, he'd reasoned.

Lil had long, brown hair and green eyes that looked almost blue in the right light. She was pretty but not beautiful, at least in a classic sense. An inch or so taller than her husband, she'd never suffered from his ongoing weight problem and had retained her perfect size eight figure even after the birth of their five children.

"Another late night? I didn't hear you come in."

"Mardi Gras," he said. "Used to love it."

"You still do. If it were up to me, this would be the last one."

"Right now, I agree with you. Hey, thanks for leaving gumbo on the stove for me. I was starving when I got home."

Lil nodded. She'd always had something on the stove for him to eat when he returned from work, and he never forgot to thank her for it.

"How's Tommy?" she said.

"He'll be fine."

Lil sat on the side of the bed and put her arms around her husband's shoulders. "Tony, when are you going to retire? With Tommy hurt and all, I've started worrying about you. I don't want to be a widow, and I can't take much more of this."

Tony didn't immediately answer because he'd heard it all before, only too often of late.

"I hear you."

"You have twenty-five years with the Department. You been eligible to retire for five years now."

"I just turned forty-six, and I'm way too young to retire. What would I do the rest of my life?"

"Raise that garden you've always wanted. Take another cruise with me, maybe to the Bahamas this time. Be home every night, safe in bed beside me instead of out on the streets. The kids are all gone now, and I want you here with me. Promise you'll at least think about it."

"I have thought about it. I'm good, maybe the best, at what I do."

"Sure you are Tony. We both know that, but you can be the best at something else. I had to hear about Tommy on the six o'clock news yesterday. No one even bothered to call me."

"I called."

"Your cell phone number isn't on the caller I.D."

"I must have used the pay phone at the hospital."

Lil ignored her husband's lame excuse, changing the subject to catch him off guard.

"I don't like our life any more. At least consider retiring."

Lil rarely showed her emotions. Tony could count the times on one hand he'd seen her cry. She was his strength, and he felt guilty as hell. He was many things. Liar wasn't one of them. Retirement seemed like something old men did. He didn't feel like an old man, or know what to say. Saying nothing wasn't an option.

"Tell me, Tony."

"I'll think about it."

"You need to think hard this time. There may not be a next time for me if you don't."

"I said I'll think about it. That's as good as I can do this hour of the morning."

Lil knew her husband well enough to know when to stop talking. Further nagging would only cause him to shut her out. She'd gotten the answer she wanted. That was all she needed. After kissing him full on the mouth, she took his empty cup and returned to the kitchen.

"You can't sleep all day. Get out of bed. Your grits and eggs are ready."

When Tony put pressure on his leg, he sank to the floor. He'd almost forgotten about his swollen knee. Pain racing up his leg brought with it instant recollection. Lillian had already left the room and had missed his soft moan. After calling the hospital to check on Tommy, he limped to the bathroom medicine cabinet where he swallowed a handful of aspirins. Cranking the water's temperature as hot as he could stand it, he stood beneath the shower until the bathroom steamed.

Tony and Lil had married early, right out of high school. She'd wanted to attend college, but their five kids delivered in quick succession had preempted any ideas of higher education. A major league ball team had drafted Tony. He'd played for only a summer in the minors, until his knee started giving him trouble.

Now, like Lil had said, he had his twenty-five. All their children had left home already, the youngest a freshman at L.S.U. When the towel dropped to the floor, he sucked in his gut and looked at himself in the hazy mirror. He didn't see an old man staring back at him. Lil stuck her head in the door, obliterating his thoughts.

"Your eggs are getting cold, lover boy. Quit admiring yourself in the mirror and come eat your breakfast."

Almost rested wasn't good enough as he drove away from home to pick up Marlon Bando, his new partner. Tommy had an apartment in the Irish Channel District, the place where they'd both grown up. Tony had driven halfway to Tchoupitoulas Street before remembering Tommy wouldn't be there. As an unhappy sense of guilt swept over him, he turned the car toward Arabi to pick up his new partner with the ridiculous name.

Arabi lay between Chalmette and New Orleans though there was little suggestion of where New Orleans ended, and Arabi began. Before Katrina, the median family income in Arabi was less than twenty-thousand dollars, most of the houses old, small, and closely spaced. The storm had flooded homes and scattered occupants, but the city had somehow rebuilt.

Now, new homes and businesses had sprung up amid the devastation, though more than a few ruined houses and F.E.M.A. trailers still remained, serving as a constant reminder of the storm's wrath. Bando wasn't from Arabi, and Tony wondered why he lived there. It was just one of the many questions he wanted answered.

When he found Marlon waiting on the curb in front of his small apartment, he realized his new partner was much younger than he'd originally thought, probably only in his mid-twenties.

"I'd invite you in, but the place is a mess," Marlon said.

"No problem. It's still early enough for coffee and beignets at Café Du Monde before we head over to the Casino."

Marlon made a face that Tony saw from the corner of his eye.

"Something wrong?"

"No, nothing."

"You don't like coffee and beignets?"

"I don't consume caffeine or processed sugar. It's okay, though. I'll just order something else."

Tony grinned. "Coffee and beignets are pretty

much all they have at Café Du Monde, and it's not far from our ten o'clock meeting."

"No problem," Marlon said.

Tony had been thinking about strong Creole coffee and sugary beignets all morning. Marlon, he decided, would have to watch him partake of the street-side bistro's excellent coffee and sugary pastries. Still, he felt guilty as he parked the unmarked police cruiser beside the banquette and planted a blue, flashing light on its roof.

Mardi Gras visitors jammed the streets all the way to Canal, swarming Jackson Square, many still half-drunk from the previous night's partying. College kids in tank tops, fraternity sweatshirts, and jeans, along with middle-aged tourists and assorted freak shows from who knew where, vied for a position in the horde. Tony didn't even notice them anymore.

Pushing through the unusually crowded outdoor café, they beat out a gray-haired couple for the last available table. Powdered sugar coated the tabletop from its former customers, and a smiling waiter in white cap and smock quickly bused it for them.

"You on vacation, Lieutenant?"

"I wish."

"I'm not used to seeing you here two days in a row."

"Duty calls Louie. We're investigating the body that washed up yesterday near the Casino."

Louie was a sallow-faced man with a prominent nose and closely spaced eyes. An ex-con, he'd managed to stay out of trouble for the past ten years. Coffee, sugar, and light banter seemed to have done the trick. Tony wondered if the combination would work for others fresh out of the slammer. He doubted it.

"Where's Tommy?"

"Guess you didn't hear," Tony said. "He got stabbed yesterday. He's out of commission for awhile. Marlon is my new partner until then."

"Hope Tommy makes it okay."

"Thanks, Louie, he'll be fine."

"Glad to meet you," Louie said, shaking Marlon's

hand. "Coffee and bennies are on me today."

Marlon stared at the dusting of powdered sugar on his hand as Louie navigated expertly through the tables of the crowded outdoor bistro on his way to the kitchen. Louie was just making small talk. Coffee and bennies were always on the house for Tony and his partner. When Louie returned with two coffees and a double order of beignets, Marlon made a face and pushed them aside.

"Could I just have a bottle of water, instead?"

Louie stared at him as if he were gazing at a crazy person. His mouth popped open, revealing a missing front tooth. Waiting to see if Marlon were kidding, Louie didn't immediately respond to his request.

"Sure thing," he said, hurrying away through the crowd again.

When he returned with a glass of water, Marlon made another face. This time he didn't say anything.

"What?" Tony said.

"It's tap water. Everyone knows New Orleans' tap water comes directly from the Mississippi and is loaded with carcinogens."

Tony started to comment, thought better of it and changed the subject. "I haven't seen you around. Where you from?"

"I grew up in north Louisiana and joined the Army after graduating from high school."

"Afghanistan or Iraq?"

"I was a M.P. at Fort Polk. Most of my time in the army was spent arresting drunk G.I.s in Leesville."

Tony grinned. "I hear that. Polk's bad as a war zone. Where you from in north Louisiana?"

"Monroe. I got a degree in criminal justice on the G.I. Bill from the university there."

Kids shouting at something down on the Moonwalk caused Tony to glance over the levee, the row of tankers and barges waiting to go reminding him of the sunken boats blocking the path to the Gulf.

"What brings you to the city?" he said, returning his attention to Marlon.

"Work, mostly. N.O.P.D. needed bodies and I needed a job."

"Most people don't start out as detectives. Whose dick did you have to suck?"

Marlon didn't take offense at Tony's words, or even seem to know they were offensive.

"I picked up some investigative experience in the Army. Chief Wexler needed someone, and you became available to break me in."

"And?"

"Well, my uncle's on the City Council, and he gave me a recommendation."

Tony thought about Marlon's explanation. It irked him to think Tommy's misfortune had resulted in his new partner's resultant good luck. It had taken him four long years before getting the nod to become a detective. He decided to let the matter drop, at least for the moment.

"Great! I guess that qualifies you."

Tony downed his coffee, wiped powdered sugar off his moustache with the back of his hand, and then headed away from the patio. He didn't bother waiting for Marlon as he pushed into the throng of people crowding the sidewalk.

"Lieutenant, did I say something wrong?" Marlon said, hurrying to catch up.

"There's someone waiting for us at the Golden Bough," Tony replied, not answering his question. "Leave the car here. We'll get there faster on foot through this mob."

Chapter Six

Jacque powered the woman to the bed in the little stateroom, forcing her face-down onto the mattress, holding her mouth and hands behind her back until she stopped struggling.

When the boat to New Orleans had gone down, he'd only time enough to release one of his hands from the cuffs. The key was still in the lock when he finally struggled out of the water and onto the muddy river bank. Thinking they might come in handy, he'd kept them.

"Don't call out and I won't hurt you," he said, cuffing one of her wrists before relaxing his grip.

The black nightgown left her lithe back and bare shoulders exposed. When he flipped her over and fastened her to the bedpost with the handcuffs, he could see she was tall, well over six feet, he guessed.

He couldn't remember the last time he'd slept with a woman. When he released his hold, she sat up, and an electric surge of pure lust stirred in his loins. This woman, so close to him that he could feel the warmth of her ample body and smell her faint perfume, had caught his feelings by surprise.

"*Hvem er du og hvorfor er du solid min mann er klær?*" she said.

She quit speaking when he raised his palm. "I don't understand what you're saying," he said. "Do you speak English?"

She stared at him with eyes the color of a Norwegian fjord, tears forming in their corners. Her feelings were clear.

"Who are you, and why are you wearing Harald's garments?"

"I'm an escapee. Your husband was tall like me. I needed his clothes."

The woman looked at him with skeptical eyes. "Where is he?"

Jacque glanced away from her hard stare. "I don't know."

"Is he dead? Did you kill him?"

"He was unconscious, though very much alive when I left him," he said.

"You're lying. If he were alive, you wouldn't be here now. The police would already be on their way to the room."

"Look, he hit his head on the sidewalk when he fell. I'm sorry. It wasn't my intention to harm him."

Jacque waited for her reaction to his deceit but got none. She was either in shock, or else didn't believe a word he said; maybe both. He wondered if it had something to do with the purple bruise on her face that looked a lot like a fist print. She also had bruises on her arms, and one on her neck.

A single tear rolled down her cheek.

"I prayed he would never return, though I didn't wish him dead."

"Did he do this to you?" he said.

"Don't touch me," she said, recoiling.

"I was just wondering what monster would beat a woman."

Her answer was a blink of the eyes. She was young, probably no more than mid-twenties. After covering her face with her free hand, she began to cry softly. Jacque removed her husband's overcoat and laid it on the bed. Stepping into the little bathroom, he returned with a damp washcloth. Sitting beside her, he began wiping her face until she pushed him away.

"Stop it!" she said.

"I'm sorry. I know you're upset."

"If you're going to kill me, then do it now and get it over with."

Her anger caught Jacque by surprise. "I've never killed anyone without reason. I need to stay here awhile. If you cooperate, I won't hurt you."

The little dog, asleep in the overcoat until that moment, began to move. The young woman's eyes grew larger when the homeless pooch poked her head out of the pile, its tail wagging. Grabbing the dog with her free hand, she began crying again, hugging it to her breast as it licked her face.

"What's your name?" she said.

"She has no name. I found her in a trash pile, trying to fight off a monster rat."

"Poor baby," she said, kissing the dog. "She looks and feels like velvet to me."

"Then Velvet she is. I'm Jacque. You haven't told me your name."

"Go to hell!" she said, glaring at him as she continued hugging Velvet.

"Look, I already know your name is Greta. I saw it in the packet of information on the table." With a cautious touch, he placed his hand on her forehead. "Your face is flushed. Are you all right?"

"I'm going to throw up."

Jacque quickly unlocked the cuff, helping her out of bed. Wobbly on her feet, she tripped before she made it to the bathroom. Jacque half-carried her to the toilet, holding her head as she vomited. When she finally stopped retching, he cleaned her face with a wet washcloth and helped her back to bed. This time, he didn't cuff her.

Velvet cuddled next to her as she reclined against a pillow and closed her eyes. When her steady breathing informed Jacque she was asleep, he touched the swollen skin behind her ear. Dampening the washcloth again, he placed it on her forehead. When he was sure she was okay, he began casing the drawers in the cabin, finding little more than a single twenty in a purse he presumed was hers. He stuffed it in his shirt pocket.

Exhausted from two days on the run, he sat in the chair beside the bed, dozing off and not waking until the ship's horn signaled midnight. Greta was still lying on the bed. Awake, she was staring at him.

"You need to kill me, or else leave. I can't abide your presence any longer."

"The swelling behind your ear. Harald must have been a heartless ogre." She hugged Velvet to her breast, not responding to his comment. "You may have a concussion," he said.

"I'm sick again," she said, grabbing her mouth.

This time she didn't make it to the toilet. Afterward, Jacque helped her back to bed, washed her face and then cleaned up the mess on the floor. She lay there, red in the face and rubbing her temples.

"Your head must be killing you. Do you have something for a headache?"

Greta didn't answer, only glaring at him. He found a box of acetaminophens in the medicine cabinet. She didn't fight him when he gave her two tablets, along with a swallow of water.

"Those should help, if you can keep them down. The best thing you can do for a concussion is to do nothing," he said. "Lie still. I'll turn out the lights."

The lamp in the bathroom provided only a faint glow to the room. Still, it was all he needed to see her on the bed. When she was again asleep, he found a coffee cup in the bathroom and filled it with water for Velvet. She drank and then promptly did her business on a paper he'd spread on the floor. When Greta awoke a few hours later, he gave her some water, and again helped her to the bathroom.

"You'll be better tomorrow," he said.

They'd repeated the process several times before he fell asleep in the chair again. When he awoke, Greta was convulsing on the bed, her eyes closed. Touching her forehead, he realized she had a fever, her nightgown soaked with sweat. Wetting towels from the bathroom, he covered her with them.

Greta's body continued shuddering as she ranted in Norwegian, and sometimes English.

"Oh *min Gud*, Harald. *Vennligst ikke drepe baby.* Why are you doing this to your own child?"

Her ranting continued throughout the night. Morning light was shining through the cabin's single porthole when Greta's fever finally broke. Removing the damp towels, he covered her with a blanket. As if realizing her plight, Velvet had never left her side. When the young Norse woman stopped struggling, the little dog jumped from the bed, running into the bathroom for a drink of water. Jacque reacted to a knock on the door.

"Room service," a woman in the hallway said.

Jacque cracked the door, smiling at the woman with a cleaning cart.

"We're newlyweds," he said. "Sorry for the disruption in your service, but we need a little privacy right now more than clean sheets. Here is something for your time," he said.

The woman nodded when he handed her the twenty-dollar bill, smiling as she pushed the cart down the hallway.

Chapter Seven

Swarms of tourists shouldered their way along the sidewalk past Café Du Monde. Joining the throng, Tony and Marlon followed Decatur to Canal Street. The going soon became easier, most of the tourists congregating as close to Bourbon Street as possible.

Tony's knee ached. When they reached Canal, the world's widest street, he was out of breath. Marlon either didn't see his distress, or else didn't care. Tony suspected the latter as he popped three aspirins into his mouth.

Gambling had long been a part of Louisiana, slot machines in the truck stops and high stakes poker games in the back rooms of local brothels where beautiful young women, many of them college students from L.S.U. or U.S.L., served drinks to their well-heeled clients when they weren't performing other duties. Legal casino gaming had finally arrived, taking a while to catch on in New Orleans. Most tourists came for the food and lagniappe, saving their gaming funds for Vegas, or closer to home in Beaumont or Bossier City.

Most legal gambling in Louisiana takes place on riverboats specially constructed for that purpose. After transportation down the river from their place of origin, they lay moored in a permanent location, never to sail again. The thought saddened Tony who'd watched ships moving up and down the river all his life. He rubbed his knee, wishing now they'd brought the car instead of walking.

They flashed their badges at the security guards after crossing the gangplank to the Golden Bough Casino. The two guards kept minors off the premises though their primary function was serving as pleasant greeters. They pointed Tony and Marlon to the security office where they were surprised by the Chief Security Officer's appearance.

"Help you?" the pretty brunette asked.

The young woman, nattily dressed in khaki pants and purple silk blouse, appeared all business. Her nametag said Venus. Her dark-eyed appeal went along with the mental picture her name invoked.

"Lieutenant Nicosia and Sergeant Bando," Tony said. "We're here about the body you found last night.

"Venus Hernandez," she said. "I was on duty when they found it."

Tony smiled at the woman young enough to be his daughter, refraining from asking how she'd managed to become the Casino's chief of security. From her name, dark hair, and olive complexion, she could have been of Mexican, or Spanish descent. Not necessarily, he knew. New Orleans was, and had always been a melting pot. Despite her name and appearance, pretty Venus Hernandez was probably a third generation resident of New Orleans, a presumption her local accent seemed to bear out.

"I'll show you where we found him," she said, starting out the door.

She led them up three flights of stairs to an outdoor, observation deck. Leaning over the railing, she pointed at the water. The riverboat was securely moored in its own cement holding basin. From their vantage, they could see much of the river, and what some locals called the Triple-C, the Crescent City Connection Bridge. Tony had things on his mind other than enjoying the colorful vista.

"Was the body found in the enclosure, or outside, in the river?" he asked.

"Outside," she said.

He began jotting details in the little notebook he always carried. "Who found it?"

"A visitor from Arkansas. He'd had too much to drink and came out on deck for fresh air."

"You questioned him?"

"I detained him until police arrived," she said. "In my mind, he's not a suspect."

Although Tony had read the report, and drawn his own conclusion, he wanted to hear the security officer's take on the matter.

"And why do you think that?"

"He was a little man and slight of build. The deceased was large, closer to seven feet than six. I'm guessing he weighed almost three hundred pounds. It's also my opinion the deceased didn't come from the casino."

"Please, explain."

"Like I said, his body was outside the holding basin when we found it. If he'd fallen from the observation deck, he wouldn't have landed outside the concrete retainer."

"Is there any other way he could have gotten down there and fallen in?"

"Customers have no access, all the doors kept locked at all times. I can't believe anyone could climb down there from up here."

She paused, as if she had something else to say. Tony picked up on her hesitation. "What else?"

"It was crowded last night. Someone would have seen a person as large as that man, running around with only his underwear on."

"His clothes were gone?"

"Except for his boxer shorts."

"If he didn't fall off the boat and drown, then where did he come from?"

Venus didn't have to think about her answer. "I'd say he floated in."

"From another boat, maybe? A tanker or tugboat out in the river?"

"The currents are too strong out there. If a person had fallen off a boat in the middle of the river, his body wouldn't have surfaced until it reached the Gulf. My guess is he entered the water from somewhere near the bank, on this side of the river." Tony nodded, having already drawn the same conclusion. "Is this a murder, Lieutenant?"

Tony already knew they were dealing with foul play. "No official report has been issued, but the man was strangled."

"Motive?"

"When we figure that out, we'll have a better idea who's responsible. My guess is someone wanted his clothes."

"Then he must be enormous. The U.S. Marshals weren't as forthcoming with their information," she said. "Is this a Federal matter, Lieutenant?"

Tony was as much in the dark as the lovely, security officer. Pointedly not answering her question, he asked one of his own.

"They examined the body?"

"Asked a few questions, took a few pictures, and then went on their way," she said with a flick of her dark mane of hair.

Tony had no idea why the Feds had interceded in what seemed a local matter. He intended to find out.

"You know a lot about police procedure."

"I have a degree in criminal science from U.N.O. and my dad was a cop with the N.O.P.D. until we moved to Baton Rouge."

"Mo Hernandez?"

"You know him?"

"We went through the academy and broke out together. Believe me, we were close. I have lots of Mo Hernandez stories."

"He retired from the B.R.P.D. last year."

News of his old friend's retirement caught Tony by surprise.

"Retired? As I remember, Mo is a few years younger than me."

"He had his twenty. Mom was on his back wanting him to leave the force. She'd become distressed about the danger. He finally gave in to her—"

Tony finished her sentence when she hesitated. "Persistent nagging?"

Tony's words cracked Venus up. When she laughed, her voice was unexpectedly husky for such a small woman.

"Sounds like you may have a similar problem. I'd like to hear some of your stories. I love cops and everything about them."

"Come to Carlucci's. I stop in most every night. You know where it is?"

"You bet I do. Dad used to talk about it. He had quite a few of his own stories."

"Mo and me killed more than a few brain cells at Carlucci's. I still manage to drink a few beers there, usually late this time of year."

When Venus smiled, Tony admired her perfect teeth, not even noticing the sudden throng of tourists that had joined them on the observation deck, one pointing to a giant oiler out in the river.

"I'll drop by next time I have a night off. I'm looking forward to it."

"See you then, Venus," he said with a backward wave as they turned for the casino's entrance.

They'd almost reached the car before Tony realized his young partner hadn't said a word during the interview.

"You were pretty quiet back there. What's your take on the body?"

Marlon moved out of the way of a group of women, yakking and laughing as they hurried toward a Lucky Dog vendor plying his trade on the sidewalk.

"I'm just a rookie," he said. "You tell me."

Tony didn't bother. He wanted to discuss the situation with someone, but decided to save his breath. His knee ached, and his feet hurt. Spotting a bus stop bench, he sat down and began massaging his sore extremity. Fishing the keys from his pocket, he tossed them to Marlon.

"Go get the car. I'll wait here for you."

Marlon fumbled the keys, dropping them to the pavement. After retrieving them, he started off without replying. When he returned with the car thirty minutes later, Tony noticed a new dent in the fender.

"You drive," he said, climbing into the passenger seat. "What's the story on the dent?"

"Someone must have clipped it while we were at the casino."

"Uh huh," Tony said.

The dent was on the driver's side, the way he'd parked against the curb. Along with everything else, it seemed Marlon Bando was also a liar. Right now, he had other things on his mind and decided to worry about his new partner at a later time.

Chapter Eight

Morning shades of purple and pink had begun replacing French Quarter neon when the ringing phone by my bed awakened me from a troubled dream. A baritone voice richly flavored with yawls, cain'ts, and idn'ts, quickly gave me instructions.

"Wyatt Thomas. You awake enough to hear me talking at you?"

"Who is this?" was my sleepy reply.

"Meet me at Antoine's in two hours and I'll tell you all you need to know."

The mystery caller slammed down the phone without waiting for an answer. Blinking away the cobwebs shrouding my crusty eyes, I climbed out of bed, wondering if I were awake or still in the middle of the dream.

My cat, Kisses, was glad I was up. Stalking outside to her feeding bowl on the balcony, and then back again, she quickly let me know she was hungry. As I refilled her food and water bowls, I glanced at the street below, tourists already passing. A late, winter bite dominated the weather. It was a dreary, gray day with no sun in sight.

Mardi Gras madness rocked the Big Easy with music playing almost everywhere, along with the distant sound of a marching band as I left my upstairs room at Bertram's and made my way to the French

Quarter restaurant for my meeting with the unknown caller.

Though tourists waiting to get into Antoine's didn't seem to mind the chill air, I was ready to seek out a heated room and have a stiff drink. If I were still drinking, that is. A waiter, composed and refreshed in his white tux, rescued me from the crowd and my dilemma, much to the ire of the others in line. Bypassing them, I followed him inside.

Taking a detour away from the main dining room, we hurried down a narrow hallway. The waiter tapped twice on a cypress door, opened it a crack, and then motioned me to enter. He disappeared down the hall as I glanced at the doorway. When I opened it and went inside, warm air whooshed around my head. The room's warmth would have refreshed me except for the cloud of harsh-smelling smoke hanging in the air.

Rich mahogany paneling, along with paintings of French, pastoral scenes, graced the windowless walls. Overhead an enormous chandelier hung from the twelve-foot ceiling. It crowned the room's only large piece of furniture: a Louis XIV desk. The imposing desk was no reproduction.

A lone man in an expensive, beige suit and yellow, silk tie occupied the desk, not bothering to stand when I entered the room. Instead, he pointed to an empty chair. A Mardi Gras mask covered with rhinestones and sequins hid his identity. At least he thought. On the desk, a plate of crawfish etouffee lay pushed aside, its spicy aroma reminding me I'd missed breakfast.

Cigarette butts lay strewn in and out of the ashtray beside his hand, indicating his disregard for the burn marks he was putting on the expensive desk. Puffing on one through the mouth-opening in his mask, he came straight to the point.

"I got a job for you, Mr. Thomas. You interested?"

"At your service," I said.

My answer must have pleased him because he slumped back into the thickly stuffed, leather chair, deflating as he exhaled smoke and watched it rise in distorted rings to the ornate ceiling.

He paused to see if I were paying attention, then said, "You know who I am?"

"No sir," I said, shaking my head for emphasis. "I don't believe I do."

My reply brought an empty chuckle from behind his mask, and it immediately drew into a hacking cough.

When he regained control, he said, "You a liar, Mr. Thomas. I can tolerate a liar. Not a fool. Tell me what you know about me and don't mince words."

I did recognize his distinctively gruff voice and thought I had even after his phone call that morning. Now I was sure. He was president and C.E.O. of the largest, local bank in New Orleans, a man that did his own TV commercials and was heir apparent to the vast Vallee banking fortune. His face was recognizable to every person within transmission range, and I was convinced it was the face behind the mask.

"You're Gordon Vallee. Most prominent banker in New Orleans. Rumor has it you're also President of the Pickwick Club."

"The Pickwick Club is secret. Tell me what you know about it."

"The City's most powerful, social organization, controlling local elections, sewage disposal, and probably everything in between. Blacks, Jews, and women need not apply."

"You a smart man. What else you know about it?"

"The Club is exclusive, impossible to buy into, as many Texas oil barons have learned. Inheritance is about the only way to gain entrance. Members are also part of the Mistick Krewe of Shiraz, the most influential club in the Carnival hierarchy."

Vallee was grinning when he removed his mask. Dark hair, graying at the temples, crowned his head and brown, liquid eyes dominated his angular facial features.

"You pass Thomas. I got a little problem and need your help."

"I'm listening," I said.

Vallee leaned forward, rested his elbows on the desk and clasped his hands together, his dramatic gesture emphasizing a diamond pinkie-ring and gold links in his French-cuffed shirt. He removed a roll of bills from his coat pocket, counted out a thousand dollars in hundred dollar bills and shoved them across the desk toward me.

"Someone is spreading lies about me. Saying I'm a passeblanc."

"Who's going to believe that?"

"In this town, you never know."

I immediately understood Vallee's problem. A passeblanc is someone whose skin is fair enough to allow them to hide their black ancestry and pass for white. The all-white membership of the Pickwick Club would not tolerate any such breach, and distress pealed like a bell in Vallee's voice.

"Lots of folks in New Orleans have black roots. It doesn't mean you're trying to pass for white."

Vallee banged his fist on the desk and glared at me. I understood his less than subtle point before he ever replied to my comment.

"Don't know about you, Thomas, but there ain't a single drop of nigger blood in this body of mine. My ancestors and I mean all of them, were lily white."

"No problem. I can document everything for you with a little time spent at the Notarial Archives."

"That ain't good enough. I want the rumors stopped and the sooner the better."

"Someone apparently has it in for you. Any idea who it might be?"

"Hell yes, I got an idea. I'm certain it's that snake Claude Sonnier. He's done his best to break me for the past twenty years. I ain't done him any favors either," he said, sending a cloud of dark smoke toward the ceiling.

"What do you want me to do besides providing you with documentation?"

"Hell, just prove I'm white." Vallee glanced at his

diamond-encrusted Rolex and said, "You got a week to take care of this for me."

"What's the rush?"

"That's when the club votes on next year's King of Shiraz. I'm the prime candidate. Now you see my problem?"

I did. Unlike Rex, which elected its annual king because of merit, Shiraz was a social club, its members occupying the rarified air of only the highest strata of old New Orleans' elite. All, or most, were also members of the Pickwick Club. Even a hint of someone less than lily white serving as king would result in a major loss of respect for the club. It was something the members wouldn't tolerate.

"Men have paid a fortune for that crown," I said.

Vallee allowed himself a smile. "Some even killed for it."

"Not you, I hope."

Vallee didn't answer. "You prove I'm not a passeblanc, and there's another thousand in it for you. Shouldn't be hard because obviously I'm not."

"And if you are, you want me to cook the results?"

Vallee didn't care for my suggestion, or my cynicism. After pounding the desk with his fist, he quickly lit another Picayune.

"Not funny, Thomas. If I thought I had an ounce of black blood, I'd kill myself, but not before I killed that bastard Sonnier first."

"I'll do my best."

"Like I said, that ain't good enough. Give me some help on this so I can defend myself. Here's my card. Call me when you get something I can use."

Taking the business card, I nodded and started for the door, hearing a bang as I grasped the handle. Wheeling around, I saw bits of broken china shattered across the desk and floor, mingled with red lumps of crawfish and etouffee sauce. Vallee had smashed the priceless plate with his fist.

I didn't miss the indication of a threat when he said, "Don't let me down, Thomas."

Lines of locals and tourists continued waiting on the sidewalk as I left Antoine's. Though tourists crowded the main streets, the Quarter's side streets remained deserted, poised for the nightly onslaught of tourists, con artists, and police. Only one old man, sweeping the sidewalk outside a restaurant, and a shine boy chasing after a lone tourist, braved the chill.

I set out to question the one person I knew might have a clue about the mystery that Gordon Vallee had presented me with. As I strolled down Royal Street on my way back to Bertram's, I passed Madeline's Magic Potions. Although I was strangely curious about what I might see behind the antique door, I just kept walking.

Chapter Nine

Bertram Picou's bar was just off Chartres Street. When I reached it, I found the radiator working overtime, the place empty except for Bertram and Lady, his ageless collie. Pulling up a stool at the bar, I relaxed, loosened my tie and let Lady lick my hand.

The place was bigger than it looked from the outside and was often filled to capacity, especially during Mardi Gras, the Jazz Festival, or any of the many other celebrations the town hosted during the year. I had no idea how old the building was, but the grooves and marks on the worn, wood floor attested to thousands of feet that had danced and trod on it.

"My man," Bertram said as he poured pink lemonade from a chilled pitcher he kept beneath the countertop for me. "You out and about awful early this morning."

"I'm up this early every morning. I had some place I needed to go to," I said.

"You back here to get in out of the cold?"

It rarely got extremely cold in New Orleans, and I could count on the fingers of one hand the times the city had seen it snow. This year was different with warmish days becoming cold nights, the humidity making high thirties feel like winter in Alaska.

Bertram's accent was straight from the bayou though so was his heart. Like my Dad used to say about him, if you tied his hands behind his back, he wouldn't be able to communicate. I sipped the lemonade before answering.

"If I were, I'd have gone somewhere else. This place is so drafty it's no wonder your customers have deserted you and gone down the street."

Bertram knew I was trying to goad him into a friendly squabble. This time, he didn't take the bait.

"This the coldest Mardi Gras I can remember. I think tourists are holed up in their hotels, calling room service and watching parades on television. They sure ain't out on the streets like they usually are."

"They just haven't gotten here yet. There are tourists out all over the Quarter."

"Well they better hurry."

"I'm here," I said, patting Lady's head and rubbing her ears.

"And you damn sure ain't down here to see my homely face. Need to borrow money?"

"Why hell no," I said. "My new client just paid me a clean grand."

Regretting the blurted reply the moment it flew from my mouth, I reached for my wallet. Bertram waited until I'd counted out five of the hundreds Vallee had given me, putting them in his extended hand.

"With that tie on and all, I should have figured that someone must have hired your scrawny ass to do something or other. Guess now I'll have to take back all those nasty things I been saying about you," he said with a smile.

"Don't put yourself out."

"I'm sorry to hear about your ex."

"Thanks. I didn't realize until I went to her wake how close I was to her family. They're taking it pretty hard."

"Hell, she never even made forty. I heard she fought the Big C hard. Life just ain't fair sometimes."

"Tell me about it. Makes me think my drinking days weren't so far out of place."

My comment caused Bertram to stare at the ceiling,

twist his mustache and shake his head. "Some of us can hold our liquor. You ain't one of those people."

He was right, and I tipped my glass to him.

"You don't need to remind me. I wouldn't be here today if it weren't for you and this pink stuff you keep sticking in front of me."

"Stop your damn whining. You know you like it."

"I never liked lemonade even when I was a kid. Now I can't live without it. Go figure."

"You didn't come here just to complain about my lemonade, or to pay ol' Bertram his rent. What else you got rattlin' inside that head of yours?"

"That's why I like you so much, Bertram. You're one smart coonass. I do need to pick your brain a bit."

Bertram winked and topped up the glass with more of the pink concoction.

"Yeah, you just about picked it clean, last time you needed information." After removing his trapper's hat, he tapped his head a time or two with his index finger. "Everyone else pays for the vegetables that come from this garden. You like some lop-eared rabbit that sneaks through the fence and just takes what he wants."

Bertram's sentences had no Rs and few Ds, and when he talked he seemed as if he were about to knock over all the bottles and glasses with his wildly gesticulating arms. The trapper's hat always topped his dark, thinning hair tied in a pigtail. To satisfy the tourist's idea of what a Cajun should look like, he always said. He needed neither the hat nor the pigtail, looking like a Cajun because he was one, his family from Terrebonne Parish in southwest Louisiana

"Hey, who's whining now?" I said. "It doesn't become you."

"And damn sure don't do me no good, either. Now what information you come for this time?"

"I got a call this morning from someone who wanted to hire me and wouldn't tell me who he was. I met him in one of those private meeting rooms at Antoine's and turns out it was Gordon Vallee. You know who I'm talking about?"

"Does an alligator drink bayou water?"

"Mr. Vallee has a little problem and hired me to get some answers for him. Seems he thinks Claude Sonnier is spreading lies around town about him. What can you tell me about Vallee and Sonnier?"

Bertram spat on the floor behind the counter, then rolled his eyes and the end of his mustache between his fingers. There was still no one in the bar except us, but suspicious by nature he took a slow look around to make sure of it before answering my question.

"Don't pay sometimes to get caught talking about people in this town, especially behind their backs."

"No one's here but me and Vallee's paying me, remember?"

"Guess that's a fact. Gordon Vallee and Claude Sonnier are two peas in a pod, far as I'm concerned. Between the two of them, they got more money than Ben Gump, and I suspect more power than most any other big shot in N.O."

"That I already know. What else?"

"Both their families big in banking. Their papas and mamas was best friends. The boys was raised next door to each other in the Garden District. Just like their parents, they was also best buddies, inseparable, by all accounts. Don't matter they don't look anything alike because people still thought they was brothers. Somewhere along the line, their friendly rivalry turned ugly. By all accounts, they hate each other's guts now."

"I've heard that. Any idea what the problem might be?"

"Don't have a clue, and I ain't sure nobody else does either, except maybe them two. What else you need? All that's just common knowledge. Stuff I'm sure you already knew."

"There's one other thing. Is Gordon Vallee a passeblanc?"

Bertram laughed and said, "Why hell no."

"No way?"

"No damn way! Where you come up with that crazy

idea?"

"I didn't come up with it. Vallee's adamant someone's trying to ruin his reputation, spreading rumors he's a passeblanc. Claude Sonnier is his prime suspect."

"That would ruin it, all right, if some of his highfalutin buddies found out it was so. Still, I ain't ever heard nothing like that."

"Maybe you know someone that has."

Bertram glanced around the empty bar again, and then poured a straight shot of Cuervo Gold for himself from a half empty bottle he kept hidden under the bar. After draining the shot, he poured another.

"Mama Marlene used to be Vallee's housekeeper, and his folks' before that. Until he fired her, that is. Claude Sonnier hired her the next day. She been working for him ever since."

The temperature outside was rising, along with pedestrian traffic on the sidewalk. When someone opened the door to check the place out, street sounds flooded the room. Bertram shook his head and grinned when some Arkansas football fan began calling the hogs.

"Hell, it ain't even noon yet. Guess you were right about the traffic out on the streets. I can already tell it's gonna get wild in here tonight."

"Do you know why Vallee fired Mama Marlene?" I asked, getting him back on track.

Bertram removed his hat, mopping his brow with a bar rag. "You got me on that one."

"You think she might know something about this passeblanc rumor?"

"Hell, she pretty much raised those two from the day they was born. If there's something to know worth knowing about them, you can bet she does."

"Where can I find her?"

"She got an apartment over in the Project. Everybody over there know her."

"Thanks Bertram. She sounds like the next person I need to talk to."

Drumbeats and bass strains of a marching band over in Jackson Square replaced the hum of the old electric fan turning slowly overhead. Bertram rested his elbows on the bar, staring at me.

"You okay about Mimsy and everything?"

"It's bothered me a bit, seeing everyone again under those circumstances. Mimsy's hair was gone because of radiation and chemo treatments, so they had her in a horrible wig. I don't like remembering her like that."

"Hell, there ain't nothing much good you can say about a funeral," he said.

"That's a fact, not to mention I had to face Father Alphonso about not attending mass in more years now than I care to count."

"How did that work out?"

"He tried to get me to confess, right then and there, and almost had a cat when I talked with Mimsy's ex."

"You mean the man that married her after you two split the sheets?"

"That's right. He's a defrocked priest now, and Father Alphonso didn't like having him around. For that matter, neither did anyone else. I was the only one that would talk to him."

"What'd he do to get defrocked?"

"Nothing that sounds reasonable to me. Seems his mother's a witch."

"Hell, so is my ex mother-in-law. You two probably had lots to talk about. I don't see how anyone can fault you for that."

"Father Alphonso did. He and Mimsy's ex Rafael did agree on one thing, though. They both think I have problems with faith."

"Do you?"

"Don't know. Father Alphonso is insisting I confess, and Rafael wants me to visit his mother's shop, Madeline's Magic Potions. It's not far from here. I passed by it today."

"And?"

"I just kept walking."

"You going back?"

Several rowdy tourists entered Bertram's before I could answer. The marching band echoing through the open door sounded closer and louder. Bertram slapped a rag across the crook of his arm, confiding one more piece of information.

"You got good ears, Cowboy, and you'll hear this soon enough. Feds are crawling all over the place, asking questions and hassling tourists. They been in here twice already."

"Any idea what they're looking for?"

"Don't know, but I'm trying to find out. Maybe you should ask your detective friend Tony. I also heard his partner got stabbed."

"Tommy? He's alive I hope."

"Barely, I heard. They got him in intensive care, so he musta got hurt pretty bad."

I finished my lemonade, patted Lady's head and started upstairs to my room. My cat Kisses would be waiting for some kitty treats. She's a talker, and I knew I'd have hell to pay if I waited much longer.

"Thanks, Bertram. I owe you one."

"Yeah," he said, killing his third shot of Cuervo before heading for the noisy tourist's table. "See you next time you need another helping of ol' Bertram's vegetables."

Chapter Ten

When Greta opened her eyes she was lying in bed, her black nightgown soaked in sweat. Jacque was beside her, holding her hand. Though slumped forward he was sitting up with his eyes closed. He opened them when she pulled her hand loose.

"You're alive," he said. "I was worried for a while."

Someone had brought a room service tray while she'd slept. Removing a silver lid, he showed her what was beneath it. The aroma wafting from the bowl reminded her she couldn't remember the last time she'd eaten.

"I got chicken soup for you. My mother used to make it for me when I was sick. I know you must be hungry so don't turn it down just because it's from me. I'll leave it on the tray beside the bed. You can eat whenever you feel like it."

More than hungry, she was starving. When he went into the bathroom and shut the door, she eyed the bowl of soup with desire, but refused to touch it. Jacque glanced at it, and then at her, when he returned.

"If you don't care about yourself, you should think about your baby. I have to go out for a bit, and I need to lock you back to the bedpost. Do you have to go to the bathroom before I do?"

Greta didn't answer, slipping into the bathroom

and closing the door behind her. When she returned, he cuffed her to the bedpost.

"I won't be gone long," he said.

When he shut the cabin door behind him, she reached for the bowl of soup with her free hand and slurped down every drop. Velvet jumped up on the bed, licking the bowl when it was offered to her, then curling up beside Greta and closing her eyes.

Whatever had caused her fever was gone for now, along with her unsettled stomach, leaving her nightgown and bedclothes damp. For whatever reason, the tall man didn't frighten her. She hoped he'd return soon and unlock the cuffs, so she could crawl under the blanket.

The little room was dark, only a dim glow from the bathroom lighting the cabin walls that were all but soundproof. She thought she heard the clamor of people somewhere in the distance, but realized it was probably just her imagination.

Jacque smiled when he saw the empty soup bowl upon returning to the room an hour or so later. Seeing her shoulders quivering, he quickly unlocked the cuffs. When she reclined in the bed, he pulled the blanket up around her shoulders and tucked her in, Velvet snuggling against her on top of the bedclothes.

"You were delirious last night. I don't understand your language, but every now and then you would speak in English."

Though Greta continued the silent treatment, at least her angry glare had dissipated. Occasionally, he'd turn around and see her staring at him. During one such instance, he thought she'd almost smiled. Seeing her now, radiant in her nightgown, he wished he'd met her under different circumstances. She was the girl in his wildest dreams. The person he never thought he'd meet. She already had him thinking irrational thoughts, and he knew it was probably the kiss of death—his death.

Greta's little cabin was ominously quiet. When

Velvet barked, they both stared at her. Jacque grinned, and he noticed Greta also did, though she quickly tried to hide it.

"She's hungry again," he said. "Or thirsty."

Turning his attention from Greta, he filled Velvet's water cup and another with hamburger from the room service tray. When the little dog finished eating and slurping water, Jacque picked her up, hugged, and kissed her.

His back was turned to her when she said, "My name is Greta."

With Kisses fed and pampered, I left my little room above Bertram's bar and took a walk, braving the Carnival crazies dominating the French Quarter. Now, I stood outside on the sidewalk, staring at cut glass and gold lettering on the ancient door proclaiming Madeline's Magic Potions, wondering if I should go in or just keep walking. Before I could do either, a woman opened the door.

"I'm Madeline. Please come inside," she said, her firm tone indicating the answer no wasn't a satisfactory response.

I followed her into the shop, waiting as she locked the door behind us and placed a closed sign in the window. Lighting was dim, air a mixture of age and incense. An old rotating fan whirred on the cabinet, setting up a tinkling crescendo when its breeze encountered a wind chime decorated with gargoyles. A black cat lay on the front cabinet, pawing a toy mouse.

Madeline had long, brown hair tinged with ample gray that touched the orange and black, crocheted Afghan draping her shoulders. Her dark dress covered even her feet and dragged across the tiles of the old shop's well-worn floor.

The droning chorus of a Gregorian chant emanated from hidden speakers, adding to spiritual feelings saturating my mind since entering the little shop. Old wooden display cabinets, filled with candles, incense, and colorful crystals divided the area. Eclectic art for sale varied from fire-breathing dragons and gargoyles to art deco prints of Elvis and Marilyn Monroe. A suit of armor stood alone in a corner.

Madeline led me through the maze to a dark room in back lined with jars filled with various secret potions. The black cat followed us, winding between my legs as I walked. Madeline sat at a small table and began shuffling a deck of Tarot cards.

"Have a seat," she said, pointing to the high-backed chair facing her on the opposite side of the table. Seeing my confusion, she stopped shuffling the cards. "You are here for a reading, aren't you?"

I shook my head. "I'm not sure why I'm here."

Madeline took my answer as a yes and continued shuffling. When tires screeched outside the shop, we both flinched at the sound of an ensuing crash. Madeline shook her head and placed the cards on the table.

When she smiled, I could see the resemblance she bore to her son. Both had long, curved noses, olive complexions, and mysterious faces often possessed by successful, runway models. Unlike her son's, her eyes were dark, not Rafael's unusual shade of gray. Her cat rubbed against my legs, and I scratched him behind his ears.

"Jinx likes you. It means you are a trustworthy person. The cards will tell me who you truly are."

It was my turn to smile. "Then perhaps you should read them for me."

Madeline nodded. Taking a long match from the cabinet behind her, she lit the two candles bordering the little table. Their flickering light seemed to meld with must and muffled chants. Tapping the deck once with her gnarly index finger, she handed it to me.

"Shuffle the cards and then cut them into seven stacks."

After following her directions, I watched as she arranged the stacks into a unique shape, flipping over the top cards of each. She studied them and then stared at me, as if trying to penetrate my eyes to see what answers my mind possessed. *Dies Irae*, a chant I recognized, began playing.

"You are in conflict and seek enlightenment. You are torn between whom to trust and what to believe. I also see something else."

I hung on her words, almost afraid she had something sinister to tell me.

"Please go on."

"Destinies have intersected. You have met a powerful person. Danger stalks him, and you are inextricably involved. It is a good thing you called when you did."

Madeline stopped talking when I shook my head. "I didn't call you."

"But—"

"I came because of your son."

"You know Rafael?"

"We were married to the same woman. He told me about you when we talked at Mimsy's wake."

Madeline reached across the table and grasped my hand. "He said he saw you there. I'm so sorry for your loss. Rafael was devastated. I wish I could have attended the wake with him, but—"

"I know. Father Alphonso. He called you a witch."

"I am a witch."

I waited for her to smile. She didn't. "This town is teeming with voodoo shops, soothsayers, and every manner of religious charlatan. Surely Father Alphonso can't fault you for making a living."

Madeline released my hand and drew back in her chair. "I'm not a religious charlatan. I have a gift and use it to help people."

"I didn't mean you, and I certainly can't see that what you do is the work of the—"

"Devil?"

I nodded again. "That's how Father Alphonso made it seem."

"All religions have roots in pagan beliefs. Catholicism is no different. Father Alphonso has no room to talk because mysticism did much to define his own religion. Still, religious persecution is rampant, even here in the City of Spirits." Madeline stood from the little table and snuffed out the candles with her fingers. "I am rude. Have tea with me and we will chat further."

Her black cat, Jinx, still rubbing against my legs, followed us out to a tiled patio in back of the shop. Like many shop owners in the Quarter, Madeline lived behind and above her storefront.

"Have a seat on the bench, and I will be right back."

As Madeline disappeared through a doorway, I sat on the park bench facing a stone fountain centering the flagstone patio. Several colorful, flower pots occupied spaces around the fountain. I heard what sounded like the fluttering of wings behind me and turned when someone spoke. At least I thought it was a person.

"Nevermore."

A large black bird, its head bobbing, sat on a perch suspended from the second-story balcony. I glanced around to see who it was that had said hello.

"Hello, I'm Wyatt. Who are you?" I asked.

The bird repeated my words.

"Hello, I'm Wyatt. Nevermore."

"You're a gorgeous and stately bird," I said, quite amazed. "Do you have a name?"

Madeline, returning from the kitchen with a pot of tea, answered my question.

"I call her Calpurnia because she's as regal as Caesar's last wife. Maybe you think I named her after the Finch family cook and maid in *To Kill a Mockingbird*." She laughed. "I named her after the Addams family's great-aunt that was burned as a witch in 1706. She learned her favorite word from some fan of Poe."

I took the cup of hot tea Madeline handed me. "Then she's a raven?"

"Yes. She calls this patio home, although she comes and goes whenever she pleases."

Jinx seemed agitated by Calpurnia's presence, his long tail moving back and forth in synchronous swipes.

"I don't think they like each other."

"Cats and birds are like fire and water. Still, these two somehow manage to coexist."

Madeline joined me on the bench. "Your son is a defrocked priest. You aren't Catholic, are you?"

"Very much so. I was once a nun."

"Once? What happened?"

"The sisters were reluctant to allow a pregnant teenager to remain in their order. Even if the father were a Father."

"Rafael's father is a priest?"

"A priest that liked idolizing women and made sure he took advantage of the situation. Enough about me. It is you that has a problem."

"Me?"

"My reading was very real."

"I don't know that I believe you."

"Because I use Tarot cards?"

"You could have told me anything. How would I know the difference?"

Jinx walked between my legs, causing Calpurnia to flap her wings. I thought she was about to fly away. She didn't. After Madeline had poured more tea, she continued.

"There are many ways to get a glimpse of the future: throwing bones, tea leaves, and crystal balls. Some Buddhists can recognize human auras, determining objectives by the color of the aura. It's called the third eye."

"Forgive me if I'm skeptical."

Madeline smiled, sipping her tea before answering. "What do you see when you look in a mirror?"

"My reflection."

"How do you know what you look like?"

"From pictures I've seen of myself, since I was very young."

"Your face in the mirror is the exact opposite of

whom you are. You think it is you because someone you trusted, perhaps your mother, told you it was so."

"What's your point?"

"What I am trying to say is we often accept things because of blind faith."

"I can't accept what you say because of blind faith as you put it."

"Suit yourself, though sometimes it is the only way to achieve an answer."

Calpurnia interrupted our conversation when she again said, "Hi, I'm Wyatt."

"She is fixated on you."

Jinx continued to rub against my leg. "So is your cat," I said.

"Do you have pets?"

"A tailless tabby named Kisses."

"Cats are independent and intelligent creatures."

"I'm not sure how you know so much about me, though what you told me rings true."

Madeline nodded and took my hand again. "Cards never lie. Heed them or suffer the consequences."

Chapter Eleven

Tony quickly learned that Marlon was ill-prepared to drive a car in New Orleans. After narrowly missing several vehicles and a couple of pedestrians, he'd slammed on the brakes, screeching to a halt as a mule-drawn carriage walked into his path. Tony closed his eyes, rubbed his forehead, and then pointed to a parking lot facing the river.

"My heart can't take much more of this. Park this thing before you kill us both."

"I'm not used to driving in the city," Marlon said.

"You're preaching to the choir here. You'll get the hang of it. Meantime, I need a few Dixies to steel my nerves."

Marlon parked the patrol car and then followed Tony to the sidewalk. The sky was beginning to darken, a late winter, early spring storm moving in from the Gulf.

"Where are we going?"

"There's a terrific little café around the corner. They got good food and cold Dixie. It's close enough to lunch, and I need a break."

Almost noon, a myriad of tourists were roaming the Vieux Carré; some were masked, costumed, and noticeably inebriated. Tony ignored them as he headed down the street. Marlon followed him into an old masonry building facing the river, and then up a short flight of stairs to a little café few tourists knew existed. The name on the door said Café Jamaica. When a large woman in a flowing, African-print dress and matching turban saw Tony, she grinned, grabbed his arm and led him to a table in front of a picture window overlooking the Mississippi river. Her bright, yellow dress had no detectable waistline, her face devoid of even a single wrinkle. She looked no older than forty though Tony knew she was probably pushing sixty-five.

"Lieutenant Tony, where you been?"

"Working like a dog. I managed to drag myself over here to get some of your delicious cooking. Marlon, this is Jamaica, best cook in New Orleans."

Marlon extended his hand, but Jamaica just smiled and slapped his shoulder.

"Glad to meet you Marlon. Where's Tommy?"

"A Chicano gangbanger sliced him up pretty bad. He's gonna be okay, but Marlon here's my partner until he pulls through."

"Damned illegals," she said. "They's starting to take over everything.

"Thank Katrina for that!" Tony said. "And the money F.E.M.A. was tossing out. What this country needs is better immigration laws."

Jamaica grinned. "Hell, Lieutenant, there wouldn't be a living soul in Nawlins if they had that law."

"Guess you're right about that. We'll have to make do till they trade in their tacos, and start liking gumbo."

Jamaica nodded. "And until they do, they's one minority we can all hate."

Marlon frowned when Tony grinned, and said, "Amen to that, sister."

"You don't have to tell me what you want to eat. I already know," she said.

Jamaica put her beefy hand on Marlon's shoulder. "You look like you can put away lots of gumbo."

"What he can't, I can," Tony said.

"You so full of shit," she said, grinning as she

signaled a waiter with her wagging finger. "Francois, bring these two gentlemen ice-cold Dixies, and two-dozen oysters."

"That your grandson?" Tony asked.

Jamaica slapped his shoulder. "That's why you're such a fine cop. You don't ever forget nothing."

"Or bad cop, depending on which side of the law you're on."

Jamaica grinned, popping his shoulder again as the Dixies and oysters arrived.

"Oysters are on me, Lieutenant."

"Jamaica, I know you're married, but bend down here and let me give you a kiss," he said.

The large woman was still grinning when she put her arms around Tony's neck, and he kissed her, right on the mouth. In a swirl of yellow cotton, she hurried away, back to the kitchen.

The café was tiny, no more than a dozen tables, all filled with happy diners, their knives and forks clinking a rhythmic tune. A barge with a tugboat pushing it appeared through wispy fog forming on the river. Tony and Marlon had the best seat in the house, a grand view through the big window.

Tony forked an oyster into his mouth, red sauce soon dribbling down his chin. Despite Marlon's concern, Tony didn't bother wiping it off as he quickly consumed half the oysters. When he noticed Marlon wasn't eating, he wiped his chin, placing the napkin on the red and white, checkerboard tablecloth.

"What?"

"I'm a vegetarian," Marlon said.

"Where the hell you from, Marlon? Oysters ain't animals they're shellfish."

"I don't eat shellfish."

Tony turned his head, staring out at the line of tourists on the Moon Walk (the path along the river named for longtime mayor Moon Landrieu) waiting to enter the day cruiser docked below. Some of them were glancing up at the darkening sky.

"Peachy," he finally said. "You gonna starve to

death in this town."

When Jamaica returned to their table, she said, "Why aren't you eating your gumbo?"

"He's a vegetarian," Tony said, answering for him. "And he don't drink, either."

"Why didn't you say so?" she said, pushing the gumbo to Tony's side of the table. "I'll get you something else."

Tony finished his Dixie, and his bowl of gumbo, and was starting on Marlon's food when Jamaica and her grandson Francois returned with something different for Marlon and more beer for Tony. Marlon smiled when she put the steaming plate in front of him.

"Smells wonderful," he said.

"My own recipe. Greens stewed with okra and fresh tomatoes, and a bowl of my famous red beans and rice, no sausage. And Marlon, I cooked everything in corn oil. I'm a vegetarian too."

Francois popped the cap off a bottle of Perrier, pouring it into a glass for Marlon.

"We don't drink river water around here, either. Enjoy," she said as she left the table, gracefully winding her way back to the kitchen.

Tony watched as Marlon tore into the meal. "Glad to see you got an appetite. I was beginning to worry about you."

"I never knew you could make vegetables taste this good," Marlon finally said.

"And you keep eating only vegetables?"

"Personal reasons."

"You wear a belt and shoes, don't you? They're made from leather."

"My belt and shoes are made out of synthetic materials. I don't exploit animals in any way."

"Whatever," Tony said, turning his chair toward the window.

When Marlon finished the last tasty morsel of beans and rice, he gazed out the window at the twin bridges partially cloaked by rolling fog spanning the river.

"I love the river, and the twin bridges are just gorgeous."

"You ought to see them at night, all lit up; two beautiful river ladies."

"They aren't far from where the murder occurred. Any ideas yet?"

"You read the report. What do you think?"

"Except for neck abrasions there were no injuries to the body. No tattoos or identifying marks. No identification. No report of a missing person."

"Nothing but a brick wall."

"Still, there are a few things," Marlon said.

"Yeah?"

"Like you told the woman at the casino, whoever killed him probably did it for his clothes. That seems plausible because the killer had to be as large as the victim, and stronger, if he killed him with his bare hands like the report indicates."

"Go on," Tony said.

"The Feds were at the murder scene last night. Why are they investigating a local murder?"

"Because they're interested in the killer, for some reason?"

"A killer that needed someone else's clothes because all he had to wear was prison garb."

"Bingo!" Tony said, snapping his finger. "We're dealing with an escaped prisoner."

"Not just any prisoner. A Federal prisoner. And what the Feds know, they're keeping to themselves for some reason."

Tony threw some money on the table. "Great food Miss Jamaica. Catch you next time."

Marlon hurried after him, down the short flight of stairs. When they reached the sidewalk, Tony bent over and grabbed his knee.

"Oh hell! I knew I should've had another Dixie."

"Try these instead," Marlon said, handing him two pills.

"What are they?"

"Naproxen. Perfect for pain. Take the bottle. You

need them more than me."

Tony didn't argue, taking the bottle and swallowing the two pills.

Light rain was falling when they exited the building and ran for the car.

"Thanks for the pills," Tony said. "Now we got some work to do, and I hate computers."

"Then take a nap, and let me do it. I'm pretty proficient with them," Marlon said.

Except for an occasional whimper from Velvet, Greta's cabin was quiet. Exhaustion had finally caught up with her, and she lay with her head buried in the pillow. When she finally awoke and got out of bed, she became ill again, rushing to the bathroom to throw up until there was nothing left in her stomach but burning acid.

"It's not the concussion," Jacque said when she returned to the bed. "It's the baby. How pregnant are you?"

"Three months."

"You sure about that?"

"I know the very minute it was conceived."

Jacque started to say something but changed his mind, popping the top on a can of Sprite he'd bought from the soft drink machine down the hallway.

"Drink some of this. It'll help settle your stomach." Jacque handed her the soda, along with several crackers. "These are always good for a queasy stomach."

"Why are you being nice to me if you intend to kill me later on?"

"I'm not going to kill you. I'd have left hours ago if I'd thought you were okay."

Jacque was telling the truth. He needed to leave; get as far away from the ship as fast as possible. He also knew something else—he should kill the young woman and dispose of her body before he did. The thought troubled him more than he cared to admit.

The psychiatrist who had worked with him in

prison had said he killed without remorse. That was mostly true. He didn't kill because he liked it. He was adept at it, a point that had not gone unnoticed by organized crime lords he'd previously worked for. Still, taking a life or even the idea of taking a life had never bothered him, at least until now.

Velvet had fallen asleep beside Greta. Reacting to her voice, she awoke and began licking her face. Greta smiled broadly. Grabbing the dog, she hugged it to her breast.

"*Min lite kjærlighet*," she said. "My little love."

Jacque stared at her. It would be so easy to kill her now. Grasp her throat and squeeze until there was no life left in her. She wouldn't even suffer much.

"Jacque."

"Yes?"

"Are you still here?"

"I'm not going anywhere."

After a long pause, Greta said, "You never told me why you're a fugitive. What crime did you commit?"

"Things I'm not proud of."

"I'm finding it hard to think of you as a terrible person. I know I should be afraid of you, but I'm not."

"I'm just someone that came from a dark and terrible place and had nowhere else to go."

"And you killed Harald."

"Yes, and if I'd known beforehand what he'd done to you, I'd have made him suffer miserably before I let him die."

"It doesn't bother you to snuff out someone's life?"

"No. Don't ask me why. I have no answer."

"How many people have you killed?"

"A few," he said.

"And you say it doesn't bother you?"

"No."

"That's hard for me to believe."

"My profession apparently troubles you much more than it does me," he said with a grin. "Soldiers in combat mow down people; father's protecting their families shoot intruders; police officers in the line of duty kill armed robbers. What's the difference?"

"I would never hurt anyone for any reason. I'm pretty sure of it," she said.

"Yes you would. You fought Harald when he attacked you. I can tell by the marks on your hands and arms. You weren't just fighting for yourself. You were protecting your unborn baby. I have no doubt you would have killed him before letting him harm your child."

"That's different."

"How is it different?"

"It wouldn't have been premeditated."

"Survival isn't a question of premeditation, it's about living another day and taking another breath."

"This isn't a jungle."

Jacque sat on the side of the bed and grasped her hand. "There is evil in the world, pure evil, and it usually appears in the form of ordinary humans, people like Harald. What else did he do to you?"

Greta didn't attempt to pull her hand free, or wipe away her tears that were now flowing freely.

"I never loved him. My father worked for Harald's father. Harald was nearly forty and had never married. I'm twenty-five."

"You were pushed into the relationship?"

Greta closed her eyes. When she opened them, she was staring at the ceiling.

"Bullied is more like it. When I told my father I wouldn't date Harald, he became very angry. He said I was selfish. He needed advancement in Harald's father's business, and said I could deliver it for him and my mother."

"I only saw him once," Jacque said. "He didn't seem that repulsive to me."

"Oh, he was an uncommonly handsome man, and well educated, but his heart was black and hard as a lump of coal. We dated until I told him it wasn't working out, and I wanted to end our relationship."

"And?"

"He told me how much he loved me and begged me

to marry him. I finally agreed."

"But why?"

"Because I was so confused. Everyone wanted the union to occur. I just got caught up in the madness. Before I knew it, the wedding plans had become a serious production."

"Still—"

Greta raised her hand to silence him. "I knew it would never work out, and I attempted to stop it. That was when he hit me the first time, and raped me. It was three months ago, the night I became pregnant."

"And then he forced you to marry him."

Greta nodded. "It was going to be the wedding of the decade. I told my mother I couldn't go through with the farce. It made her cry. She didn't understand. Like my father, she thought I was just being selfish. She begged me to reconsider."

"You didn't tell her what he'd done to you?"

"I didn't think anyone would believe me. I'm not sure I believed it myself. When we were in public, Harald was the nicest man in the world. When we were alone, he was like a different person."

"So you were badgered into the marriage."

"I didn't know what else to do. All my friends thought he was the catch of the century. I couldn't tell them he was a violent ogre."

"And nothing changed after the wedding?"

"We spent the first night of our honeymoon in a hotel, in Stavanger. Within hours, he'd slapped me so hard I thought he'd broken my nose. I spent my wedding night locked in the bathroom, praying he wouldn't break down the door."

"Why didn't you call the police?"

Tears streamed from Greta's eyes. "I just couldn't. My mother and father were counting on me. I felt so trapped. When we arrived here in New Orleans, things got worse. Harald's moods grew darker, and he became even more aggressive than before. There was nothing I could say or do to lessen his aggression. He said I was dirty, and he didn't even want to touch me, much less sleep with me."

"It's okay now."

"When he left, I called my parents and told them to come for me. They must have sensed the desperation in my voice because my father is now on his way here. To bully me into going back to Harald, I have no doubt."

Jacque pulled her close to him. "Harald's gone, and he'll never bother you again."

"Jacque," she said when her tears finally stopped flowing. "Will you sleep with me tonight?"

"I would be honored," he said, feeling the depth of her pain and seeing it in the crystal blue of her sad eyes.

Chapter Twelve

I spent the next morning at the Notarial Archives researching Gordon Vallee, and all of his relatives. New Orleans possesses a vast treasure trove of public information gathered since 1734. No place on earth has kept better or more detailed records and historical documents.

The archives contain a wealth of mortgage and demographic information—maps, plats, birth records, deeds, and examples of architectural and cultural history. To call it priceless is to minimize its irreplaceable historical significance.

Before Hurricane Katrina, I needed only to visit the repository, moved from the basement of the Civil Courts some years prior to the disaster, to get whatever information I had sought. Everything changed after the killer hurricane, including control of the invaluable mine of information. It didn't matter because it was still my first place to go when I was searching for information, no matter how obscure.

I quickly learned two things: Gordon Vallee and his nemesis Claude Sonnier were among the City's elite; both, by all accounts, had lily white lineages with not a bit of black blood as far back as I could find. Making copies of all relevant documents, I placed them in a folder to give to Gordon Vallee. Barring a surprising discovery the historical documents would be enough to prove Vallee's ethnic background. After replacing a thick leather-bound index book, I set out to visit Mama Marlene.

Before the killer hurricane, New Orleans had a secret area most tourists never saw—an interior barely hidden beneath a thin layer of wealth and replete with squalor and poverty. Such was the Iberville Project, once the site of Storyville, New Orleans' old red light district.

In the words of an old jazz musician, "Storyville was wide open."

What he meant was within the few blocks of a precisely drawn area, activities such as gambling and prostitution, though still illegal, wouldn't be prosecuted by local police. Because of its wide-open reputation, people visited from all over the world to sample the city's hospitality. Visitors to Storyville spread the word about jazz, the new music genre born in New Orleans, to all parts of the world. Because of Storyville, jazz quickly became a musical standard.

Storyville no longer exists, shut down by puritanical influences, perhaps the U.S. Navy, as some have suggested, during World War I. It was leveled to make room for the Iberville Housing Project. The Project became synonymous with drugs and gang crime. For years, police would only go into the Project during the day, and then only with a large contingency of well-armed police. Like the rest of New Orleans, Katrina changed the face of the Iberville Project.

The Project isn't far from million dollar homes owned by wealthy occupants on the far end of Bourbon Street. Before Katrina, I would have feared for my life had I gone there. With various drug gangs now permanently relocated to Dallas, Houston, and Kansas City because of the disaster, the danger was mostly gone. At least for the moment, I wasn't worried about visiting Mama Marlene.

When I stepped off the Canal streetcar, seagulls, winging toward Lake Pontchartrain dotted the sky over the project. They looked like blips of moving white against a motionless, pale-blue, canvas backdrop. The first person I asked told me where to find Mama Marlene. The old woman answered the door on the first knock, her dark hair seeming to thwart her age.

"I'm Wyatt Thomas," I said, handing her a bouquet of faded hothouse flowers I'd purchased from a vendor on Canal. "Are you Mama Marlene?"

"I am," she said in a scratchy voice wracked by too many cigarettes. "Do I know you?"

"I'm not selling anything, I promise. I do a little work for Mr. Vallee. He asked me to stop by and check on you."

"He did? Please come inside." I regretted having told a half truth to the old woman as I slipped past her into the apartment's tiny living room. She led me to a threadbare couch. "Sit down. Can I get you something to drink?"

"No thank you. Are you okay?"

"Got a bit of a cough," she said.

Mama Marlene pulled a pack of Camels from the flowered blouse draping her shrunken chest. Popping one out of the pack with a practiced flip, she rolled it between her lips. When she eyed the vintage Zippo on the coffee table beside a dirty ashtray, I got the hint and picked it up, using it to light the cigarette for her. Her long draw resulted in an expelled cloud of gray smoke, and a hacking cough that emanated from deep in her lungs.

"These things are gonna kill me one of these days. Don't matter much because life wouldn't be worth living without them." She looked at me again and said, "Why'd you say you was here?"

"Mr. Vallee wants to know if there is anything you need."

"Does he? He could have come by and found out for himself. I fed him, dressed him, and wiped his little butt until he was old enough to do it himself."

Mama Marlene took a long drag on her cigarette, and it sent her into another coughing jag. When she finally regained her breath, she drank from a glass of water sitting on the coffee table.

"I'm so proud Claude saw fit to hire me when Gordon let me go. Can I get you some water?"

"No thanks, I'm fine. Mr. Vallee never told me why he let you go."

"He's so sensitive sometimes. Got mad at something I said."

"Would you mind telling me what he was so sensitive about?"

"My old memory's gone south lately. I just can't remember."

"Do you have family of your own?"

"Besides Gordon, I got Vincent."

Mama Marlene's answer, or at least the way she said it caught me a bit off guard.

"Gordon is your son?"

"I raised him, didn't I?"

"Yes you did. Is your husband dead?"

When Mama Marlene laughed at my question, it sent her into yet another coughing jag, smoke billowing out of her mouth like a smoking cannon. After another drink of water, she remembered my question about her husband and tossed her head.

"A mean one, him. Vincent caught the old man slapping me, and he whipped him. Ain't seen the old fart since."

"Your son Vincent, he lives here in the city?"

"He got a house over in Bywater. He check on me most every day."

"What does he do for a living?"

"Vincent's in construction. Got family of his own now. They's light-skinned, like me."

"You're Creole,"

Mama nodded, smiling proudly. "I probably got more white blood in me than you do."

"Wouldn't surprise me," I said, grinning at her overtly racist statement. "You never know who's black or who's white around here."

"Ain't that the truth? Sure I can't get you a glass of water."

"Well, if it's no bother."

"Ain't no bother," she said, standing from the couch with some difficulty. "Ain't the best water in the world. Least it's wet," she said as she returned and handed me a glass.

"Like you said, it's wet, and it tastes good."

Mama Marlene grabbed the TV remote on the coffee table and turned on the television, a daytime soap crackling into view.

"You just keep talking, you. My soap's on, and I try to never miss it. What'd you say your name was?"

"Wyatt. Is there any chance that either Gordon or Claude is Creole?"

Mama averted her gaze from the TV a moment and frowned at me. "Them two boys is both white as the Pope. Why you go and ask such a thing?"

"Just curious," I said. "This is New Orleans. Even the Pope might be part black if he grew up around here."

"Ain't that the truth?" she said.

"Well then?"

Mama ignored my suggestion and turned her attention back to her soap.

"Both of them boys went to the best schools and never wanted for a thing. They's kings of this city. You know that."

A dozen or so pictures populated the mantle of Mama Marlene's fake fireplace. All of the people in the pictures were white.

"You have lots of great photos. Who are all these people?"

"The person on the left is Gordon when he was a baby, and his mama and daddy."

Who are the two girls?"

Mama Marlene beamed. "They's Gordon's twin daughters, Desire and Dauphine. Ain't they pretty? I helped raise them up, too. The boy in the picture beside them is Sonny Sonnier, Claude's boy. He and Dauphine got married last summer."

"Gordon's daughter is married to Claude's son?"

"You didn't know?"

"Must have slipped my mind. The girls have unique names."

Mama's shrunken cheeks formed into a toothless grin.

"The Vallee's was expecting a boy. When they had twin girls, they was lost for names. Gordon had an old street map of New Orleans. He picked Desire and Dauphine, two streets off the map. That's what they named them."

"Do the girls know?"

Mama grinned. "They ain't got a clue. They still think they was named after French royalty because that's what their daddy told them."

"Gordon and Claude aren't close any longer. Do you know the reason why?"

My question seemed to agitate her because she put another Camel in her mouth and lit it without waiting for me to do it for her.

"I'm sure they got their reasons."

Mama Marlene crossed her thin arms as she puffed on the cigarette. If she knew the cause of the conflict, she wasn't going to talk to me about it.

There are sixty or seventy parades during Mardi Gras season, many of them going up Canal to N. Rampart before turning back toward the river. One of the parades had just reached the nearby intersection and was making the turn, the blare of trombones and hollow banging of bass drums sounding like a sudden bayou thunderstorm.

"How do Claude and Gordon handle their kids being married?" I asked, changing the subject.

"They both still live in the houses where they was born, next door to each other in the Garden District. When they have a family function, they just pretend each other don't exist."

"I can tell the subject disturbs you."

"Tried to talk to them about it. Claude don't even want to hear it and gets mad anytime I say something about it. Gordon just think of me as a crazy ol' nigger woman."

"And not his mother?"

Mama Marlene turned her attention away from her favorite soap opera, stubbed out her Camel, palmed another and put it between her lips. I grabbed the Zippo and lit it for her.

"He just don't know," she said, unexpected tears welling in her eyes.

Mama soon began coughing again, and I hurriedly filled her water glass from the tap in the kitchen. I had a feeling I'd learned as much as I was going to for the day. When her hacking finally ceased, I started for the door.

She smiled and nodded when I said, "I'll tell Gordon you're doing okay."

"Give him my love and tell him I miss him," she said as I shut the apartment door behind me and headed for Canal Street.

Hurricane Katrina had changed many things. For one, it had shut down most of the streetcars, at least for a time. One remaining after the storm was the Canal Street Line that connects the riverfront with many of the cemeteries. The end of the parade procession was passing, second liners strutting and marching after it. I joined them for a little stroll.

The weather was warmer when I reached the intersection of Canal and Bourbon making my sports coat almost too warm to wear. I found one of the few remaining pay phones inside a drug store and called Gordon Vallee's cell phone. He answered on the first ring.

"You asked me to call you when I had something to report."

"You calling from a pay phone?"

"I'm not big on new technology."

"Great! I hired a dinosaur. I'm at Brannigan's on Decatur. How far away are you?"

"Just around the corner."

"Then get over here. I'm waiting for you."

Chapter Thirteen

The first thing Jacque saw when he awoke the next morning was Greta's bare back. She was still asleep. If he were going to kill her, now would be the perfect time. She wouldn't even know it was he applying deadly force to her neck. It didn't matter because he couldn't bring himself to do it.

Velvet had awakened him, shuffling paper in the bathroom. Now, she was nosing around the little cabin for something to eat or drink. Finding nothing, she jumped on the bed and licked his face.

Jacque slipped out of bed and filled two coffee cups, one with water and the other with milk. He then fed Velvet some left-over beef tips. The night of intense love-making with Greta had left him ravenous. He realized as much when his stomach growled.

Opening the cabin door, he found a Times Picayune lying on the diamond patterned carpet. The front-page story was about the body of a large man found floating near one of the casinos. Deciding not to worry about the implications, he put the paper on the bathroom floor for Velvet. Greta smiled when she opened her eyes and saw him sitting at the table looking back at her.

"I'm hungry, but I feel the sickness returning. I don't think I could keep anything down."

"I got you another Sprite from the machine down

the hall, and there are crackers left over from last night. They should help keep your stomach calm, and give you a little nourishment."

Greta took the soda and crackers, placing them on the nightstand without taking as much as a bite or sip.

"I have something I want to tell you. Thank you so much for last night."

"Thank me? I should be thanking you."

"You don't understand," she said. "After Harald, I was afraid I could never have feelings again for a man, except hatred, maybe. Last night, you proved me wrong, and that I am still a whole woman."

"I'm happy you're happy," Jacque said, sitting beside her on the bed. "I have a problem. I thought I was safe here. A story in this morning's paper says Harald's body was found. It's a matter of time before the police trace him to the ship. I can't stay here much longer."

"You said the authorities agreed to put you into Witness Protection after you testify against your old bosses."

"That agreement was made before I escaped. All bets are off the table now."

"You just saved yourself from drowning. It wasn't your fault the boat sank. Why not just turn yourself in?"

"Because the police know I killed Harald, or at least they will."

"I'll tell them that you were protecting me," she said.

"They wouldn't believe you."

"Then let me come with you. We could be together forever."

"Our forever wouldn't last long. You have two lives to think of now. I can't let you go with me."

"I promise I won't slow you down," she said.

"No, I don't want people connecting us. I'm so glad you called your father to come for you. You need help and support. I can't offer either to you."

Greta began crying again for the first time in many

hours. Velvet jumped on the bed and into her lap. Hugging the active dog, Greta stroked her head.

"A nightmare just ended for me. Now, after I've found someone I love, you tell me you are going away, and I'll never see you again."

"Your pregnancy is causing strong emotions. It's true we're connected. It's not love."

"Pardon me, but I know what love feels like. Don't you have any feelings for me?"

Jacque hesitated a moment and then looked away before speaking.

"Emotions are a weakness, and they will get you killed. I haven't had any since my mother died—at least until now."

Greta squeezed his hand tighter. "Then you do feel something."

"Yeah, and it scares me. I'm not used to looking out for anyone except myself. Now, I believe I can tell you my darkest secret. You and Velvet are the only two beings on earth I trust."

"Then let us come with you."

"Emotions aside, I have a promise to keep."

"What promise?"

Jacque looked away and closed his eyes. "One I can't forget. I also need money, and Harald didn't have much on him."

"It's in the ship's safe. They took his thumbprint as identification. He let me know he was the only one that could retrieve it."

"I should have guessed as much," Jacque said. "Aren't you the least bit hungry?"

"Don't worry about me; I'll eat the crackers. You must be starved. There's a buffet on the upper level. Why don't you get something to eat?"

"Will you be okay?"

"I need a shower and to do a few girl things. Velvet and I will be okay until you return."

She smiled when he said, "Fine, but I'll miss you."

Jacque was halfway down the hallway when he turned around and went back to the cabin. He opened the door to hear Greta singing a Norse tune in the shower—a happy tune. Shutting the door gently behind him, he started toward the buffet on the upper level.

When he walked outside for the first time in many hours, he found it was dark again. Until that moment, he hadn't realized how tired and desperate he'd been. Darkness calmed his nerves a bit. The empty feeling in his stomach indicated he first needed to satisfy his hunger. Then he would explore the ship and find some money.

Foot traffic on the ship was sparse. Either something was going on, or else many of the passengers had gone ashore to celebrate Mardi Gras firsthand. Possibly a combination of both, he thought as he climbed the stairs to the buffet. He found a table with a splendid view of fireworks going off over the river.

The buffet was worth the wait, and he filled his plate with enough food for two men. Not counting calories, he returned for dessert twice. Everyone seemed in a festive mood, many of the passengers in costumes.

"Where's everyone going?" he asked when a young man dressed as a pirate bumped into his table.

"Mardi Gras celebration in the main ballroom. They have masks at the door," he said.

Jacque finished his coffee and then followed the crowd down the hallway to the entrance to the grand ballroom. After putting on the mask the man at the door gave him, he pushed his way into the crowded room. He was instantly engulfed in a sea of noisy people, also in masks, drinking and pretending to be part of Carnival madness outside the ship.

The jazz trumpeter on the bandstand hit a sour note as Jacque worked his way through the crowd, hoping to meet some drunk flashing wads of cash, or an otherwise easy target. Being at least a head taller than anyone else in the room, he could easily see what was going on around him. As he scanned the crowd, he noticed a man reaching beneath his shirt for a large bill. Catching a glimpse of his money belt, Jacque began working his way toward the man, hoping he wouldn't move away before he got there.

Reaching the bar, he sidled up beside a middle-aged couple, elbowing the man standing beside them as he did. With a glance at Jacque, the jostled man moved away to a different spot in the large hall. Intent on the couple standing beside him, Jacque barely noticed.

Neither of the two people was wearing a mask. Both could have passed for late thirties or early forties. Their stone gray hair gave them away the man's a long crew cut and the woman's extending barely past her ears. Their clothes were casual, though obviously expensive. They were speaking in a language Jacque thought was German. He spoke a few of the only words he remembered from his tenth grade German class.

"Wie geht es Ihnen?"

The man with wire-brush, gray hair smiled. *"Wir sind gut. Sie sind aus Deutschland?"*

"That was the only German I know," Jacque said, speaking in English. "I'm from Stavanger, Norway but live here in the States now."

Both of them smiled and the woman said, *"Jeg er norsk, fra Stavanger. Jurgen og jeg bor der nå."*

"I'm sorry. My mind was somewhere else," Jacque said.

"I said we live in Stavanger. Jurgen is a petroleum engineer working in the North Sea. I grew up in Norway, and he swept me off my feet when we met."

"I'm Harald Gjertsen. Where are your masks?"

"My purse," the woman said. "We're saving them for later."

"I'm Jurgen. This is my wife Anna. We are going to Bourbon Street in a little while and take in some of the local craziness."

"It's rampant in the French Quarter this time of year," Jacque said. "Most locals don't even bother going there."

"I'd buy you a drink, Harald, but everything is free. What are you having?"

"A Dixie," he said as a bartender appeared.

The smiling young man dressed in white smock and black tie brought him a Dixie beer and champagne cocktails in plastic cups for Jurgen and Anna.

"We're sorry to have to drink and run, but Mardi Gras beckons," Jurgen said.

"*Farvel*," Anna said with a wave.

Jacque watched as they moved away through the crowded room, waiting a moment before following them. When they reached the door, he noticed the woman turn and look. Seeing his head above the crowd, she tugged on her husband's arm and said something to him. It didn't matter. He knew they were on their way to Bourbon Street. He also knew an alleyway they would probably pass.

Jacque didn't take a taxi or even the streetcar to the nearby French Quarter. He knew of back alleyways, and shortcuts not even the locals knew existed. A brindle alley cat didn't bother moving when Jacque passed him in the darkness. Both were creatures of the night, Jacque as much in his element as a jaguar stalking his prey through a grove of tropical bamboo. He wasn't even out of breath when he joined the army of revelers on Bourbon Street.

"Hey Shaquille, dunk one for us," someone called from a balcony.

Used to comments about his height, Jacque didn't even turn to look. He hadn't experienced the madness of Mardi Gras since his years as a homeless teen. When he melded into the mass of middle-aged tourists and inebriated college kids, it was as if he'd never left. Tonight, he had other things on his mind as he stepped around a street musician, singing and collecting coins and bills in his beaten-up, old guitar case.

If Jurgen and Anna started their tour of Bourbon Street at the intersection with Canal, the couple would reach the dark alley in less than an hour. Jacque would be waiting for them and had a plan to get their attention.

Jurgen and Anna appeared through the crowd just as Jacque had anticipated. When Jurgen passed the alley, Jacque grabbed his arm and yanked him into the darkness. As Anna watched, Jurgen pulled a pistol from his belt and pointed it at Jacque's head.

With no time to wonder where a foreigner had obtained a weapon, Jacque batted Jurgen's hand into the air, sending the first bullet skyward. Grabbing his wrist, Jacque squeezed it until the German winced in pain and released the pistol.

Jurgen was kicking and fighting when Jacque wheeled him around toward the old masonry wall, put the pistol to his head and pulled the trigger. His hands were on the money belt before Jurgen's heart had stopped beating.

The noise on Bourbon Street was overwhelming, but everyone heard the two bullets fire. Anna rushed to her husband's side as people in the crowd began screaming and trying to get out of the way of the man moving in their direction. Jacque just pushed them aside, not bothering to run.

Greta met him at the door, hugging him when he entered. "I've been worried. Where have you been?"

"I'm back now."

She didn't let go of his arm until they sat together on the bed. "Velvet is anxious. She's been pacing the floor."

"She's like me, and unused to being cooped up in a tiny space. I'll take her down to the dock for a walk."

"Yes, but hurry back. I missed you."

"I missed you too," he said, kissing her forehead. "I'll be right back."

Jacque spirited the dog out of the ship and to the street facing the Mississippi River, lights from the boats out on the water flickering like fireflies. When Velvet had finished her business in the bushes and returned to him, wagging her tail, he started toward the ship.

Cop cars with flashing lights and blaring sirens stopped him from going further. He didn't know why or how, but someone had tipped the cops to Greta Gjertsen's cabin. As much as his head and heart ached, he and Velvet couldn't return to her.

Chapter Fourteen

My visit to the Notarial Archives, and then to Mama Marlene's apartment had answered many questions. I'd found no evidence Gordon Vallee was a passeblanc. I'd performed such background checks for banks, insurance companies, and for prospective employers many times.

None of those businesses ever expected any more information than just the facts. Still, I knew Vallee wouldn't be happy. He'd see, as I'd already seen it would make little difference to a rumor monger bent on sullying his reputation.

I strolled the short distance to a little French Quarter, Irish Pub on Decatur Street. I knew the place. During an unusually low point in my life, I'd frequented it on an almost daily basis.

Another parade was passing on Basin Street bass instruments of a marching band rattling windows as a clamoring crowd revved up for another night of parties and festivities. Three men in dark masks and plumed hats, dressed as musketeers, hurried past me on their way to Bourbon Street. Pigeons fighting over a discarded hotdog didn't bother flying away.

Brannigan's featured an old wooden countertop with worn, though comfortable stools, the attractive female bartender looking familiar as she read a paperback by the dim light of a neon beer sign. Several regulars sitting at the bar, drinking Guinness and exchanging stories, didn't glance up when I walked behind them.

Many of the barflies were aspiring poets, artists, and writers. Would-be only because most would be too inebriated when they finally got home to do much writing or painting. I knew, because that was the story of my own life for longer than I cared to count. I found Gordon Vallee at one of the three booths backing up to a weathered brick wall. Someone was with him.

I slid into the circular booth next to a young woman as the clack of breaking balls sounded from a nearby pool table. The red-headed woman behind the bar apparently recognized me and quickly brought a Black Jack and water, placing it in front of me with a knowing stare. Gordon's voice returned my attention from the lovely bartender.

"This is my daughter Desire."

"I'm Wyatt," I said with a nod.

"I know. Dad's told me all about you."

"There's not much to tell."

Desire flashed me a world-class smile. "Oh I think you're being modest. He didn't tell me how cute you are."

"If he'd told me how good looking you are, I wouldn't have believed him," I said, countering.

Desire had long, brunette hair with lightened highlights. Like her Dad's, her limpid, almond-shaped eyes were dark as Pirate's Alley at midnight. She wore ankle-length boots and a low-cut dress that revealed ample cleavage, strong calves, and shapely thighs. I'd noticed her great legs when she'd scooted to make room for me.

Pearls highlighted Desire's royal neck, gold hoops dangling from her earlobes. As her name implied, the attraction I felt for her was strong and immediate. She was beautiful, and it took me a moment to stop gawking. Her amused smile told me she was used to awkward reactions her beauty caused.

"My daughter's a model, though I guess you knew

that already," Gordon said.

As I gazed at her, I recognized the striking face I'd seen on covers of celebrity magazines at the newspaper shop where I get my Times Picayune. Grabbing her hand, I gave it an impulsive kiss.

"I've seen your pictures. I'm relieved because I can't imagine two women in the world as beautiful as you."

Desire jerked her hand away and playfully slapped my cheek. "I know this is an Irish pub but stop the blarney or I'll have to leave."

We both stopped grinning and turned our attention to Gordon Vallee when he said, "Get your dick back in your pants, Thomas. My daughter ain't a piece of meat."

Desire grinned and rolled her beautiful eyes when I said, "Sorry."

"We got business here. Now tell me what you found."

"I checked your ancestry at the Notarial Archives. You have no black ancestors, at least of record."

Gordon's shoes cost more than the thousand dollars he'd paid me. His diamond, pinky ring and expensive Rolex made the bartender's eyes pop. That, along with the crisp Bennie he slipped into her blouse when she brought our drinks insured him we wouldn't be overlooked. He snickered at my comment about his genealogy.

"Maybe I should take my thousand dollars back, Sherlock."

"That's all you paid Mister Thomas? Cheap, cheap!"

"Shut up, Baby Doll. I don't need no sass from your ass."

Desire grinned at me. "Dad may act like a grizzly. He's just a teddy bear."

"Yeah, well I should have whipped you two girls when you were little, but your mother would have killed me if I had of."

"Not to mention Mama Marlene," Desire said.

Gordon frowned and pointed a crooked finger at his beautiful daughter.

"Don't mention that old nigger woman's name around me."

Desire's smile disappeared. Turning her knees away from her father, she crossed her arms tightly against her chest.

"Stop using that derogatory word. I'm your daughter. I don't deserve your disrespect."

Gordon glanced at me, seeking solace. "You know what I'm talkin' about, don't you Thomas?"

"Sorry, I'm on Desire's side on this one."

"If you ain't on my side, then give me my thousand dollars back and get the hell outa here."

His words infuriated Desire. "Give the old fucker his money. I'll pay you."

"Who the hell you callin' an ol' fucker?"

Desire got in his face and said, "If the foo shits—"

"Baby Doll, why you want to act like this?"

"Don't touch me," she said, again turning away.

"I said I'm sorry."

"Then quit acting like a thoughtless pig."

"I am the way I am, and too old to change now."

"Lame excuse and you know it."

"I'm sorry, Baby Doll. I'll bite my tongue off before I ever say that word again."

"You mean it?"

"Cross my heart and hope to die."

"Even when I'm not around to remind you?"

"You heard what I said, and that's what I meant."

Desire's demeanor lightened noticeably. Grabbing his head with both hands, she put lip marks on his forehead.

"Now pay Mr. Thomas every penny he deserves, you old cheapskate."

"Fine."

Gordon pulled the enormous wad of cash from his jacket pocket and began counting bills across the table.

Glancing up, he said, "Don't try to give me this

money back, you hear?"

I could only nod; the thousand dollars he'd given me was already spent.

"Take it," Desire said. "The old bastard will make you earn every red cent of it."

"Ain't no use arguing with her," Gordon said. "She got a head hard as the cement banquettes over on Canal."

"Yeah, well I wonder who I got that from."

When Desire hugged him, I felt like a bit actor in a long-running play. When the bartender brought more drinks, my pain continued. Oblivious to the one I'd left untouched she delivered another without comment.

"Now tell me what else you learned," Gordon said.

"I visited Mama Marlene."

"And why the hell did you do that?"

"A skilled investigator checks out all the leads. I know Mama Marlene, for all practical purposes, raised both you and Claude Sonnier. I also know you had a falling out with her and that she's working for Sonnier now. Why exactly did you fire her?"

"None of your business."

"Maybe, but it's important to the investigation."

Gordon glanced at his daughter, perhaps to gauge her reaction to what he was about to say.

"The old woman had worked for me long as I can remember and my Daddy before that. She's old and started confusing things.

"She told Dad she was his mother," Desire said.

"You don't think she was speaking figuratively?"

Gordon glared at his daughter before answering. "Her belief and what's the truth are two different things. I couldn't take the chance someone might believe her."

Desire's frown had returned, along with her folded arms and crossed legs.

"You promised you'd buy her a little house of her own in a nice suburb. Pay her a monthly pension."

"And let that no-good, bastard son of hers end up with it? No way!"

"At least get her out of the project. You owe her

that much."

"I don't owe her nothing. I let her go one week, the next she's working for that snake Sonnier."

"For the life of me, I don't know why you and Uncle Claude are locked in an absolutely crazy feud."

"Well, Baby Doll, that ain't your problem."

The two seemed more like an old, married couple than father and daughter. If I hoped to glean any useful information from our conversation, I needed to change its course.

"Let's get back on point. How did you first learn about these passeblanc rumors?"

"I was in the locker room at the country club when I saw someone had wrote Gordon Vallee is a passeblanc on a steamed up mirror."

"That's not much. Anything else?"

Gordon shook his head. "Jake Reynolds, one of my V.P.s at the bank overheard a conversation at the club. The story is going around."

"Did you recognize the writing on the mirror?"

"Why hell no!"

"Then I need a list of club members."

"No can do. I never even seen one myself."

"Then how about an excuse to mingle with some of the members? Ask a few questions in confidence."

Gordon leaned back, putting his hands behind his head, staring at me for a long moment as if considering something. A horse-drawn carriage passed outside on the street, the horse's hooves clomping against mortar and old bricks.

"I'm having a little costume party at the house a few nights from now. Mardi Gras, you know, with lots of associates and influential people. Don't make a fool of me."

"I'm a pro, Mr. Vallee. No one will even know why I'm there."

"He can come as my date," Desire said.

"Fine, now I got someplace I need to go. You coming Baby Doll?"

"I'll catch a ride with Wyatt."

Vallee dropped two hundreds on the table. On the way out, he stuffed another note in the pretty bartender's blouse. Desire and I pretended not to notice.

"He didn't seem too worried about leaving you here with me," I said.

"He probably has a date and doesn't want me with him anyway. You haven't touched your drinks."

"I have a little problem with alcohol," I said.

"The bartender's gorgeous, and prettier than most of the runway models I work with. She knew which drink to bring you without asking, and she's been staring at us since you came in."

"I was a big tipper during my drinking days, though not quite like your dad. I still had a practice then, and New Orleans lawyers are well paid."

"You're a lawyer?"

"I don't practice anymore. I got disbarred for shoving a client."

"They can't disbar you for that, can they?"

"The man was as influential and powerful as your dad is. He said I threw him out my office window. I didn't, of course. It doesn't matter because the story stuck and grew. I was reeling from a failed marriage and rampant alcoholism. I didn't even put up a fight."

"And now you're an investigator."

"Some people think I have a knack for it."

"How long have you been sober?"

"I quit counting after the first year."

"You don't miss it?"

"Every time someone lights a cigarette, I want a puff. When I smell whiskey, which in this town is virtually every hour of the day, I want a drink."

"Your ex didn't take you back once you sobered up?"

"She'd remarried by then. I attended her wake two days ago. She died of cancer."

"Oh Wyatt, I'm sorry."

Desire scooted close enough I could feel the warmth of her gorgeous body. When she draped her arms around my neck and cradled me to her bosom, my memories of Mimsy faded, replaced by carnal lust. We quickly became locked in a passionate kiss that continued until the bartender placed fresh drinks in front of us. When she sighed, and then began speaking to us in a Scottish accent, we glanced up at her.

"Your father paid for your drinks and told me to leave the tab open as long as you want."

With a frown and toss of her long, red hair, she left our booth in a huff.

"I think she's jealous," Desire said.

She was probably right. Now, whiskey-soaked memories began flooding my brain. I'd done much more than drink at the little Irish pub. Chrissie and I'd been a number for a while. I'd stopped seeing her for no real reason when I quit drinking. Though she probably didn't expect one now, I decided I owed her an apology and an explanation for my erratic behavior.

"Oh holy hell! My alcoholism resulted in lots of displaced memories. Her accent just reminded me of one. Excuse me a moment."

Chrissie was a real looker, unused to being the second best-looking woman in the place. As she polished a glass with a bar rag, her blue eyes stared a hole in my forehead.

"I have something I need to say. My brain was addled when I quit drinking, and it caused me to do many things I wouldn't do now. Sorry I never called to explain."

My eyes rolled with a resounding pop when she slapped me. The patrons sitting at the bar watched with rapt attention, not speaking but smiling and snickering.

"Wyatt Thomas, you're a heartless prick. Go back to your fancy floozy, and don't ever knock on my door again at two in the morning when you need a shoulder to cry on."

Desire was grinning when I returned to the booth.

"She's not just jealous; I think she's in love with you."

"My face doesn't think so. Maybe we should go someplace else."

"We can't drink on Daddy's money someplace else."

"At least I won't have to worry about a pool cue across the back of my head."

"You're funny. I like that in a man."

"I'm glad someone does."

We left Gordon's money on the table and headed for the door, trying not to make eye contact with Chrissie. I needn't have worried as she was busy hustling a pitcher of beer to two men playing pool in back.

Chapter Fifteen

Mardi Gras revelers had begun filling sidewalks and streets as we left the Irish pub. Bertram's wasn't far away. Holding hands, Desire and I headed toward Rue Chartres, a winter bite still in the air.

We found the place crowded with regulars and tourists, every table full. When Bertram saw Desire and me coming through the door, he motioned for us to join him at the bar. A Cajun band was jamming on the tiny stage. People from different states and probably as many countries were sweating the band and swaying to the music.

"I saved the best two seats in the house, thinking you might come up. Cowboy, this must be your cousin because she's way too pretty to be your girlfriend."

"Desire, this is Bertram Picou, owner of this fine establishment."

Bertram leaned on his elbows and smiled as he stared at Desire. "You so damn pretty I could look at you all night long. Where you from, girl?"

"Right here in New Orleans."

"Makes sense to me. I always said, there ain't no prettier girls in the world than right here in N.O."

"Bertram's guaranteed not Irish. Doesn't matter because he's still got more than his share of Blarney," I said.

"I like him. He's cute. Who belongs to this gorgeous

collie?"

"That's my Lady," Bertram said.

Lady lay behind the bar at Bertram's feet. Realizing she was the subject of conversation, her tail began thumping against oiled hardwood. When Desire vaulted over the counter in her short skirt, she earned wolf whistles from throughout the bar. Kneeling beside Lady, she gave her a hug. Lady's wagging tail indicated she was as taken by the pretty young woman as we were.

"You're the one that's beautiful," Desire said.

"And smart as a whip," Bertram said. "She likes you."

"The only female here that does," I said. "I'd say there's trouble in paradise for a bunch of husbands and boyfriends if they don't get their eyes back in their heads."

"Can't say I blame them," Bertram said. "You climb over the bar in that short skirt again, and you'll start a riot. Hell, you so pretty, you're likely to anyway. What you drinking?"

"I'm crazy about Margaritas."

Bertram showed her the exit from behind the bar and opened it for her.

"Good choice. Ol' Bertram here mixes a mean Margarita, and I don't mean from no damn machine."

Desire climbed up on the stool beside me, earning her more than a few wolf whistles. Ignoring them, she clutched my hand.

"Why did he call you Cowboy?"

"Long story."

"I have all night."

"Most people don't realize it, but there are cattle ranches all over Louisiana, especially near the Texas border. My cousin's parents had a ranch, and I used to spend my summers there. I learned about horses and cows long before I had a girlfriend."

I grinned when she said, "Well I'm glad you like girls now."

Bertram soon returned with Desire's Margarita

and lemonade for me. His waitress and main squeeze Shirley was working the floor. When she shot him a dirty look, he excused himself to help her.

"I love this place. I can't believe the bras, panties, and underwear hanging from the rafters."

"Inhibitions are easy to lose in the Big Easy."

With a wicked grin on her pretty face, she kissed me and then began working her own underwear down her legs and pulling them over her boots. With a squeal, she tossed her thong panties into the rafters. For a moment, I thought Bertram's prediction of a riot might come true.

Every man in the crowd who had witnessed the act was right on point. Soon, angry wives and girlfriends were herding their husbands and boyfriends toward the front door.

"Ain't you a little cold?" Bertram asked.

"No, I'm hot," she said.

"Well wrap this around you anyway," he said, handing her an ankle-length, feather coat he kept on the coat rack behind the bar. "Otherwise, I'm gonna lose lots of money tonight."

Desire grinned and wrapped herself in the frizzy coat. The effect was startling. She looked even sexier, if such a thing were possible, in the eye-popping, rose-colored garment.

"This is Gordon Vallee's daughter."

"Well thank God she took after her mama and not her daddy," Bertram said. "You look awful familiar."

We all turned when someone behind us said, "World's most famous supermodel. A million hits a day on her internet fan site."

"Desire, this is Father Rafael Romanov."

Rafael didn't look like a priest, resplendent in an expensive suit, polished shoes and London Fog topcoat. He took the empty stool beside Desire.

"What can I get you to drink, Padre?" Bertram asked.

Rafael raked long fingers through his dark and curly hair. It wasn't the first time I'd noticed his hypnotic, gray eyes and long, hooked nose.

"Turkey and water, please, and make it a double. Tonight, I have a powerful thirst."

"Are you really a priest?" Desire asked.

"Yes I am, although Wyatt forgot to tell you I'm defrocked. The Mother Church no longer recognizes me."

"What the hell did you do?" Bertram asked as he returned with Rafael's drink.

"I fell in love with a woman for one thing. My mother is a witch, for another. Oh, and I'm also a gypsy."

"If you abandoned the church for someone, then she must be a wonderful woman."

"She was brilliant, and beautiful. Ask Wyatt, he knows."

"Rafael married Mimsy, my ex. He was with her when she died."

"I'm so sorry," Desire said, grabbing and squeezing both of our hands. "I was raised a Catholic. Can you hear my confession? I have so much sin."

"How can a girl as young as you have so much sin? I would be happy to hear your confession, if we only had a confessional."

"There's an empty booth in back," she said.

Rafael nodded, and he and Desire hurried away through the diminished crowd to a booth in back of Bertram's bar.

"So that's Mimsy's husband? What does he do now?"

"He works as a rent-a-priest for a cruise line here in the city. He's apparently making more money than Midas."

"Good," Bertram said. "Then I'll make him pay for his own drinks."

Desire and Rafael, smiles on both their faces, soon returned to the bar. Noise on the street outside grew louder, and more people soon began returning to Bertram's.

"I confessed to the sins I've committed, and to

those I intend to commit. If I die tonight, I will be okay in the eyes of God."

Rafael ignored her obvious delight, turning his attention to me. "Mother tells me you took my advice and consulted her."

"I was also raised Catholic, and taken aback by a few things."

"Such as?"

"Calpurnia, for one thing, and Gregorian chants playing in the background."

Rafael smiled. "Calpurnia's an exotic pet, I'll admit. You apparently haven't delved into Catholic mysticism. Many believe the chants reflect the key tones used to create the universe."

"Is it true?" Desire asked.

"Catholicism began during a time wrapped in paganism and darkness. Although it has evolved, its roots are different from the way the modern church wants it to appear. Will you visit Madeline again?"

"Is my soul in danger?"

"All our souls are in danger. She told me something about you."

"Tell us," Desire demanded.

"She called you a Traveler."

"What does that mean?" I asked.

"If you don't already know, then maybe you need to search your soul."

"I want to visit her," Desire said. "Will you take me?"

"He'll take you," Rafael said, answering for me. "Cats can never overcome their own curiosity." Killing his drink, he dropped a hundred-dollar bill on the counter and pulled his topcoat over his shoulders. "Your drinks are on me. Adieu my friends. I have spirits to attend, and I must join them."

We watched him walk out the door, disappearing into endless, Mardi Gras revelry.

"He is such a nice man and has the strangest eyes."

"I've only known one other person with eyes like

his. Since he's also a Catholic priest, I don't think they're related."

"Wyatt, what's a Traveler?"

"A nomadic Irish person, though I think Madeline has another definition."

"Like what?"

"Someone who knows things."

"A sixth sense?"

"Something like that."

"Do you?"

"I think I'm more like Rafael's cat. I have a healthy curiosity, and my mother used to tell me it would get me into trouble someday."

"Has it?"

"More than once. Now I'd better call a cab for you."

"No way. By midnight, the Quarter will be packed with masked crazies. That's where I want to be. Walk with me down Bourbon Street?"

"Why not?" I said. "I don't mind spending a few more hours in the company of a beautiful woman."

Smiling at my compliment, she said, "I need to visit the powder room first. Will you wait for me?"

"You already know the answer to that question."

She soon returned with the frizzy coat wrapped tightly around her. Leaning over the bar, she gave Bertram a kiss as Shirley stared across the room, giving her the evil eye.

"Can I borrow your coat?"

Too busy waiting on customers who'd begun pouring in from the streets, Bertram winked as we walked out the door.

Desire and I left Bertram's, heading for the lights of Bourbon Street. Participation in the first Mardi Gras after Katrina had proved sparse, with few tourists wanting to party in a recently devastated city. Several years later, things had changed. We could see as much as we approached the epicenter of the celebration.

Tourists and revelers crowded the sidewalks, flashing neon beckoning as we neared Rue Bourbon. I had attended Mardi Gras many times, since I was too young to remember. It didn't matter. The sights and sounds still excited me. Upon reaching Bourbon Street, we waded into the insanity.

Fun seekers, many in masks and wild costumes, crowded streets and balconies of the surrounding, second-floor apartments, rentals, and hotels. Everyone, it seemed, was inebriated, or else working on it. Desire and I pushed our way onto the crowded street.

"Can you smell it?" I asked.

"Smell what?"

"Pot, antiquity, and pure adrenaline excitement; I smelled it the first time my parents brought me here. I can still smell it."

Revelers on the balconies were calling to the women in the streets. It didn't take them long to spot Desire. A young man in a red University of Alabama sweatshirt was the first to yell at her.

"Show us your tits and I'll throw you some beads."

Desire was happy to comply. When she opened the gaudy coat, I realized she was totally naked beneath it, dressed only in her boots and pearls. Beads and dollar bills began raining down on our heads, the gallery in the balconies erupting with encouraging cheers. With her coat still breached, she put her arms around me and stuck her warm tongue in my mouth.

"Oh Wyatt, I'm so hot," she said when she finally pulled away.

"Hey, you just sent my thermostat into the danger zone. I don't want to spoil the party, but you better shut your coat before we get mobbed by a gang of horny college boys."

I didn't wait for her to comply, pulling the coat tightly around her. She flashed me a drunken smile when I scooped up a handful of beads and draped them around her neck.

"You earned them."

The crowd had a mind of its own and soon began moving us forward in a slow but steady stream of shoulders and hips, propelling us like an unbridled current in a human river. Bars, restaurants, hotels, souvenir shops, and strip clubs lined both sides of the narrow street—a loud combination of flashing neon, jazz, blues, raspy-voiced barkers, and the ever-moving mass of people dulling our senses with Bourbon's droning dissonance.

No one in the crowd managed to avoid seeing Desire. Before we'd walked a block, she'd flashed hundreds of people, earning her dozens of beads that draped her neck, both inside and outside the garish coat.

"Buy me a Hurricane?" she said.

Many of the bars and restaurants sold cocktails and specialty drinks directly to people passing on the street. I bought Desire a pink Hurricane in a large green cup that advertised the name of the establishment. After a healthy pull on the red straw, she offered me a drink.

She grinned when I said, "You're enough to send me over the edge. I don't need any help from a rum bottle."

A strip show barker called to Desire as we walked down Bourbon Street. The skinny man had a day-old growth of dark stubble on his chin, tattoos up and down his bare arms, and a cigarette dangling from his lips. We could see a half-naked dancer on stage inside.

"Get in here you hot babe. It's amateur night, hundred dollars to the best amateur dancer in our contest, and I can guarantee you're a shoo-in to win."

Desire tugged my wrist. "Come on, Wyatt. I want to go inside."

As she rushed past the barker, he grabbed my arm. "Two drink minimum," he said. "Forty bucks up front."

After handing him two twenties, I hurried through the noisy club in search of Desire, not waiting for him to stamp my hand. She was laughing and talking with two dancers dressed only in gaudy bras and revealing g-strings. Before I could say hi, they'd pushed her up the steps, a Bob Seger ballad blasting from the jukebox.

Halfway through the song, the red coat came off

her shoulders and onto the stage, the mostly drunken crowd pounding their tables, whooping and cat-calling. Even some of the other dancers began throwing dollar bills. Desire loved it, blowing kisses to the crowd as she scooped up loose bills littering oiled wood. I earned a round of boos when I pulled her off the stage, retrieved the coat, and wrapped it around her.

"You're a natural," I said. "This town hasn't seen moves like that since Blaze Starr danced in Uncle Earl K's lap."

"I want to perform again. I know I can win the hundred dollars."

I grinned. "There's no doubt in my mind about that. If we don't get out of here before someone recognizes you and calls your dad, he'll have my head, though not before he has my nuts."

I had to pull her back out to the street, a waitress yelling at us because we hadn't touched our drinks, and the barker carping because he said we still owed a cover charge. They both gave up when we disappeared into the madness. I finally managed to pull her out of the slow-moving torrent.

"I've never been so hot in my life. Make love to me," she said.

Opening the frizzy coat, she pulled me to her, unzipping my fly and groping my private parts like someone possessed. It was then we heard gunshots. The roar of approaching sirens soon followed, along with masses of frightened revelers attempting to swim against the human river moving past us.

We backed against the wall as a very large man banged into us, a pistol in one hand, and money belt in the other. When our eyes locked, he pointed the gun at my forehead.

"Pow," he said before disappearing into the crowd.

Chapter Sixteen

Nearly midnight and long past his normal bedtime, Marlon yawned as he ducked beneath yellow, crime tape cordoning a circular swath of Bourbon Street. Tony, preparing to question a beat cop, didn't seem to notice.

A patrol car sat askance in the road, its motor running, headlights beaming and distinctive blue lights flashing. Four cops on horseback were controlling the curious crowd, not allowing them to get too close to the scene.

"What's the story here?" Tony asked, showing the young man his badge.

"A tall man accosted a couple and robbed them. When the victim pulled a gun, the thief grabbed it and shot him. The victim's wife was with him when it happened."

Not far away, someone was sobbing and ranting in a foreign language. Tony turned to see an E.M.T. attempting to calm the distraught woman.

"Who are they?"

"German couple here on a cruise. The victim had a money belt. The thief took it and got away through the crowd."

Tony's forensic team had already begun combing for evidence when another car with flashing lights bulled its way through the crowded street. The lights on the car weren't blue. Two men in dark suits quickly exited and showed Tony their badges.

"I'm James Landry, U.S. Marshal's office. This is my partner Matt Rivera. Pull your people off the case. We're taking over this investigation."

Landry had a full head of graying, red hair and angry, green eyes. Rivera, his muscular partner, looked as if he'd be more at home in a football uniform than the blue jacket pulled a little too tightly across his broad chest. Landry, four inches taller than Tony, stared down at him, invading his space. Tony took a step backwards.

"On whose authority? I need to hear something from someone besides you before I call my team off the case. Until then, we're not going anywhere."

"This is a Federal matter. That's all you need to know."

"I hear your gums bumping. Now I'm telling you; this is my turf. I don't know you from Adam."

"What's your name, mister?"

"Homicide detective Anthony Nicosia, N.O.P.D. Last I heard local police have jurisdiction over local murders."

"Yeah, well this one's different."

"Mind telling me how?"

"You're an insolent bastard. If this were the Army, I'd have you up on court martial tomorrow."

"Well it ain't the Army, it's the Big Easy in case you didn't know. Now you better get me some answers, or I'm going to have my men arrest you."

"I could take your head off, Nicosia," James Landry said, leaning so close that Tony could smell garlic from the chicken he'd just eaten.

"Give it your best shot," Tony said.

Realizing his bluff wasn't working, Landry backed off and called a number on his cell phone. Tony was soon speaking to Chief Wexler.

"Hold your ground until the rest of Landry's team arrives and then turn the crime scene over to them. We got orders directly from Washington."

Tony handed Landry's cell phone back to him. "What's going on here?"

"You don't have a need to know."

"Why are you cutting us out of this investigation? We can help you do whatever you want."

"Like what, maybe loot the body as some of your men did after Katrina?"

Landry's words were more than Tony could handle. Smacking him across the face, he knocked him backwards onto the pavement. Diving on top of him, he locked his fingers around his thick neck. It took Landry's younger partner, and three beat cops to wrestle him off the larger man. When they did, Landry bounded off the pavement, shouting and pointing an angry finger at Tony.

"You crazy son of a bitch! I'll have your badge for this." By this time, Landry's gang of U.S. Marshals and his forensic team had arrived. Tony's anger briefly abated, and he turned to his own people without replying to Landry's threat.

"Everybody stop what you're doing. The Feds are taking over this investigation. Stand down and turn your evidence over to them."

Tony's forensic team began packing their gear and turning over their samples. Tony crawled under the crime tape, followed closely by Marlon Bando.

"You're going the wrong way," Marlon said.

"We're not done yet. I'm gonna question the wife of the victim."

"But the Marshals have the case now. You heard what they said."

Tony turned with a frown, hands on his hips. "Why the hell didn't you help me out back there?"

"They're the Feds. What could I have done?"

"Help me kick that big motherfucker's ass, for one thing!"

"I had no authority."

"Authority my hind foot! Partners cover each other, no matter what. Don't you even have a clue what I'm talking about?"

Not waiting for an answer, Tony walked away. Marlon followed him to the ambulance where an E.M.T. was still trying to convince the wife of the victim to go with him to the hospital. She was an attractive, middle-aged woman with graying hair and blue, Scandinavian eyes.

"Ma'am, I'm Lieutenant Nicosia, N.O.P.D. Do you speak English?" When she nodded, he said, "Can I get your name, please?"

"Anna Schumacher. Is my husband—"

"Sorry, Mrs. Schumacher. Maybe you can help us catch the responsible person."

Tears flowed from the woman's eyes. "What else can I tell you that I haven't already said?"

Marlon looked confused when Tony asked, "Did you recognize the man that shot your husband?"

"Yes. He was on our cruise ship."

"A passenger?"

The woman nodded again. "He is so tall, he is hard to miss."

"How tall?"

"I'm five-six. He towered over me."

"Did you or your husband ever speak to him?"

"About two hours ago, at the bar on the ship."

"Which ship?"

"The Scandinavian Queen. We've been stuck in port for several days, waiting for authorities to clear the shipping channel.

"You're from Europe. Why did you start your cruise in New Orleans?"

"We intended to spend a few days here, after the cruise returned from the Bahamas, and before we returned to Stavanger."

"So the man that accosted you and your husband was someone you recognized from the Scandinavian Queen."

"The ship had a Mardi Gras celebration in the main ballroom, the place crowded, only standing room near the bar. Jurgen was afraid to leave our money in the stateroom, so he kept it with him in a concealed money belt. I noticed this man watching us. Jurgen said I was foolish, but I'm sure he saw him take money from the belt to leave a tip for the bartender."

"And he approached you. What did he say?"

"He was exceptionally genial, although he seemed—"

"Phony?"

"Yes. We told him that we were living in Norway. He said he was also from Norway. He was lying."

"How do you know?"

"While my husband is German, I am a native Norwegian. He is an engineer that works for an oil company in the North Sea. We met in Stavanger. The man did not have a Norwegian accent. I said something to him in Norwegian, and he didn't respond."

"Did he say where he was from?"

"No, but I'm pretty sure he ordered a local beer with a distinctive label."

"A Dixie?"

"Yes," she said.

Katrina had severely damaged the Dixie brewery. Looters had stolen or destroyed much of the brewery's equipment. Tony continued to drink the beer, pretending it was still brewed in New Orleans and not by arrangement with a brewery in Wisconsin. Its label hadn't changed, and it helped Tony conceal his fantasy as truth.

"Did he introduce himself?"

"He said he was Harald Gjertsen. I remember because I have a cousin whose last name is Gjertsen. He must have realized I was suspicious because he said he was raised in the States and didn't speak Norwegian very well."

"And you think he saw your husband's money belt."

The woman nodded again. "I'm sure of it."

"What were you doing on Bourbon Street?"

"Jurgen wanted to experience a little of Mardi Gras madness."

"Harald Gjertsen followed you off the ship?"

"I saw him in the crowd behind us. He surprised us in the alleyway and told Jurgen to give him the money belt. He didn't know my husband had a pistol."

"Your husband pulled the weapon? You just flew in from Norway. Where'd he get it?"

The woman glanced at the sidewalk. "He bought it at a pawnshop. I told him that we didn't need it."

"Too late to worry about it now. What happened when your husband pulled the pistol?"

"It didn't frighten Gjertsen, or whoever he is. He just pushed it away, causing Jurgen to fire into the air. When Jurgen tried to fight him, the man took the pistol away and shot him."

Memory of what happened next caused the woman to cradle her face in her hands and sob.

"I'm sorry about dragging you through this, Mrs. Schumacher. What happened next?"

"He yanked the money belt loose and ran away."

"Where did he go?"

The woman pointed toward the crowd, up Bourbon Street.

"He's a monster! Jurgen was bleeding. He just kicked him away."

The E.M.T. led Anna Schumacher to the ambulance as Tony grabbed his cell phone and started up Bourbon Street, Marlon hurrying to keep up.

"Poor woman," he said.

"Her husband experienced more of Mardi Gras madness than he'd bargained for."

"Where are we going?"

Tony didn't reply, holding up his hand as someone answered his cell phone call.

"Bonnie, send some men to the cruise ship Scandinavian Queen. Find Harald Gjertsen. Bring him in for questioning and tell the officers to cover their asses. This guy's a killer."

"We might be stepping on toes here," Marlon said.

"Shut the fuck up!" Tony said.

Flipping the phone shut, he began walking against

the crowd, flashing his badge as a warning for people to get out of his way. He stopped at the first bar they came to, pushed the protesting barker aside and entered. The seedy bar smelled of stale smoke and spilled drinks, a young, blonde stripper with clouded eyes gyrating slowly on a small stage to the tune of a sad, country ballad. Ignoring the losers sitting at the pussy bar, he spotted someone he knew.

"Hey Cowboy, I didn't know you liked strip clubs."

"Lots of things about me you don't know, Lieutenant."

"Maybe I don't want to know."

The bar's flashing strobe light reflected off Desire's coat causing Tony to do a brief double take.

"Miss, you're way too young and innocent to be hanging out in a strip bar with this perv."

"I pulled him in against his will. I want to dance, but he won't let me."

Tony gave Desire a look, glanced at Wyatt and then back at her again. Marlon stood behind them. From the stunned expression on his face, he'd also never been in a strip club, the young woman on stage perhaps the first naked female he'd ever seen.

"I'm Wyatt."

"Marlon Bando."

Marlon's clammy hand felt like a limp fish. "What are you doing here, Tony? I didn't know you were a voyeur."

"Lots of things you don't know about me, Cowboy. We're looking for someone. There was a shooting down the street. You seen anyone in the last hour or so that's six-seven or taller?"

"Matter of fact, we did. We heard some shots. Next thing we knew, this tall guy, in a big hurry, bumped into us. He was carrying a pistol and money belt."

"Did you get a good look at him?"

"You know me, Tony. I never forget a face."

"Then I hate to disturb the rest of your evening, but I need you to come down to the station with me. Sounds like you got a close look at our perp. Maybe you can help us put a name on him."

"What about Desire? Can I at least send her home?"

Tony shook his head. "What if she saw some things you forgot? This won't take long."

"Famous last words," Wyatt said as he threw some money on the bar, grabbed Desire's hand and then followed Tony out to the crowded sidewalk.

Chapter Seventeen

Tony had Marlon drop him off at his house, and told him to come for him at eight thirty the next morning. Lil met him at the door with a smile and a cold Dixie.

"It's late. You didn't have to wait up," he said.

"If I didn't, I'd never see you."

"It'll get better. Carnival's almost over."

Lil followed him down the hall as he removed his coat and drank the beer.

"You thought about our discussion yet?"

"I thought about it," he said.

"And?"

"And I'm still thinking about it."

"It's getting late, Tony, and I'm not talking about what time it is."

Tony wheeled around and faced her, raising his hand to indicate a time out.

"All right, already. I've had a long day. I'm beat. Can't we have this discussion tomorrow?"

"Fine," she said, heading for the bedroom. "There's chicken and rice on the stove, and more beer in the fridge. I'm going to bed."

Tony and Lil sat at the table in their small kitchen. It wasn't even eight yet when Marlon knocked on the door.

"Who could that be this early?"

"My new partner, and I don't even have my pants on yet."

Lillian opened the door and greeted the young man. "I'm Tony's wife Lil. Come in. He's not quite ready. Have you had breakfast?"

Marlon shook his head. "No ma'am, I don't usually eat breakfast."

"An awful habit for such a young man. What's your name?"

"Marlon," he said, following her down the hallway.

Tony was working on his breakfast of bacon and eggs. Lil frowned when he didn't bother acknowledging Marlon's presence.

"Tony, it's Marlon."

"I see that," he said.

"Take a seat at the table. Can I get you a cup of coffee?"

"No thanks. I don't drink coffee."

"Orange juice, then?"

Marlon nodded. "That would be nice, thank you."

"Bacon and eggs?"

"I'm watching my cholesterol."

"Probably wise," Lil said. "Are you from around here?"

"No ma'am. I grew up in Monroe and went to school there."

"Married?"

"Single. I haven't met a woman I'm compatible with."

Lil frowned and gave Tony a dirty look when he said, "Surprise, surprise."

"Toast?"

"Without butter, please."

"Chief Wexler must think highly of you, picking you to replace Tommy."

"Yes and I don't know why," he said.

Tony smirked and said, "Influential uncle, maybe?"

Marlon didn't respond to the insult, but Lil did. When she flashed her husband a dirty look and shook her spatula at him, he just grinned and kept eating his bacon and eggs.

Tony let Marlon drive when they finally left the house, and he quickly rued the decision. New Orleans drivers are horrible. Marlon was even worse, narrowly averting two accidents before they were a mile down the road. Tony just shook his head, put a hand over his eyes, and took a deep breath.

"Where to?" Marlon asked.

"Julia Street Wharf."

Tony rolled his eyes when Marlon asked, "Which way is that?"

"Go over to Canal, turn right and then head toward the river."

"You sent officers to the ship last night."

"Yeah, well it's no surprise Harald Gjertsen wasn't there. We need to find out what the cruise line knows about him."

"Is there even an outside chance Gjertsen is our killer?"

"Gjertsen is the victim that washed up at the Golden Bough, the person posing as Gjertsen our killer. Wyatt Thomas identified him for us last night."

"We learned in police science classes that eyewitness descriptions are usually unreliable."

"Well this is the real world, Thomas a pro. There's a problem, though. The person he identified, Jacque Leguerre, is supposed to be in Federal prison."

"Then that's the reason the Feds are all over town. Leguerre's the escapee we talked about."

"If so, then he must be someone pretty important."

"Why don't we just give this information to Landry and let him and his people handle it?"

"Number one, New Orleans is our town. Number two, they obviously don't have a clue how to find this guy. Number three, you work for the N.O.P.D, not the Feds. This is our responsibility."

"You're the boss."

"I'm not your boss, I'm your partner. Don't you

have the foggiest idea what I'm talking about?"

Marlon kept driving and staring straight ahead. He finally said, "I'm doing the best I can."

"Partners should be closer than brothers, anticipate problems and cover each other's back. Stay with me on this one. I know where I'm going with it, and I didn't just fall off the turnip truck."

Marlon turned on Canal, and they soon reached the Julia Street Wharf where they found the cruise ship Scandinavian Queen docked. After a short hike to the cruise ship's business office, a permanent building near the water's edge, they waited in front until the cruise director joined them. The young man, dressed in white uniform with brass buttons, had surfer blonde hair, bronze tan, and a perpetual smile. He shook Tony's hand a bit too enthusiastically.

"I'm Ted Delany, cruise line personnel director, at your service."

"I've never seen so many passengers. Looks like you got a real cluster fuck on your hands."

Delany nodded. "N.O. is our home port. Every cruise includes two days here in the city. The shipwreck in Southwest Pass has us jammed up."

"Just what we need. Mardi Gras on steroids!"

Delany's smile faded. "Couldn't have happened at a worse time. My people are about to drop trying to keep up with everybody."

"Welcome to the club," Tony said. "You familiar with the passenger named Harald Gjertsen?

Delany motioned Tony and Marlon to join him behind the counter where he accessed the ship's database on a company computer.

"This is our home port. We embark from here to Cancun, Aruba, and the Bahamas. Every cruise includes two extra days in New Orleans. Like a two for one vacation. We've been waiting now for three days to leave port."

"Are the passengers ready to mutiny?"

"No, but like I said, we've been working overtime to keep them happy."

"And Gjertsen?"

"From Norway. He and his wife flew in three days ago. We have lots of passengers, many of them from Europe. I don't remember all of them. I remember Gjertsen because he was unusually tall. He and his wife were friendly, but they kept to themselves."

"I didn't know until this morning he had a wife."

"Her name's Greta. When your people came by last night, they found her in their cabin."

"She okay?"

"Totally traumatized, and who wouldn't be? They took her to Charity."

For a moment, Tony forgot the hospital hadn't reopened since suffering severe damage during Hurricane Katrina. Its status was still in limbo.

"Why'd you let them take her there? She's no derelict."

"Just kidding. It's closed. Remember? Anyway, it wasn't that dreadful."

"You shitting me? If you're dead broke, maybe. Three hots, a cot, and no jailer."

Delany grinned. "Sorry about the bad joke. Her father flew in this morning from Norway to take her home. They're staying at the Monteleone."

"Then she's likely to survive until we question her. Meantime, we need photos, emergency contact numbers, everything you got."

As Tony and Marlon left the business office with the package of information given to them by Delany, they met the redheaded U.S. Marshal and his beefy partner. It was the first time Tony had noticed the younger man. His dark hair was cropped short like an Army recruit and his nose slightly canted, as if broken on more than one occasion. When James Landry saw them, he blocked their path.

"I told you to butt out of this investigation. You must be even dumber than I thought."

"Hey, we got a killer running loose around here. You can't stop the N.O.P.D. from protecting our citizens and tourists."

Landry started to say something, but thought better of it.

"This is sensitive."

"Then let us in on it. We're crossing the same ground here. We can help."

Landry shook his head. "The identity of the person we're after can't be compromised."

"You mean Jacque Leguerre?"

Landry's frown returned. "How the hell do you know that?"

"Someone near the murder scene last night identified him."

"And you weren't going to tell me?"

"I'm telling you now."

"Who else knows?"

"Just me and Marlon."

Landry started to reach for Tony's jacket, thought better of it, backed up and took a deep breath.

"Okay, Nicosia. This information I'm going to give you is confidential. Understand me?" Tony nodded. "Leguerre was a mob hit man, scheduled to testify against his former bosses in exchange for our promise to put him in Witness Protection. He somehow managed to escape."

"Peachy! Just what we need! Another murderer on the streets."

"He's a sociopath, not a psychopath."

"Yeah, then why did he escape, and why is he still killing people?"

"Doesn't matter. We got bigger fish to fry here."

"I'm listening."

"His testimony will bring down some high-ranking mob figures. We were trying to spirit him into the City, up the river in the boat that sank in Southwest Pass. We recovered all the bodies except his."

"You got to be kidding me. There are so many cross-currents and undertows out there no one could have survived."

"Leguerre did, and now he's here in New Orleans."

"Then why didn't you tell us?"

"I told you why. We have reason to believe organized crime has infiltrated the N.O.P.D."

"That's crazy."

"Maybe, but if the bad guys find out now, I'll have your heads."

"Meanwhile, he's already killed two more people."

"He kills without remorse and is strong, almost beyond belief."

"Sounds to me like he needs a bullet between the eyes; not Witness Protection."

"We're in agreement on that one, but it's not my call, or yours either. Right now he's off limits. It's essential we capture him alive and unharmed, so he can complete his testimony. Got me?"

"We're hip."

"Fine, then raise your right hands. I'm swearing you in as temporary U.S. Marshals."

"You shitting me? Is that legal?"

"You bet your sweet ass it is, now raise them."

Curious tourists watched as Tony and Marlon right hands raised, swore an oath of allegiance. After exchanging business cards and turning over the file from the Scandinavian Queen, they started up the sidewalk.

"Are we U.S. Marshals now?" Marlon asked.

"Don't have a clue. I know an assistant Federal district attorney that will, though."

"What now?"

"Since we're on the dock, let's stop back at the casino and find out if the young woman we met yesterday has learned anything new to tell us."

Tony's knee was bothering him again when they reached the Golden Bough, and Marlon had no trouble following him up the gangplank. A smiling Venus Hernandez soon joined them, dispensing with handshakes and hugging Tony with enthusiasm. Lacing her arm through his, she smiled when he explained why they had dropped by.

"I was just thinking about you," she said.

"In a good way, I hope."

"This is my night off. I was going to stop over at Carlucci's, and hoping you'd be there."

"You bet I will."

"What time?"

"How about eight?"

Venus hugged him again, and then planted a soft kiss on his cheek, maybe a little too close to his lips. Marlon didn't miss his partner's smile and reddened face. Neither Venus nor Tony noticed he was noticing.

"Can't wait," she said, waving as they descended the gangplank on their way back to the car.

Clouds began covering the sky, an early spring chill once again in the air. Tony had forgotten his sore knee during the visit with Venus Hernandez. The walk back to the car caused him to remember again. When he slowed to rub his knee, Marlon's ensuing question caught him off guard.

"Forget something, Lieutenant?"

"Like what?"

"You didn't ask Miss Hernandez if she has anything new for us."

"We'll have plenty of time to ask her tonight at Carlucci's. Right now, we need to get over to the Monteleone and interview Greta Gjertsen."

Chapter Eighteen

Despite Lieutenant Nicosia's promise, it was early morning when Desire and I finally left the police station. I barely suppressed a yawn as the sun began peeking over the buildings. When we reached Canal Street, I whistled for a cab. Desire just kept walking.

"You may as well stop whistling. I'm not ready to go home yet."

"I've kept you out all night. I don't want your dad to get the wrong idea. He might kill me."

"Or fire you. Isn't that what you're really worried about?"

I flashed an indignant frown. "Not so. I care about people's sensibilities."

"Dad is about as sensitive as a gator feasting on a floating carcass. Besides, he won't fire you. I have him wrapped around my little finger."

"Still—"

Desire held up a palm and shook her head. "We got sidetracked last night. You know we have business to attend to."

"There's nothing I would like better, but—"

"No buts. I'm naked under this coat, my dress at Bertram's. I can't go home like this even if I wanted to. And I don't want to."

"But—"

"I said no buts. Quit whining, and then take me to

your place. I need a shower and so do you."

I grinned, not wanting to win the argument. The streets were still wet with rain. The storm had passed, so we continued walking without bothering to hail a cab. As we neared Canal, the sun was little more than a splash of yellow finger painted across the sky. Cottony clouds left over from the early morning rain floated past, breathing life onto the canvas.

"Okay, just keep your coat closed, or we're liable to find ourselves back at the police station."

"It's Mardi Gras. There'll be dozens of half-naked people on the streets by noon. You know that."

"Maybe, but it won't be noon for hours. Right now, the only people out and about are bunches of elderly tourists. I'm sure their old hearts couldn't endure the spectacle of seeing a girl as pretty as you with all her clothes off."

"Spectacle, huh?"

"You know what I mean."

"Quit grumbling," she said, squeezing close enough to me that I could feel the warmth she radiated. "You know you love it."

A streetcar rumbled past, screeching to a halt at a passenger stop to pick up some tourists on their way up St. Charles Avenue, or maybe the Audubon Zoo.

"I'll like it better when we're alone in my room and not crossing the widest street on earth."

Desire cinched the coat tightly around her waist, then put her arm around me.

"Just shut up," she said.

When we reached Bertram's bar, there was no one there except him and Lady. Desire caught Bertram by surprise when she stood on her tiptoes, bent over the counter and kissed him on the mouth. When she pulled off the red, feathery coat and handed it to him, his dark eyes grew wide, and his mouth dropped.

"You're a sweetie Bertram. Thanks for letting me use your coat."

We both watched as she strutted, stark naked up the staircase. Bertram winked and grinned as he tossed me her dress.

"Got you a hot one there, Cowboy. Better take care of her before she realizes what a lemon you are. And take this," he said, tossing me Desire's dress. "Shirley found it in the lady's room last night."

Snatching it from midair, I started up the stairs. When I caught up with Desire, she seemed as relaxed and casual with her nudity as if she were alone in her own bedroom. Except for the silly grin on her face, that is.

She laughed when I said. "You're breathtaking. Have you thought about a career in modeling?"

She didn't respond to my compliment. "Don't you ever lock your door?"

"I have nothing worth stealing, except my cat."

My tailless cat met us at the door, arching her back and winding between our legs. Desire whisked Kisses off the floor, hugging her against her bare breasts.

"Who is this sweet kitty?"

"Her name is Kisses, the only girl in my life before I met you."

"I don't believe a word you say. I've known movie stars who aren't as sexy and handsome as you."

As if she'd visited my apartment many times, she plopped down on the bed. I wasn't the only one taken by Desire. Kisses jumped up on the bed and began kneading dough on her chest.

"Looks as if my cat likes you better than she does me."

"I don't think so. You impressed me at the police station last night."

"And how did I do that?"

"The way you went through the mug shots and identified the person we saw. I wouldn't recognize him if he walked through the door right now."

"His eyes," I said. "I couldn't forget those eyes."

Desire sat up and patted my cheek. "You're a fascinating man Wyatt Thomas. Now, how about that shower?"

"Through that door," I said, pointing

Desire peeked inside the bathroom. "I don't like wasting water. You need a shower, too. Why not join me?"

She didn't have to twist my arm.

There's nothing quite as exhilarating as a new love affair. Desire and I lay naked on my little bed, staring out the second-story patio that was green with ferns hanging from the covered roof, and draping almost to my antique, wicker settee, and the large, potted plant where my first cat Bob was buried. Tourists bustled by on the sidewalk below, so close we could almost hear their conversations. Desire glanced up at the slow moving ceiling fan over the bed.

"I love your apartment, and I'm pretty sure I love you," she said.

She grinned when I said, "I'm glad I didn't disappoint you."

"You're pretty good for an older man, and you already knew you wouldn't disappoint me."

"I'm not much older than you are," I said, my feelings slightly miffed.

"You remind me in a lot of ways of my dad, except I know you're not a racist."

"Hey, it's the south. You can't get away from it down here."

"I'm from down here, and I'm not that way. You and Bertram aren't either. After a couple of serious arguments, Dad quit trying to persuade me. Now he just pretends I'm the same as he is. Dauphine, on the other hand—"

"Your sister's a racist?"

"I'm not sure what she believes. She worships Dad. When he's around, she tries to act just like him. If she only knew."

"Knew what?"

"I can't tell all my secrets. Sorry, I spoke out of turn."

Letting the comment drop, I squeezed her hand and asked, "What about your mom?"

"She is originally from New York and modeled long before me. She called her agent and landed me my first job."

I grinned at her story. "Like they were taking a real chance by giving you a shot."

Desire ignored my flippant remark. "Mom met Dad on a photo shoot in Jackson Square. She doesn't have a bigoted bone in her body. She even gets along with Cayenne."

"Cayenne?"

"You'll meet her at the party."

"Okay then. What about Claude? Do you know why he and your dad hate each other?"

"I call him Uncle Claude because they were like brothers growing up, even if they don't look anything alike."

"What does he look like?"

"Tall, with brown hair and fair skin like you. You've seen Dad. If he's not a Creole, he's missing a good bet."

"Your dad favors the Vallees, Claude the Sonniers. That's not so surprising," I said.

"Except that Claude looks more like the son of my grandparents than Dad does."

"What about Claude's wife? Does she get along with Gordon and your mom?"

"Uncle Claude has been divorced for years now. When you see him with Mom, you'll think it's them that are married. They can't keep their hands off each other."

"Your dad doesn't mind?"

"Hey, are you on the clock or what? If you are, then stop it. You can work on Dad's job when I'm not here."

"Sorry."

"Besides, we were talking about his blatant racism."

"I wouldn't know you now if it weren't for your Dad's quirks."

"It's crazy, though. Mama Marlene is more like his mom than Grandmother Flo ever was. I loved them both dearly, but my grandparents were socialites, and spent little time, from what I understand, raising Dad."

"Dauphine is your twin sister. I thought all twins were exactly alike, even in the way they think."

"So much for what you know about twins."

"What's the story?"

"Dauphine and I are different as night and day. If we were states, she'd be red, and I'd be blue. We're not even identical. You'll know when you see her."

"Does her kowtowing to please your father make her his favorite daughter?"

Desire smiled. "Dad's always liked me better. Don't ask me why."

I watched as she sat on the edge of the bed, smoothing dark hair draping her graceful shoulders. When she walked to the patio door, the room's dancing shadows set up by the ceiling fan highlighted her body like a Goya painting. She opened the sliding door and went outside.

Stretching her arms, she said, "I like being naked, and love it when people look at me."

"Then you must be happy all the time."

A car passing on the street below screeched its tires, slowing for tourists who had seen Desire on the balcony, and were gawking up at her.

"You better get back in here before you cause a wreck, a riot, or both."

Desire did a spin on one toe, waved at the throng of tourists who had begun gathering under the balcony, and then hurried back into the room. Excited by her exhibitionistic performance, she dived on the bed, sprawling her lithe body on top of me.

"I'm wondering. Do you love me, even just a little bit, Mr. Thomas?"

"I like you a lot, Ms. Vallee. You're beautiful, and I'm not just talking about your face and body."

She rested her elbows on my chest and stared at me with hypnotic eyes.

"Do you believe in God?"

"I guess so. Why do you ask?"

"Because I'm wondering. I've always liked bad boys,

and you're a little too good. It just seems you must be intensely religious."

Her comment made me feel like laughing. What escaped my lips was only a titter.

"I believe in a greater power, though I've had a problem with organized religion now for years."

"Are you Catholic?"

"Raised that way, though I'm presently estranged from the church."

"Father Rafael is such a passionate man. He said you are lost, and seeking a higher power."

"Did he? What else did he say?"

"He got the strangest look in his eyes when I was confessing my sins. He said I was an innocent."

"Oh?"

"He said he had the gift of second sight, something he'd never told anyone, including his own mother. He said even though I don't know who I am right now, someday I will."

"How strange," I said.

"That's all he would say. Wyatt, I want to meet his mother Madeline. Maybe she can explain what he meant. Will you take me to see her?"

A car horn blaring at pedestrians on the street below almost drowned out my reply.

Chapter Nineteen

Tony and Marlon left their car in a parking lot, taking the Riverfront Streetcar to the French Quarter. They walked the short distance, avoiding as best they could the many drunks and partiers already crowding the sidewalks, to the old multistoried hotel that was a fixture of the city.

"Shouldn't we have called first?" Marlon asked.

"Sometimes it's best just to show up, before the person you intend to question has time to consider what they're going to tell you."

Marlon followed Tony to the front desk where he flashed his badge at the counterperson whose nametag said Don.

"We need to speak with Greta Gjertsen, one of your guests. Can you ring her room for us?"

The man behind the counter had a full head of gray hair, with mustache to match. He glanced up at Tony with a wry grin.

"Guess at least a few of you came back to town after Katrina."

A muscle in Tony's lip twitched, displaying his only response, other than a frown, to the man's comment.

"Not funny. Just buzz Ms. Gjertsen for us."

"Could, but she's not in her room."

"You keep personal tabs on all your guests?"

"Not usually. This one you can't miss. She's every

bit of six-three and looks like a young Ingrid Bergman."

"Movie buff, huh? If she's not in her room, where can we find her?"

"She and her old man went into the Carousel Lounge about an hour ago. You can't miss them because he's taller than she is"

"Not their first time?"

Don shook his head. "They practically closed the place last night."

Tony nodded and started to walk away. Thinking better of it, he turned and saluted the man.

"Thanks for the info, Don. You ever get tired of this place you might try the N.O.P.D. We're always looking for alert employees."

Delivered with a frown, Tony's advice sounded sinister instead of helpful. Don took it that way, rapidly losing his grin as he turned his attention to a pile of loose papers on the counter.

"Fucking asshole," Tony said as he opened the door to the Carousel Lounge.

"What'd he do?" Marlon asked.

"We're N.O.P.D. This town would be in chaos without us. We should be treated with respect."

Marlon's jaw dropped when they entered the lounge. A circular bar, topped with a sparkling crown imprinted with smiling Mardi Gras characters, highlighted the darkened room. The tables and booths surrounding the bar were empty. Two people were there, kibitzing with the bartender. Marlon could see they were both tall. Tony approached the young woman.

"Ma'am, are you Greta Gjertsen?"

The man beside her turned on his stool. "Who wants to know?"

Whipping out his badge, Tony said, "Lieutenant Anthony Nicosia, N.O.P.D. I have a few questions for Ms. Gjertsen."

"Greta is not in the proper frame of mind to discuss her ordeal," the man said.

The woman was tall, the man even taller, dark hair

graying at his temples. He spoke excellent English with only a slight accent Tony presumed was Norwegian. He guessed his age at fifty-something. From the way he'd slurred his words, he'd probably been at the bar awhile.

"You Ms. Gjertsen's father?"

"Yes I am. Now I told you—"

Tony raised his hand, cutting him off. "Look, we need a statement from your daughter. Marlon and I can join you, sit at the bar, drink a Dixie and take it now, or she can come downtown with us and do it there. Your choice."

The man opened his mouth to say something, thought better of it, and then turned to his daughter.

"Are you okay to talk with this man, *min lite kjærlighet?*"

"I'm fine, Papa."

Greta Gjertsen swiveled in her high-backed stool and smiled. She was stunning, with ash brown hair, pale blue eyes, and as Don had said every bit of six-foot-three.

"I'm Greta. This is my father, Bruse Bakken. Please, join us."

They were drinking martinis; Greta's words were slurred much like her father's, causing Tony to wonder how many drinks they'd already put away. He didn't ask, taking the stool next to her. The bartender arrived to greet them.

"Lieutenant Nicosia, I haven't seen you in a while. Couple of Dixies?"

The man was about Tony's age, dressed in white shirt, black vest and *fleur de lis* tie. He smiled and stroked his chin.

"You got an excellent memory, Marvin. Dixie for me, and a bottle of water for Marlon, my partner."

"Sorry about Tommy. Hope he's okay."

"They don't come any tougher than Irish Channel tough. You already know that, Marvin."

The friendly bartender smiled and nodded, walking away to get their drinks. Tony returned his attention to the stunning Norwegian woman.

"Marv and I go way back. You okay?"

When she nodded, her smile disappeared, tears forming in her electric eyes.

"I'm fine," she said.

"Sorry for your loss. I can't bring your husband back. Maybe, with your help, I can catch his killer."

Greta began to weep, resting her head on his sports coat and dampening it with her tears. Tony patted her shoulder.

"It's okay. I got five kids, two boys and three girls. I know how it is when one of them is hurting."

"The man was a monster," her father said.

"He raped you?" Tony asked.

Greta Gjertsen shook her head. "He didn't hurt me."

"The animal should be shot down like a mad dog," Greta's father said. "Harald's parents are coming to recover his body."

Tony glared at him, and then showed Greta a mug shot. "Is this the man?"

"Yes."

"He held you captive?"

"It wasn't that way."

"I'm not sure what you mean," Tony said.

"I can't explain," she said, motioning Marvin to bring her another martini.

"Don't you think you should take it easy on the alcohol?"

"Stop badgering her," Greta's father said. "She's a grown woman who has gone through a terrible ordeal. She can drink all night if she wants."

Marvin brought the martini and placed it in front of her. She pushed it away and continued to cry at Tony's next comment.

"Even if it's bad for your baby?"

"What did you say?" Bakken demanded. "Greta's not pregnant." When Tony didn't answer, he stared at his daughter. Greta lowered her head as tears continued welling in her eyes. "Greta?"

Though she wouldn't meet her father's stare, she began nodding her head.

"Bring her some water, Marvin," Tony said. "And take the drink. She's done with it."

Greta's father had her arm, trying to get her to face him. "How long have you been pregnant?"

"Three months," she said.

"You were expecting during the wedding? How could you?"

"That's about enough, Bakken," Tony said. "Take your hands off her."

"She is my daughter, and I will talk to her any way I like."

"No you won't."

Bakken banged his fist against the bar. "You cannot tell me what to do."

"Oh no? How would you like me to cuff you and drag you downtown? Would you like to spend the night in the slammer with a bunch of Mardi Gras drunks? You're gonna find out in about two seconds."

"You have no authority."

Tony glanced at Marvin, polishing a glass as he listened intently to the conversation.

"Marvin, would you kindly tell Mr. Bakken here what I can, and cannot do?"

Marvin took the martini from Bakken's hand. "I don't know where you come from, but here in New Orleans it don't pay to piss off the N.O.P.D."

Bakken opened his mouth, as if to reply. Seeing something in the bartender's eyes made him change his mind. Standing to leave, he turned to Greta.

"Greta, let's go."

"You go ahead," she said.

"I will see you upstairs," he said.

Before he had exited the bar Tony's words halted him. "I'm going to check on your daughter every day until she leaves town. Like you said, Mr. Bakken. Stop badgering her. Get my drift?"

Bakken didn't have to answer. The look in his eyes told Tony everything he needed to know.

"Ms. Gjertsen, I hope I didn't scare you."

Greta smiled for the first time. "Lieutenant, I don't believe you would hurt a fly, and I'm not afraid of my father either. He never even spanked me when I was little. Mama would have killed him," she said, grinning again.

"I'm glad to hear that. I'm also glad you survived your ordeal with Jacque Leguerre. He's a wicked man, and I'm sorry you had to endure him."

"He never threatened me. He even had a young dog with him."

"A dog?"

"A shepherd mix with black and auburn markings. She was a beautiful and intelligent animal."

"He had a dog with him?"

"Yes, a wonderful dog."

Tony glanced at Marlon who, along with Marvin, was listening.

"Did he tie you up; keep you locked in a closet or bathroom?"

"No, he was a perfect gentleman."

"Doesn't sound like the man we're looking for," Tony said. "Did he say where he was going; tell you anything about what he intended to do?"

"He said he was leaving town after he took care of some business."

"What business?"

Strobes of light reflecting from a neon bar sign danced in her long hair when she shook her head.

"He would not tell me."

Tony touched her wrist. "Greta, are you afraid he'll come back and hurt you? Is that the reason you're not telling me anything?"

"No, he never threatened me. Something he said made me feel sorry for him."

"Yeah, and what was that?"

"He said he was just someone who had come from a dark and terrible place. I am sorry about one thing," she said.

"Tell me."

"He was going to leave Velvet with me. He'd taken her for a walk when police came to my room."

"And you wanted her?"

Greta nodded. "I felt she understood all my problems."

Tony slid off the stool, his nod informing Marlon to do the same.

"Thanks, Ms. Gjertsen. I got no more questions right now. Take care of your baby."

Tony pulled a twenty from his wallet, trying to give it to Marvin. "Your money's no good in here," the red-headed bartender said. "Next time, don't stay away so long."

"Why are we leaving?" Marlon said as they exited the bar. "She knows more than she's telling us."

"She told us all we need to know," Tony said, bending to rub his knee.

"What's the story on Marvin? You seemed to know him pretty well."

"Ex-cop. Took a bullet in the leg trying to stop an armed robbery. Now he's too gimpy to continue policing."

"I'm so sorry," Marlon said.

"Don't feel sorry for him. He makes more money than you and me, and he don't ever have to take another bullet again trying to protect somebody."

Chapter Twenty

Desire and I finally managed to get out of bed and venture from the room. Bertram's business had picked up, and he was busy waiting on customers. Tourists stood in the doorway, trying to decide if they should eat something before they began partying. I grabbed Desire's elbow, reining her in before she walked out the door.

"You want one of Bertram's Margaritas before we go?"

"Not now," she said, giving Bertram a backwards wave as she led me out the door. "I'm already drunk on your love."

As I followed her down Chartres, I realized we hadn't eaten since we'd met. It must be love I thought as I followed her through the meandering tourists crowding the street on both sides. Overhead, fireworks burst into smoky, cascading color.

"I'm starving. Let's get something to eat," I finally said.

Desire glanced at me with a grin. "You'd think you've been chopping wood or something."

"Or something," I said. "Never mind, but you may have to give me mouth to mouth later on."

When I rubbed my stomach, she said, "You're such a baby. All right, I can probably eat something myself."

It was New Orleans, so it took almost no time

finding a place to eat. The little café wasn't old, though the building it occupied was. Two walls of the café were open to the outside, overlooking Jackson Square, affording its patrons the opportunity to people watch while they ate. Most of the diners were doing just that.

I was soon hunkered down, working on a muffaleta, Desire mostly picking at hers as she gazed out the open café at portrait artists plying their trade, a clown with curly hair juggling hard boiled eggs, a mime, his face painted white, and scads of tourists, many clad in costumes. Pigeons, vying for crumbs on the bricks, didn't seem to notice there was a celebration going on. Desire tugged my attention away from the sandwich.

"Have you ever been inside St. Louis Cathedral?"

"Of course I have. My grandparents used to take me there for Mass every Easter and Christmas."

"Grandparents? What about your parents?"

"A long story and I'm much too happy to talk about it right now."

"Please?" she said.

"It's a beautiful day, and Carnival in the Big Easy. Next time it's drizzling rain and I feel like being depressed for a few hours, I'll tell you the story."

"Spoil sport. I've lived in New Orleans all my life, and I've never been inside the Cathedral."

"Never?"

"No one ever took me, and I've always been too intimidated to go by myself."

"No need for intimidation. They're friendly; I promise."

"Then will you take me when we finish eating?"

"Better than that. I'll give you a guided tour."

My promise to show Desire the Cathedral made her anxious as if I'd promised a chocoholic a tour of a candy factory. She practically dragged me out of the little café.

The most imposing edifice in all of New Orleans, the Cathedral was likely the most photographed. Desire released my hand, hurrying inside. I found her waiting for me, gazing through open doors at the wide passage of black and white tile that led past the pews to the impressive altar.

"This is the oldest Catholic cathedral in continuous use, in North America," I said in my best tour guide's voice.

That was the end of my guided tour, Desire already staring at paintings and filigree designs on vaulted ceiling and beautiful, stained glass windows. Three nuns dressed in full habits were near us, kneeling and praying.

"What are they doing?" she asked.

"Performing the Stations of the Cross. There are fourteen of them scattered around the Cathedral, and probably every other Catholic church in the world. They symbolize Christ's journey to Calvary, and his crucifixion."

"I'm Catholic, but I can count on one hand the times my parents took me to church. So they're performing a ritual?"

"One as old as the religion itself. The leader of the group announces the name of the station and gives a statement of praise. The others respond. The leader reads a recitation. They'll pray, say a Hail Mary, and then move to the next station."

"But what does it mean?"

"They're demonstrating their faith, and maybe praying for something they feel strongly about."

"Like what?"

"I don't know. It could be most anything."

The nuns were dressed in white robes that rippled and flowed, causing their every move to seem almost choreographed.

"They look like a flock of angels," Desire said.

She glanced at me when I said, "Maybe they are."

"Do you think they'd mind if I joined them?"

Desire's question caught me by surprise. The impression I had of her was more of a beautiful model strutting down a Paris catwalk than that of a young woman engaged in serious worship with a group of nuns.

"I'm sure they won't mind. Knock yourself out."

With a mile-wide smile, she hurried to join the sisters, looking somehow acceptable, even dressed in boots and abbreviated skirt. They welcomed her, quickly instructing her in the ritual. She was soon praying and reciting, even joining in on hymns sung between stations. The journey took more than an hour Desire smiling and hugging herself as she strutted up the aisle toward me.

"That was the most awesome experience I've ever had," she said as we exited the Cathedral and rejoined the madness of Mardi Gras. "I've never felt so much at peace in my life."

"I'm glad. Do you still want to go to Madeline's?"

"Now more than ever," she said, grabbing my hand again and pulling me through the dynamic throng suddenly engulfing us.

"What's in your hand?" I asked.

"Rosary beads. The sisters gave them to me. They also shared something else."

"Like what?"

"Their wisdom."

It wasn't far from Bertram's to Madeline's Magic Potions. Madeline met us at the door, almost as if she were expecting us. She immediately clutched Desire's hand.

"Rafael was right. You are an angel. Please come in."

"How did you know who I am?"

"Rafael is a poet, and his flowing couplets could describe only you. I knew who you were the moment I saw you."

As she'd done the first time I met her, Madeline locked the door behind us. Like a child in a toy store, Desire spread her arms and twirled through the eclectic shop. When she spotted Jinx, she picked up the large cat from the cabinet and hugged it.

"What a gorgeous cat."

"Some people think black cats are unlucky."

"How could such a beautiful creature be unlucky?"

As before, the lighting was dim, Gregorian chants constructing a dramatic cloak of background music melding with the peal of gargoyle wind chimes. Motion of the fan set flames of Madeline's many candles into a dance of flickering lights amid mingled odors of candle wax, perfume, and antiquity. For a moment, I wasn't sure we hadn't stepped through a portal. Maybe we had.

"I asked Wyatt to bring me here," Desire said.

Jinx followed us through Madeline's shop crowded with potions and oddities to the room in back where she'd read my tarot cards. This time, she didn't bother opening the deck.

"You don't have to tell me why you came, child. I know you have questions that are vital to you. Perhaps my crystal ball can provide the answers."

The room was dark, lighted only by a single candle that popped and sputtered like a smoldering caldera. When she removed her crystal ball from its decorative box, the orb glowed like a living being. I could almost feel power emanating from the crystal's interior as she placed it on the table.

"This crystal ball was cut from a quartz seam in a Romanian coal mine. The fire you see is caused by reflections from veils in the quartz, though some say it's because the solid rock is alive."

"It is alive. I can feel it," Desire said, her gaze focused on the polished sphere.

Desire was right. The glowing ball reflected light from the candle, setting in motion dancing rainbows of color that permeated every corner of the dark room.

"My mother gave it to me," Madeline said. "Without the gift of vision she also gave me, her teachings would be for naught."

Madeline cupped her hands around the crystal, frowning as she stared into its glow. Monks, chanting in the background, caused her motions to seem like a choreographed production. If they were, it was effective, music, antiquity, and the hypnotic crystal ball causing me to lose track of time. Time seemed halted as I stared at the visual sparkler, its insistent fire burning a hole in my brain.

Madeline began to hum; not a tune but the sound of a resonant vibration coming from somewhere deep in her throat. I noticed her dark eyes, locked open and unblinking, reflecting flashing sparkles from the surface of the ball. When she finally spoke, it was in a much deeper voice that seemed to emanate from someone in a deep trance.

"You are both Travelers. Your paths have crossed many times in the past."

When Desire started to say something, I touched her arm and shook my head. She drew away from my touch as Madeline continued.

"Though your paths have crossed, the time you spent together has never been for long. I see," she hesitated, "I see—"

The voice that wasn't Madeline's droned to a stop, and she pushed the crystal aside, turning her head away from the light.

"Are you okay?" I asked.

"Please, put this away for me."

When I hoisted the crystal, its weight surprised me. I returned it to its case. Madeline didn't turn back around until she was sure I'd accomplished the task.

"What's the matter?" Desire asked.

"I'm unable to complete the telling of your fortune."

"But why?"

Madeline's hands quivered, and she shook her head. "Sometimes the future is best left untold.

"It's not fair. Is something terrible about to happen to me?"

"I can't tell you, please—"

"Desire's right," I said. "Paint it in the best light, but tell us what's going to happen."

Madeline stood from the table, whisking Jinx into her arms, stroking him as she walked to the door.

"Let's have tea in the courtyard."

We followed her to the patio, all of us blinking in bright sunlight. Desire and I waited on the park bench while Madeline prepared tea.

"Hello, I'm Wyatt," Madeline's raven said from her perch, alarming Desire who hadn't noticed her.

"Her name is Calpurnia," I said.

"Hello, Calpurnia. I'm Desire."

"Hello, I'm Wyatt. I'm Desire," Calpurnia said.

"You have to take care what you say around her," Madeline said, returning with a teapot and three cups on a tray. "She repeats everything she hears."

The roar of an afternoon parade, just reaching its terminus over on Canal, caused Calpurnia to flap her wings and lift off, briefly, from her perch. A trumpet blared, signaling the end of the long parade and many marchers with tired legs. Madeline poured our tea.

"Now tell me what my future brings," Desire said.

"Sometimes there's no easy way to say something or diplomatic way to phrase it."

"It's okay, just tell me."

"A curse rests on your family. You will reach a crossroads, the route you choose the only option you will have in the matter."

"A family curse? Is it terrible?"

"The crystal ball doesn't lie."

"Then what can I do?"

Madeline squeezed Desire's hand. "There is nothing you can do about the curse, though kismet isn't always certain. Sometimes God changes his mind."

Chapter Twenty-One

Not far from the Eighth District Headquarters, Carlucci's was the watering hole of choice for many of the cops in the neighborhood. Every now and then, an unsuspecting visitor would wander in. None of them ever stayed for long.

Still early when they reached Carlucci's, Marlon wrinkled his nose at the reek of years of accumulated cigarette smoke. Pool balls clattered, and a cue ball bounced across the floor as their eyes adjusted to pervading dimness. Aaron Neville's voice resonated from the jukebox in the corner, singing, "*You musta put the voodoo on me.*" Someone was tapping a foot and clapping, keeping time with the music.

Mike, an ex-beat cop, began pouring two pitchers of Dixie when he spotted Tony coming in the door, He didn't bother putting his cigarette in an ashtray. When the ash dropped on the countertop, he brushed it off, onto the floor.

"How many glasses you gonna need tonight, Lieutenant Tony?"

"Don't know yet. Who all's here?"

"The usual crowd."

"Great," Tony said. "Take two pitchers to their table and more when they run out. I'm expecting someone, and we'll be sitting in the corner at a table of our own."

"Doc ain't gonna like that. He's been gunning for a rematch since the other night when you beat him six games in a row."

"No darts for me tonight. He'll just have to live with it."

"Bidness?"

"You could say that," Tony said.

"Hey Tony!" a voice called from in back of the room hazy with cigarette smoke. "You been ducking me?"

Doc Warner, one of the cops sitting at their usual table, motioned Tony to join them.

"Come on, Marlon. I'll introduce you."

Warner rushed to greet them. Chief of Technical Services and Support, he was so small his people called him Bilbo behind his back.

"Where you been? You owe me about ten games of darts."

"Yeah, and you still owe me about ten bucks from the last time we played. Doc, this is Marlon Bando, my new partner until Tommy gets better."

"Hey, Marlon. Sorry about Tommy, Tony."

A cute woman with short blond hair hugged Tony, her eyes tearing as she rested her chin on his shoulder. Tommy and Donna Fonteneau often dated, and she'd visited him at the hospital every day since the stabbing.

"I know you're worried as me about Tommy," she said.

"He's going to be fine. You need to stop worrying."

"You okay?"

"No, but there's nothing much I can do about it. Marlon here's filling in."

Donna gave Tony a sisterly kiss on the cheek, and then patted Marlon's shoulder.

"Glad to meet you, Marlon. I'm Donna."

Mike brought the beer as Marlon and Tony pulled up chairs at the table. Jon Do, youngest son of Vietnamese immigrants, scooted his chair aside to make room for them, banging into his best friend Ernie Martinez in the process. Paul Portie, looking much like a nineteenth century Creole, except for his uniform, shook Marlon's hand.

"Better watch your partner," he said with a grin. "He's a troublemaker."

"Yeah, well don't believe a word this one says," Tony said, glancing at his watch. "Marlon's going to visit with you guys tonight. The daughter of an old friend is joining me. We're going to sit by ourselves and discuss old times."

Everyone at the table issued a collective groan.

"Daughter of an old friend? Uh huh!" Ernie said.

"Is meeting her more important than our dart game?" Doc Warner asked.

"Wait'll you see her. You'll see."

"Hey, I'm jealous. We don't need to call Lil, do we Tony?" Donna asked.

"Don't even think about it. Marlon don't drink or smoke, and he ain't real bright. Otherwise, he's a pretty decent guy."

Marlon winced at Tony's rude remark, even though he'd said it with a grin and a wink.

Donna squeezed Marlon's shoulders a bit more than sisterly. "You're pretty cute. We'll take care of you, maybe even corrupt you a little. You don't mind sitting with us, do you?"

"Watch her, Marlon," Ernie said. "I don't see a wedding ring on your finger."

"I'm single, guilty as charged."

"Well you're a step up from these usual reprobates I have to drink with. Will you join us while Tony visits with his old friend's daughter?"

"I've got no place else to go," he said with a smile.

"Great," Tony said. "I'll order more Dixie."

He left the table before Doc Warner could protest further. Paul, Ernie, and Jon were drinking Dixie beers, and whiskey shots, their libidos already stoked and lubricated. Marlon didn't complain when pretty Donna linked his elbow with hers. Doc Warner didn't let him wallow in her attention for long.

"You play darts, Marlon?" he asked.

"Never tried, to tell you the truth."

"Come on, I'll teach you," he said, grabbing Marlon's arm and wrestling him away from Donna.

"Tony looks lonely over there all by himself," Ernie said.

"He's been a little standoffish lately," Paul said.

Donna was watching Marlon and Doc toss darts at the bull's-eye target on the wall. Mention of Tony caused her to rejoin the conversation.

"He's been that way ever since Tommy got stabbed. I think he's going through a crisis."

They stopped what they were doing and stared when Venus Hernandez entered the bar, still dressed in khakis and flashy purple blouse.

"Wow!" Ernie said. "I could stand a little of that crisis myself."

"Middle-age crazy is what it's called. My uncle had it bad a few years ago. Started dating a younger woman and even bought a red Corvette," Paul said.

"I don't know about a new car, but that babe's young enough to be his daughter."

"Maybe she is," Donna said. "You seen her lately?"

Venus spotted Tony in the corner, smiled and waved.

Tony pulled out a chair as everyone's eyes locked onto her. Even Doc and Marlon halted their game of darts and stared.

"Wow is right!" Jon said. "She's a knockout."

"I'll say," Paul said.

"Put your tongues back in your mouths," Donna said, her arms tightly crossed. "You're embarrassing me."

Doc returned to the table from the dart game.

"You finally find someone you can beat?" Donna asked as Marlon sat next to her.

Everyone laughed, including Marlon, when Doc Warner shook his head. "You'd better stick to detective work, son. You'll never make it on the pro dart tour. What's the story on Tony's girl?"

"She's Chief of Security at the Golden Bough

Casino. We met her while investigating the murder victim that washed up there the other night."

"She's gorgeous," Donna said. "I'm jealous."

"What a bod! I'm in lust," Jon said.

Paul guffawed. "If she's Chief of Security at the Golden Bough, she wouldn't give a peon like you a second look."

"Who says? She obviously likes cops. I'm a cop."

"Older cops it seems to me," Doc Warner said.

"Hell, Jon," Ernie said. "You know what they say about female cops. She can probably out arm wrestle you."

"That's about enough," Donna said. "What are you drinking, Marlon?"

"I'm okay. I have to take Tony home tonight."

"Tony can take care of himself," she said, scooting closer to him as pool balls clattered.

Venus had barely sat down when she glanced over at the other table and made eye contact with Marlon.

"Your partner looks lost. Doesn't he know those other people?"

"He is lost, and he always seems to have that deer in the headlights look."

"He's cute. Maybe we should ask him over to sit with us."

"Don't do that. He'll be fine."

"What are you drinking, ma'am?" Mike asked, appearing through the haze of cigarette smoke wafting toward the ceiling.

"Abita and a cold mug," she said.

"You got it," he said as he headed back to the bar.

Someone had fed a handful of quarters into the jukebox, J.J. Cale's bluesy guitar, and smoky voice combining in a rock ballad. His words were barely discernible above the clatter of pool balls, rattle of pinball machines, and whiskey talk of the bar's patrons.

"Let's join the group," Venus said.

"I thought you wanted to hear some Mo stories," Tony said.

"You can tell me over there. I've wanted to join the group at Carlucci's since I was thirteen. Please?"

Venus grabbed his hand, leading him to the other table. Talk suddenly stopped, everyone all eyes and ears.

"I'm Venus Hernandez," she said. "My dad, Mo, was an N.O.P.D. cop until we moved to Baton Rouge. He told me all about this place. May we join you?"

Doc shook her hand. "Glad to meet you, Venus. Mo was a friend of mine. How's he doing?"

"Retired and fishing most of the time."

John grabbed chairs from another table, arranging them to make room for Venus and Tony. Venus pulled the chair next to Marlon, sandwiching him between her and Donna.

"I'm Paul. What you drinking, Venus?"

Mike arrived with her Abita and cold glass before she could answer.

"Abita's my favorite," she said.

"Tony only drinks Dixie. When he's buying, that's what we all drink," Jon said.

Donna grabbed an unused glass and filled it with beer. "Dixie's fine with me," she said, downing half the contents of the glass.

"Smart girl," Tony said. "Mike, bring us two more pitchers."

Someone had recharged the jukebox, and the Neville Brothers' *Fire on the Bayou* was playing in the background.

"And a round of slippery nipples for everyone," Venus added. "And put it on my tab. I'm buying."

"All right!" Ernie said.

Paul chimed in. "That's what I'm talking about."

"Amen, brother," Jon said.

Tony wasn't as enthusiastic. "Whoa! Last time I drank a slippery nipple, I almost got a divorce."

Venus grinned. When she rested her hand on his thigh, an electric shock shot up his leg.

"Maybe this time you'll succeed. Anyway, one won't hurt."

"It's not the first one that worries me," he said.

Mike knew enough to add grenadine syrup to the recipe in order to create the nipple in the slippery nipple. He brought a round for the table, including one for himself.

"*Salud*," Venus said, raising her glass.

They drained their glasses, the table top cracking like rifle shots when they slammed them against its Formica surface.

Venus did more than that, licking the nipple from the bottom of the shot glass, a performance that earned appreciative whistles from John and Ernie. Tony grinned and emulated her performance, and then drank Marlon's he'd refused to touch.

"Keep them coming, Mike," Venus shouted. "I feel like getting snockered tonight, and everyone may as well join me."

"I hear that," Paul said.

Donna grinned and leaned against Marlon. "You're kinda cute. You got a girlfriend?"

Marlon could only shake his head.

"He is cute," Venus said. "Shy guys are always the best in bed."

"Oh ho!" Donna said. "Then you may have to take me home tonight."

"Don't let her scare you, Marlon," Ernie said. "Word on the street is she can't hold her liquor."

Donna grinned. "Maybe I need to call your wife and have a little talk with her."

"Peace," Ernie said, raising his arms in sign of surrender.

Tony frowned at the sexual innuendos being bandied about the table, and then grinned as Venus returned her attention to him. When her hand clutched his leg, perhaps a bit too close to his private parts, he didn't protest.

By the fifth shot, no one at the table felt any pain. Doc Warner begged off first and went home, followed by Ernie Martinez and Paul Portie. Jon Do had one more shot before deciding he should also leave while he was still able to stand. No one was left at the table except Donna, Marlon, Venus, and Tony.

"You ready to go yet, Lieutenant?" Marlon, the only sober one at the table, asked.

"Not yet. We still have lots to talk about. I'll take him home," Venus said.

Donna's head was drooping. "Someone needs to give me a ride. I was carpooling with Paul."

"Marlon can take you," Tony said. "Pick me up at the house tomorrow?"

Marlon's nod was his only response.

Most of the bar's patrons had gone home when Venus and Tony stumbled out the door to the dark parking lot in back. She led him to her white Cadillac with a vanity plate that said "TATAS YAYA". Once in the car, she crawled over the console, into his lap.

"I'm so hot, I can't stand it."

Tony's deft hands had already unbuttoned the purple blouse and gotten under her sexy bra. He stroked her nipples as her long tongue probed his throat.

Her voice was husky when she said, "Fuck me, baby. Don't make me wait."

Chapter Twenty-Two

Much later that night, Venus drove Tony home. Before letting him leave the Cadillac, she put her hand between his legs and squeezed. It didn't matter if his neighbors saw him. They were used to having him come and go at all hours. Lil wouldn't be as forgiving if she'd known what was going on.

He tried blinking away the steady light shining through slats in the living room window. His head felt as if someone had exploded a nuclear device inside it, and the resultant firestorm had spread all the way to his stomach. Though Lil had left red beans and rice on the stove, he'd been too drunk to eat anything. He fell asleep on the couch without removing his clothes.

The aroma of bacon and eggs coming from the kitchen next morning carried with it a wave of nausea and almost unbearable guilt. He rushed into the bathroom without saying good morning, glad he did when he looked in the mirror and saw Venus' lipstick on his shirt collar, his clothes reeking of her perfume.

Stripping, he wrapped the clothes in a towel. He'd take them to the laundry on his way to work. Hoping Lil wouldn't see the hickey on his neck he took a long shower, trying not to worry about it. His pleasant memory of Venus made him feel even guiltier than he already did. Lil was waiting for him when he walked in the kitchen. She wasn't smiling.

"Have too much to drink last night?"

"The boys were letting off steam. I got carried away."

"You could have called. Where were you?"

"I flopped at Paul Portie's house. He finally got me up and drove me home."

To Tony's relief, Lil didn't question his lie.

"It's been a long time since you've stayed out all night, even during Carnival," she said.

"I told you what happened and where I was. This Carnival's been tough on me. I needed a few drinks to get my head on straight."

Lil stared at him, frowning, shaking her own head. "Sometimes you amaze even me, Tony."

Usually, during such confrontations with Lil, the less he spoke the better off he was. Remembering this from their last argument, he tried to act accordingly.

"Next time, I'll do better. I said I was sorry. What more can I do?"

"Tony, you're wearing me out," she said.

"What? I'm just doing my job, and it ain't an easy one. You know that."

"Then maybe it's getting too hard to handle. Maybe it's time to leave it. That's all I'm trying to say, Tony. Breakfast's ready when you are."

"Great. Maybe some eggs and coffee will make my stomach feel better. Now, if I just had a new head."

Lil glanced at the ceiling. "You are incorrigible; you know that, don't you? I'll get you some aspirins."

"You're an angel. I'll be there in a minute."

"Save your sweet words. I'm not listening."

Lil glared at him when she placed the plate of fried eggs, toast, and sausage, and two aspirins on the table in front of him.

"I'm feeling a little sick at my stomach," he said, glancing at the eggs.

"Good. I hope you feel like hell. Maybe it'll help you realize how I feel when I'm waiting for you to come home at night, not knowing if you're alive or dead. You think it's fair to me, Tony?"

"Look, I told you what happened, and I said I was sorry. Can we drop it now?"

Lil didn't immediately respond. He thought she was through. She wasn't.

"Tell the truth, Tony. Did you do something wrong last night you need to tell me about?"

"Just my job."

"I may as well stop wasting my breath. You'll never change, will you?"

The doorbell rang before Tony had a chance to respond. Lil returned with Marlon Bando who simply frowned, nodding when Tony gave him a wave.

"Tony said Paul Portie gave him a ride home last night. Were you in a hurry the reason you left him at Carlucci's?"

Marlon glanced at Tony and then back at Lil. "I had some reports to file. I hope I didn't cause you any trouble. If I did, then I'm sorry."

"Thanks, Marlon. I trust you, and that's all I needed to hear," Lil said.

The morning had turned cloudy, a damp front moving in from the Gulf. Tony spirited the bundle of clothes out of the house and to the car, hiding them behind his back.

"Throw me the keys," he told Marlon.

Tony tossed them back to him soon as he'd stowed the incriminating bundle in the trunk of the patrol car. Marlon drove out of the neighborhood, onto a main street before slowing.

"This way," Tony said, pointing. "Hey, thanks for covering for me in there. Lil was on my case pretty good."

"I don't lie very well."

Tony let the remark drop, trying to change the subject. "You get any from Donna last night?"

"She was drunk."

"It's all right. You can tell me."

"Nothing happened, and even if it had, she and I

are both single."

"What's your point?"

"You aren't. That woman was making a play for you last night, and you weren't resisting very well."

"That's crazy. She's half my age."

"Some women like older men, and it's obvious she likes cops."

"You're way off base here."

"You're married to a wonderful woman. I should be so lucky."

"Butt out! I don't need your advice."

Marlon continued staring ahead, tapping his finger on the steering wheel without commenting. Tony's window was open, and the sound of a car crash ahead of them tightened the tension. Gentle rain began dotting the windshield, and Marlon switched on the wipers.

"Where to?" he finally said.

"The Federal Building on Poydras. We have an appointment to talk to someone about this deputy thing. Someone with answers. He'll join us in the coffee shop when we get there."

When Marlon and Tony reached the Federal building on Poydras, they took the elevator to the basement. Waiting in the coffee shop of the fourteen-story structure, neither spoke until a man in a blue-striped suit joined them.

"How you doing, Eddie boy?" Tony asked, standing to shake the younger man's hand.

"I'm good. I was wondering when you'd call." Since Tony didn't introduce Marlon, the man in the blue suit extended his hand. "I'm Eddie Toledo. You must be Marlon."

"Eddie's the assistant, Federal District Attorney here in N.O. He's my drinking buddy. Where you been, Eddie? Haven't seen you down at Carlucci's lately."

"Things are busy around here. I haven't had much free time."

A handsome man with brown hair cut a little too long Eddie Toledo walked with a slight limp and spoke with a New Jersey accent.

It was after ten and the coffee shop empty, except for the cashier and the three of them. Blocked by tons of concrete from Mardi Gras craziness, it was the first time in many days that Tony had managed to forget the event. The elevator door opened with a whoosh. Seeing he was on the wrong floor, the passenger never stepped out of the cab.

"Sit down, Eddie. I'll buy you a cup of java," Tony said.

Eddie continued standing. "I know why you're here. Let's get right to it."

"We need to ask you a question."

"The answer is yes, you're both deputized, U.S. Marshals now."

"Then it's true?"

"Not only is it true, if Landry's instruction weren't enough for you, I have something pertinent to convey. You find out anything about Jacque Leguerre you tell Marshal Landry or me first. And Tony, that means Chief Wexler too."

"You know that puts me in a serious conflict of interest with the N.O.P.D."

Though Toledo never raised his voice, his dark eyes stared bullet holes through Tony's head.

"That's your problem, not mine. Leguerre's testimony will be the culmination of years of blood, hard work, and the loss of at least two undercover agents. Losing him now is not an option."

"I didn't realize how serious you fellows are taking this."

"Deadly serious. Don't fuck it up for us or, I swear, friends or not, I'll take you down myself. Ca pish?"

"I'm starting to get the picture," Tony said.

"You sure about that? I wouldn't want you to think I didn't warn you."

"You're coming in loud and clear."

"Good. That's what I needed to hear."

Eddie did an about face and exited without another word. They watched him punch the up button on the elevator and then ignore them until the cab arrived.

"Now what?" Marlon asked.

"Pardon me for feeling like hammered shit and not thinking too well right now. I didn't get much sleep last night."

Marlon handed the cashier some money, poured coffee from the urn, returning with it to the table.

"Sugar or cream?

"Black's fine."

"I can get you a doughnut."

Tony glanced up at Marlon, trying to determine if there was any hint of sarcasm in his voice. Hearing none, he just shook his head.

"What I need is eight hours of uninterrupted sleep. Since that ain't gonna happen anytime soon, I'll make this coffee do. Got any other bright ideas?"

"I've been thinking about it."

"Yeah, well tell me."

The Feds know Leguerre is in the area. Doesn't matter. It's clear they don't have a clue where he is, or even where to look."

"Go on," Tony said, suddenly interested.

"Landry, as you say, didn't just fall off the turnip truck. He's in a bind. Instead of going through channels, he has tapped you and me."

"Don't you think it's mostly just to keep us from interfering with his investigation?"

"I think there's more to it than that."

"We don't know any more than they do."

"Yeah we do. We know the territory, and they don't. Men went A.W.O.L. all the time when I was a M.P. at Polk. We almost always found them because they usually went straight home. You could take it to the bank."

When Tony finished his coffee, Marlon took the empty cup and returned to the urn for a refill. Tony nodded his thanks.

"Let's assume you're right. Everyone knows he's from N.O. What else?"

"I was listening to what Ms. Gjertsen said.

Leguerre's got a free pass with the Feds. All he has to do is testify. Why not just do it and get it over with?"

"You think he wants to see his family first?"

"Maybe he has other reasons." Marlon said.

When the elevator door opened again, an attractive young woman in a leather skirt entered the snack room, putting coins into the candy machine. Neither man noticed, Tony staring intently at Marlon.

"Problem is there's no record he ever grew up around here," he said.

"Leguerre must be an alias. It doesn't matter because we have plenty of other info on him: his age, skin, hair, and eye color; not to mention he's six-ten."

Tony tapped the table twice, and then took his cup to the coffee urn for a refill. He returned to the table with a bottle of water for Marlon.

"What else?"

"He's been spotted twice near the docks. Runners return to places where they were most comfortable."

"Go on," Tony said.

"He's so big he probably played sports in high school. Let's run what we've got on him in the computer and see what pops out."

"Why haven't the Feds figured this out?"

Marlon took a last drink of water before screwing the cap back on the bottle.

"Don't know for sure. Maybe their profiler had a lousy day and made an erroneous assumption. Maybe it's led them in the wrong direction. Whatever, we ought to be able to figure it out."

Tony slammed the rest of his coffee, stood from the table and started for the elevator.

"I don't have a better idea, so let's go check the computer."

Chapter Twenty-Three

Neither Desire nor I knew exactly how to take our meeting with Madeline as we exited her little shop. Desire's personality had become thoughtful, her smile having gone somewhere else. When we reached Canal, I whistled for a taxi.

"I can't take a cab," she said. "I haven't any money."

Fishing in my jacket, I found one of the Bennies her dad had given me.

"This is the smallest bill I have."

Desire snatched it from my hand. "Dad will give you another."

A green streetcar, tourists snapping pictures from the windows, clanged its bell as it turned off Canal, and headed up St. Charles Avenue.

"I'm not worried about it," I said.

She gave me a kiss, and then stared at me with her mesmerizing eyes, as if she had something pressing to say.

"I'm having dinner tonight with Dauphine and my mom. I want you to join us."

"Okay."

"Why are you grinning? This is serious."

"I can tell by how you're looking at me. What's the problem?"

"We're going to a restaurant in the Quarter, on Bourbon Street. It's Mom's favorite place. We do this every year during Mardi Gras, and I've never taken a boyfriend before."

"Then maybe you should go without me," I said. "I don't want to spoil the tradition."

"That's the point. I've never had a boyfriend I cared enough about to take. Now, since I do, this will be the perfect time to introduce you to Mom and Dauphine."

"Are you sure you like me that well?"

"I don't just like you. I'm totally infatuated with you. I've never felt this way about anyone. How could you not know?"

"We're still just working on our first date."

"That's my point. We haven't been apart for more than ten minutes since we met at the Irish bar. I'm planning to go home and change clothes, and I'm already thinking about missing you. Will you miss me?"

"You know I will."

Desire took my hand, squeezing it a bit too tightly as she spoke. "Madeline was right. We have known each other before, maybe in a parallel universe."

"I believe it. I know I've seen you in my dreams more times than I can count."

She smiled and kissed my hand. "That's sweet, but it sounds like a pick-up line."

"I've already picked you up, and I don't need to come up with a line. What I said is true."

"You're serious?"

"Seriously serious."

"You know, Wyatt Thomas, I think I love you, though I'm not totally sure. You're so damn good looking I may just be lusting after you."

"No one's ever done that before."

"Now you are lying," she said with a grin. "I may have to punch you."

"Why don't we just go back to my room? We can both unload some of our lust."

"Later. Right now you have a job to do."

"Oh, and what's that?"

"Impress Mom and Sis."

Desire left in the cab, heading for the Garden District after leaving me with instructions on where to meet her, what time, and what to wear. She was right about one thing. I began missing her the moment she'd disappeared up St. Charles Avenue.

Desire had given me instructions to meet her at a restaurant on Bourbon Street named, aptly enough, Rue Bourbon. The downstairs part of the restaurant served sumptuous meals at a reasonable price. The service was outstanding, the drinks better, or so I'd been told. I'd eaten there once with my friend and business partner Mama Mulate.

Not many tourists or citizens know there is also a restaurant on the building's second floor. Probably because it's exclusive, and so expensive people like me would have to take out a loan to eat there. That's assuming you were invited. Tonight I had my invitation.

Per Desire's instructions, I wore khakis, a light blue dress shirt, and my navy blazer. There was apparently a reason for the request. A waiter dressed in black, except for his white jacket, spotted me when I walked in the door.

"Are you Mister Thomas? Then follow me, please," he said when I nodded.

He led me through the crowded bistro to a small elevator, punched in a secret code, and then motioned me inside when the door opened. On the second floor, he led me through a less crowded and much more eloquently appointed dining room.

We didn't stop there, going out on the patio overlooking Bourbon Street where we found Desire and two other attractive women. Desire smiled when she kissed me. Putting her arm through mine, she wheeled us around to face the two women.

"Mom, this is Wyatt Thomas, the man I told you about."

"Call me Junie Bug," the woman said, shaking my hand. "Every one else does. This is my other daughter, Dauphine."

"I stand corrected," I said.

Junie Bug, Dauphine, and Desire all stared at me. "And why is that?" Junie Bug asked.

"Because before this very moment, I wouldn't have believed there was another woman in the world as beautiful as Desire. Now I know there are at least two more."

They smiled, though didn't seem the least embarrassed by my shameless flattery as they were all apparently used to being considered attractive. The waiter, a true professional, never cracked a smile, just clearing his throat to get my attention.

"Sir, what would you like to drink?"

"Lemonade if you have it; water if you don't."

"Here, Wyatt, sit next to Mom and me."

The three women were drinking cocktails, Dauphine and Desire martinis, Junie Bug a vodka tonic.

"You don't drink, Mr. Thomas?" Dauphine asked.

"Wyatt, please. I'm an alcoholic. One mixed drink and I'd be hanging from the railing by my ankles."

Dauphine wasn't sure what to make of my comment. Junie Bug laughed and touched my wrist.

"There are lots of alcoholics in New Orleans. Most of us just don't admit it."

"I'm afraid I had no choice. For me, it was either stopping cold turkey, or start living with the winos over on Camp Street."

Everyone laughed; their appreciation of my humor likely stoked by the result of imbibing several cocktails before I'd arrived. Bourbon Street rocked; masked revelers pouring out of bars or coming from the parade that had just ended up on Canal. We could barely hear the dulcet tones of the string quartet playing just inside the café's open door.

"I know you work for my husband. What else do you do, Wyatt?"

"I'm an information junkie. When a client has questions, I can usually find answers for them. I'm adept at it."

"Are you a private detective?" Dauphine said.

"I've been called that, although I don't have a P P.I. license."

"You could get in trouble for that," she said.

"Someone would have to complain. No one ever has."

I wasn't lying when I'd complimented Junie Bug and Dauphine on their looks. Unlike Desire's dark tresses, her mom's hair was ash blond and stylishly short. Dauphine's hair was long as her sister's though also ash. Their eyes were even different colors, Desire's dark and Dauphine's hazel like her mother's.

Junie Bug reminded me of an actress from the silent era whose name I couldn't remember. Like Desire, Dauphine was a classic beauty with high cheekbones and expressive eyes.

Hair dye and contact lenses were possibly responsible for two of their physical differences. I couldn't explain the difference in their skin colorations as easily. Dauphine and her mother had pale skin, Desire's olive as if she were from Corsica. Though obviously sisters, it was just as clear they weren't identical. The waiter interrupted my musings.

"Drinks for the ladies and pink lemonade for the gentleman."

"Thank you," I said. "Most places don't stock pink lemonade."

"Rue Bourbon stocks whatever their clientele desires."

The three women smiled when a handsome man joined us. With a wave and flashy smile, he grabbed a chair beside Dauphine, broadcasting his drink order to the attentive waiter.

"I'd like a tall glass of vodka, a little ice, and company of three gorgeous women. You must be Wyatt," he said. "I'm Sonny, Dauphine's husband."

Sonny Sonnier was dressed in Scottish wool, British leather, and Chinese silk, his socks probably more expensive than my whole outfit. He had more diamonds on his fingers than most dowager heiresses. He also looked enough like Dauphine, with brown, curly hair and hazel eyes, to be her brother.

Happy to see him, Dauphine gave him an enthusiastic hug when he turned and kissed her.

"I'm not disturbing anything, am I?"

"You got here just in time," Junie Bug said. "Mister Thomas was trying to sweep us off our feet."

"Then he's a better man than me if he can accomplish that feat."

"Sonny's a banker, like Gordon, and his dad."

"You work with your father?" I asked.

"I work with Gordon," he said.

"Don't ask," Junie Bug said. "Our little feud makes no sense to anyone, except maybe Claude and Gordon."

"You have any idea who might be trying to smear Mr. Vallee?"

"Gordon said he hired you. Are you on the clock now?"

"Sorry," I said.

Sonny didn't let it drop. "Everyone at the table knows who's behind this smear campaign."

Chastised by his comment, I could only answer, "Oh?"

The conversation concerning her husband had suddenly become contentious, and Junie Bug didn't like it. "Now is not the time, nor the place to discuss this matter. It's Carnival in the Big Easy, an occasion for things other than sniping at each other."

Duly admonished Sonny said, "Sorry, Mom."

The waiter appeared with Sonny's tall vodka and fresh drinks for everyone else, including more lemonade for me. Sonny killed his drink in one long swallow and raised a finger for another. When it arrived, he drained it quickly, like the first one, and then stood from the table.

"Gotta go. I'm meeting some high rollers from Texas. Don't wait up for me, Dauphy. We're shutting the town down tonight."

Before leaving, he walked around the table, saying something only I could hear.

"My dad's the responsible rumor monger. No pun intended, but you can take it to the bank."

Desire interrupted my thoughts as I was wondering why he felt the need to tell on his father, even if it were true.

"Dauphy, do you and Sonny have a little problem? It seems he's shutting the town down most every night lately."

"Desire, don't harass your sister. You can see she's upset."

Desire did see. Moving around the table, she engaged Dauphine in a long hug, neither of them smiling.

"Oh, my poor sister, you deserve better than that asshole," she said.

"Desire, stop it this moment. You're prying in your sister's business."

"We're twins. Her business is my business."

A man walked up behind us, a tall glass already in his hand.

"Am I intruding?" he asked.

"Claude, join us. Sonny just left. Wyatt, this is Claude Sonnier, Gordon's nemesis."

"Pleased to meet you," I said.

Claude and Gordon may have grown up together, but, as Desire had said, they looked nothing alike. Claude was taller, his brown hair the same color as Sonny's, except with an added hint of gray. He seemed to possess a perpetual smile, and a mouthful of expensive teeth.

"Uncle Claude, this is my date, Wyatt Thomas."

"You must be special," he said. "Desire's never brought along one of her beaus to our yearly get together."

I didn't have time to comment. The crowd on

Bourbon Street below us had reached an explosive crescendo, partiers moving shoulder-to-shoulder, drunks throwing beads and dollar bills from the balconies. The noise level had already exceeded ear-splitting decibels when a group of college boys spotted Desire, Dauphine, and Junie Bug.

"Three babes on the balcony," one of the young men called.

"Hey girls, show us your tits, and we'll throw you some beads."

"Those boys are sure bustin' a rug," Claude said. "Raise their temperatures a little bit, and show them your tits Junie Bug."

"Yeah, Mom, do it," Desire said.

"You got an awesome rack, better than most twenty somethings," Dauphine said. "Show those horny college boys your gorgeous set," she said, echoing Claude and Desire's sentiments.

To my amazement, Junie Bug wobbled to the railing surrounding the balcony, pulled her blouse from her black pants, and then raised it over her breasts. She wasn't wearing a bra. Desire, Dauphine, and Claude, cheered and applauded as beads, tossed from the crowd, began covering the terrace.

"You still got it, Junie Bug," Claude said, hugging her when she returned to the table.

"Mom's built like a brick shithouse," Desire said.

"I'm not blind," I said. "Maybe I should forget about younger women and make a play for her."

Desire was grinning when she made a fist and shook it at me. "You do, and I'll knock you off this balcony."

Claude was drinking vodka tonics, just like Junie Bug. Drinks continued to flow, no one seeming to slack off. My stomach was starting to growl when the waiter brought some snack crackers. Before long, Desire, Dauphine, and their mother were all flashing revelers on Bourbon Street, Claude laughing and egging them on.

"We're having fun now," he said. "I'm glad Gordon

hates this place."

Claude, I noticed, was more than familiar with Junie Bug, kissing her neck and copping a feel every chance he got. Junie Bug was all smiles, either too drunk to care, or else liking the attention. Desire, excited and grinning as she nuzzled closer to me, didn't seem to mind either. Dauphine just shook her pretty head, wriggled her nose, and crossed her eyes.

"I thought we were going to eat something," I said, whispering into Desire's ear.

"When Mom's drinking and having fun, she doesn't like to eat and lose her buzz."

"Oh," I said. "What about the rest of us?"

"You're not going to starve," she said.

"No, but if I don't stop smelling the aroma coming from the restaurant, I may have to swipe a piece of French bread from someone's table on my way back from the men's room."

"That's what you get for not drinking your calories like the rest of us."

"You're right," I said. "I deserve my fate."

"Mom," Desire said, quickly forgetting about my hunger pains. "Do you believe in spirits?"

Junie Bug wrestled away from the ever-more amorous Claude Sonnier.

"Stop it Claude, or I'm going to punch you."

"Mom," Desire said.

Junie Bug sat up straight and combed her fingers through her hair. "Why do you ask, Baby Doll?"

"Wyatt and I visited a psychic today. She got me to thinking."

"You visited a seer and didn't invite me?" Dauphine said.

"We didn't plan it; we just went on a whim. This mysterious gypsy woman named Madeline had a crystal ball, and used it to tell our fortune. Real crystal, not something made of glass."

"What did she say?"

"She said Wyatt and I were lovers in past lives."

"What else?"

"She said there's a curse on our family, and I was approaching a crossroads, the direction I take determining my future."

When Junie Bug dropped her drink, it shattered on the concrete floor, startling everyone.

"Mom," Dauphine said. "What's the matter? You're white as a ghost."

Junie Bug didn't answer. Her face had grown suddenly pale, her eyes wide, and mouth agape.

Chapter Twenty-Four

Someone from the wait staff hurried out and began cleaning Junie Bug's spilled drink. Desire and Dauphine rushed to comfort their mother. Claude got into the act, daubing her forehead with his handkerchief he'd dipped in his glass of water.

"I'm okay," Junie Bug finally said, brushing them all away. "I just had a moment."

"You sure, Junie Bug? You still look pale," Claude said.

The waiter had brought another round of drinks. Junie Bug grasped hers in both hands, sipping it until color began returning to her face and lips.

"Mom, what happened?" Desire asked.

"I don't know. You said something, and I just blanked out."

"I was telling you about our visit to the fortune teller, and what she told us."

"Mom," Dauphine said. "Did something Desire said upset you?"

Junie Bug nodded. "Yes."

"What?" Desire demanded.

"It's not so much what you said, it was the subject matter. It caused me to remember something that happened long ago."

"I wasn't trying to frighten you."

"It's okay, Baby Doll. What you said reminded me

of an incident that happened to your father and me, many years ago. Something I'd long forgotten, or maybe suppressed."

Desire glanced at Dauphine and then back at Junie Bug. "Tell us."

"I can't. You wouldn't believe me anyway. I'm not sure, after all these years, I believe myself."

A cheer went up from the street below as a couple of college girls flashed their breasts to the drunken party throwing beads and dollar bills from a balcony. No one in our group seemed to notice.

Junie Bug grinned when Dauphine said, "You're not leaving this table, or having another drink until you tell us the whole story."

"Let's eat something first, and then I'll tell you what I remember. Can we all get gumbo?" she asked the waiter.

"Yes ma'am," he said, hurrying off to enter the order.

Despite threats from her daughters, Junie Bug refused to explain what had upset her until she'd finished her gumbo. I didn't mind, eating all of mine and what Desire hadn't eaten of hers. Junie Bug finally wiped her face with a napkin, placed her spoon on the table, and sipped her vodka tonic as the rolling tempo of a jazz band resonated from an open door, somewhere below us.

"Years ago, just after your father and I married I nagged him to move out of his parents' house and into a place of our own. There was an old Creole residence in the Quarter that had lain vacant for years. Gordon, or maybe someone in his family, knew the person that owned it.

"The three-storied building didn't look like much from the outside but was downright fantastic on the inside. The house had carved, mahogany doors, beautifully accented walls finished with hand-made, crown molding you don't see any more. Black and white marble covered some of the floors, and there was intricate ironwork everywhere.

"The building was tall. From the roof, you could see all the way to the Mississippi River and much of the French Quarter. A lovely courtyard, complete with fountains and palm trees, connected the main house to the slave quarters located in back.

"The large house was furnished with expensive furniture that must have come from France and Spain during a different century. The whole place was beautiful, and I thought I'd died and gone to heaven."

Dauphine raised her hand taking the chance that interrupting Junie Bug might spoil her retelling of the memory.

"Why had it stayed vacant for so long?"

"At the time, I didn't even think about it, I was just so happy to be out from under your grandparents' roof."

"I don't remember Gramps and Nana being so horrible," Desire said.

"Oh no, they weren't. Gordon and I were young. I just wanted us to have a house of our own."

"Quit interrupting," Dauphine said. "Let Mom tell the story."

"You girls stop bickering, or I'm going home right now and never finish it."

"Mot-her," they both said at once, drawing the word into two syllables.

"Anyway, as you can tell, I was enthralled with the house. Claude was still Gordon's best friend at the time. He hadn't married Lucille yet, and he was living with us in a room downstairs."

Dauphine looked at Claude, who was holding Junie Bug's hand as she talked.

"You and Daddy lived together under the same roof? I don't believe it."

Claude flashed her one of his patented smiles.

"Like your mama said, we were still best friends then. Hell, Gordo and I had some of the same girlfriends growing up. When he'd get tired of one, I'd take her for awhile, and vice versa. Besides, I didn't get in their way."

"No you didn't," Junie Bug said. "As I remember, you were out on the Quarter most every night, doing who knows what all."

"I was out on the town the night you're talking about."

"Who's telling this story, you or me?"

"You are my dear. Please proceed. I won't interrupt again, I promise."

"What night? What happened?"

"Gordon and I had gone to our room late that night. We were lying in bed when we heard something banging around downstairs. Wind chimes hanging in the courtyard all began chiming at once, as if the wind had suddenly picked up.

"Music from the chimes stopped almost soon as it had begun. It was summer. The old house had air conditioning, but it didn't work well. I remember because sweat was trickling down my neck, my peignoir damp.

"The room suddenly became cold, as if we'd stepped into a meat locker. The drops of perspiration between my tits cooled so fast they sent a cold chill right down my spine. Then we heard something moving downstairs. The curtains didn't totally block out light from the streets. I looked at Gordon. He was also wide awake."

"Someone's downstairs," I said. Your father said, 'Must be Claude, returning from his safari.' Go see, just to make sure, I said.

"The stairway was outside our bedroom door. Gordon went out, and stared down the stairwell. I kept waiting for him to say it was Claude. He didn't. He just stood in the darkness staring downstairs.

"What is it, I called? When he didn't answer, I joined him in the hall."

"Tell us what it was," Dauphine demanded.

"It was dark. There were no lights except those flashing in from the street, through the curtains. We didn't need lights to see what we saw. A disembodied head, lit up like a glowing watch dial, floated up the stairway toward us."

Dauphine squealed. "Mother, you're lying."

"What did you do?" Desire said.

"I was squeezing Gordon's hand so hard, I know it must have hurt him. He grabbed my arm, pulled me back into the bedroom and shut the door. 'Did you see what I just saw?' he asked me.

"I could barely speak and was shaking like a leaf. The temperature had warmed again, and no spook came through the door.

"Gordon, please tell me what we just saw wasn't a ghost. 'I think we were both dreaming,' he said. The same dream? 'It happens,' he said. How do you know? 'What else could explain it?'

"I had no answer. We were both exhausted from days of partying and trying to keep up with Claude. I fell asleep and didn't awaken until the grandfather clock outside our door clanged twelve times. I was shivering, the room icy cold again. I thought my heart was going to burst out of my chest. I didn't have to look to see Gordon was also awake, staring at glowing apparitions standing in front of our bed.

"We sat up and stared, too frightened to move, and not knowing what else to do. I was shivering, all the light and noise from out on the street gone, replaced by a blue, flickering aura, and a piercing whine that sounded almost like a human scream.

"There were five ghosts, two females, one a girl, and three men. They were all transparent and electric blue as Bourbon Street neon. They hovered at the foot of our bed staring at us. Their feet weren't touching the floor. It was the ghosts of five black souls, two of them on crutches, and all in chains. From their sad expressions, they were in terrible pain."

"My God, Mother! What did you do?" Dauphine asked.

"Gordon and I were frozen in place, watching as they extended their hands. The ghost girl floated toward me, reaching for me. When I tried to touch her hand, it just dissolved away. They just flickered and were gone."

Junie Bug grew silent, Claude no longer holding her hand, his own arms and legs tightly crossed, his smile gone. Dauphine rushed around the table and hugged her mom. Desire quickly joined them, holding the vodka tonic to her lips until she took a sip.

When color began returning to her face, Desire asked, "You and Daddy saw five ghosts, for real?"

"Yes."

"What did you do?"

"Gordon got out of bed and put on his pants. 'Come on,' he said. 'Let's get the hell out of here.'

"I barely had my shoes on, and I think we forgot to lock the door as we hurried to our car parked on the street. We didn't tell your grandparents because we didn't think they'd believe us. Hell, we didn't believe it ourselves."

"You were there, Uncle Claude," Desire said. "Did you see the ghosts?"

"Not really. Gordon came by the next morning. Told me what had happened and said he and your mother were moving back with your grandparents."

"Claude didn't believe us, thought we were crazy," Junie Bug said.

"I was enjoying myself way too much to move away. I convinced Gordon to sublet the house to me."

"Gordon was still frightened, and told Mama Marlene what had happened. She hired a voodoo woman to visit the mansion," Junie Bug said.

Dauphine glanced at Desire. "Daddy had Mama Marlene hire a voodoo woman?"

"Yes, and Gordon consulted a Catholic priest."

"This sounds like the start of a bad joke. You can't be serious," Desire said.

"Oh I'm serious, all right."

"What did they find?"

"You'll have to ask Gordon and Mama Marlene. It's been so long, and I was so relieved to be out of the place, I can't remember now."

Dauphine wasn't satisfied with her answer. "Uncle

Claude?”

"I have to tell you, I didn't believe the story, though I could tell Gordon and Junie Bug did. Someone recommended a priest who knew about such things. I consulted him on a whim more than anything else."

Dauphine stared across the table. "And you didn't see the ghosts?"

"When Gordon and Junie Bug moved out, I took their upstairs bedroom. I'd met a lady about that time, and had convinced her to spend the night with me. When we woke up the next morning, I stepped into something thick and sticky on the floor."

"What?" Dauphine asked.

"Black slime, stinking to high heavens. It seeped between my toes and was everyplace, in the bathroom, on the walls, down the stairs—"

"Oh my God!" Desire said.

"My lady friend went into hysterics. I just grabbed a few things, and we got the hell out of there. I hired someone to pack up my stuff and move it for me."

"What about the priest?"

"He'd already convinced me to let him perform an exorcism at the house."

Dauphine squealed. "You have to be kidding. Did he do it?"

Gordon nodded. "He told me the spirits were gone. I don't know because I never went back into the house again."

With our festive mood ruined by Gordon and Junie Bug's tale, our dinner party wound down quickly. The celebration on Bourbon Street was still going strong as we left Rue Bourbon, on our way to my apartment.

"I can't believe Mom never told me that story before now."

"As traumatic as it sounded, I'm sure she did her best to forget it."

"I want to talk to Mama Marlene; find out what she knows about it," she said. "Will you take me?"

"I'd like to visit her, too, but not tonight. It's late,

and she's asleep. Besides, she lives in a dangerous part of town."

With a grin, Desire kissed my cheek. "This whole town is dangerous, or haven't you figured it out yet?"

"We can visit her later."

"Fine, but whatever you do, don't go see her without taking me with you."

The noise of the mob on Bourbon Street died away as we turned on a side street and headed for Chartres. Suddenly engulfed in darkness, we heard the dismal horn of a tanker anchored in the river.

A bunch of rowdy drinkers were raising the noise level in Bertram's. As we walked up the stairs, I spotted Detective Tony Nicosia, sitting at the bar, talking with Bertram. He wasn't alone, an attractive woman beside him. Since it was late and I had my own beautiful lady with me, I didn't stop to say hello.

Chapter Twenty-Five

It was well after dark as Venus and Tony walked down the hospital corridor to Tommy's room. Several days removed from the stabbing he'd recovered faster than anyone could have imagined. Now, he was out of the I.C.U. and in a room of his own. Tony opened the door slowly, peeking in to see if he were awake. He was, propped up in bed watching television.

"Hey, we came to visit. You look way better than you did three days ago."

Tommy still had an I.V. in his arm, and wires attached to a device that monitored his heart rate, blood pressure, and who knew what all.

"Well, look what the cat drug in," he said.

"Glad to see a smile on that ugly mug of yours again. Tommy, this is Venus Hernandez. She's Mo Hernandez's daughter. Mo is an old friend of mine."

"Glad to meet you, Tommy," Venus said. "You feeling okay?"

"Like an old pincushion, but better than I did yesterday. At least now I think I'm going to survive."

"We brought you a few things," Tony said.

"An oyster po'boy, I hope. I'm getting tired of green beans and plastic chicken."

"Can't help you there. The gift shop downstairs only had magazines, flowers, and knick knacks. I know you don't care much for flowers and knick knacks, so I got you a couple of magazines."

The blinds for the room's lone window were open, neon from a nearby restaurant flashing a colorful prism of light on the television screen. Tony cranked the slats shut as Venus' cell phone rang.

"Gotta catch this call. I'll be back."

Both Tommy and Tony were silent a moment, the only sound in the room the dripping I.V. and whir of hospital instruments.

"You look good," Tony finally said. "You need anything?"

"What the hell you doing, Tony?"

"What are you talking about?"

"Donna's been here every day. She told me all about your little scene over at Carlucci's the other night."

"What scene?"

"You know damn well what I'm talking about. You were sitting with the gang, and that girl was all over you. Donna said she couldn't believe where you had your hands, or the fact your little sweetheart was eating it up."

"That's crazy."

"You the one that's crazy. Are you trying to get a divorce?"

"I'm not trying to do anything. Just a little fling, that's all."

"Little fling my ass! Everyone is talking about it. How long do you think it'll be before Lil finds out, if she hasn't already?"

By now, Tommy was sitting straight up in bed, obviously agitated. Tony glanced around to see if there were anyone listening to their conversation.

"Look, I already know I'm in a little deep here," he said. "I also know I need to break it off. I just haven't found the right way to do it, yet."

"You and Lil have been married almost forever. She's the best woman in the world. You gonna just let it all go by the wayside?"

"I hear you, Tommy. You ain't even the first person

to rake my ass over the coals about it. I'm not sure about anything right now, and what I need is help."

"Take my advice. Make a clean break; the sooner the better."

"If I broke it off with her now, it would kill her. I'm convinced of that."

"Tony, you're full of yourself. Who do you want to hurt the most, her or Lil? Break it off with her. If I didn't have these tubes and wires attached to me, I'd get out of this bed and kick your ass right now."

Tommy's face had grown red, worrying Tony. When the blood pressure reading on the instrument began to rise, it set off an alarm, filling the room with discordant noise. Tony quickly flipped the off switch, returning the room to silence again.

"Okay, I get your message. Now calm down or we'll have every nurse and doctor on the floor in here."

"You're gonna do something about it, aren't you?"

"Yes."

"You sure?"

"Tommy, you got my word. Now get off my back, will you?"

"Fine," Tommy said, drawing a deep breath and leaning back against the pillows.

An ambulance was pulling up to the entrance of the emergency room below, its siren droning to a halt. Tony waited until the sound died away.

"I'll figure this out," he said.

"Good. Don't make me have to kick your ass."

Venus reentered the room as Tommy finished his sentence.

"Did I miss something?"

"I just said this hospital food chaps my ass."

"We'll bring you an oyster po'boy next time we come by, won't we Tony?"

"You bet. When are they springing you from this place? The partner they assigned me is getting on my nerves."

"Yeah? What's the matter with him?"

"He has a degree in criminal science and thinks he

knows everything."

"Watch it," Venus said. "I've got the same degree."

Ignoring her, he said, "The only police experience he's ever had was in the military police at Fort Polk."

"How'd he qualify to be a detective?" Tommy asked.

"Don't get me started. He has an uncle on the city council."

Tommy winced and turned away when Venus grabbed Tony's arm and squeezed.

"You're being too harsh on Marlon. He's trying his best, and he's obviously intelligent."

Tony stared at Venus a moment before returning his gaze to Tommy. "I'm sorry, but he's an egghead."

Seeing she was getting nowhere, Venus crossed her arms and stopped talking.

"Give him a chance, Tony. It'll be awhile before I'm up and about again," Tommy said.

"As if I had a choice. We better go and let you get some rest. I'll bring you back that po'boy tomorrow you hear?"

Venus and Tony reached the darkened parking lot, halfway to her car before either of them spoke.

"Where to?" she said.

"I need a drink. Maybe a couple or even three."

"Carlucci's?"

"Nah, I'm a little tired of that place. Besides, tonight I want something stronger than beer."

Bertram's was rocking when Venus and Tony entered the bar on Rue Chartres. Except for gentle rain dampening the sidewalk, the weather was perfect, prompting lots more pedestrian traffic than on prior days. Bertram's was filled to near capacity, Shirley busy delivering pitchers of beer. A zydeco band had fired up on the small stage, playing a resounding rendition of "My Calenda". When Bertram spotted Tony coming in the door, he had two of his regulars slide down to make room for him.

"Where you been, Lieutenant? Ain't seen you here in a while."

"Been busy. Bertram, this is Venus Hernandez."

"You so young and pretty. What you doing out with this old man?"

"You kidding? Tony's not old."

"Maybe not. What you having, honey?"

"I feel like a Margarita," she said.

"Good choice. Ol' Bertram here mixes the best Margaritas in town, maybe in the whole world. No machine here. I mix every drink with my own hands. You don't need to tell me what you're drinking, Lieutenant."

Bertram reached beneath the counter and produced a bottle of Dalmor Scotch from which he proceeded to pour Tony a straight shot.

"You got a memory like an elephant," Tony said.

"Maybe better. What brings you two to the Quarter?"

"We just saw Tommy in the hospital."

"I heard about the stabbing. How's he doing?"

"Good. Another month or so and he'll be good as new. Don't know if I can take another month with my new partner or not."

"Yeah? What's the matter with him?"

"Tony thinks he's a nerd," Venus said.

"Ain't nothing wrong with that. We all got a little nerd in us. What else is wrong with him?"

"He just don't get it. You know what I mean?" Tony said.

"Can't say as I do. Kill that shot and I'll pour you another. Maybe after two or three, we'll start getting to the bottom of things."

Venus sipped her drink. "Hey, this is the best Margarita I've ever had."

"Told you," Bertram said. "Pardon me a minute while I take care of them two drunks at the end of the bar. I'll be back."

The world's biggest block party was going strong, the noise level in the bar hitting record decibels, and even louder out on the street. On the dance floor, a woman dressed as Cleopatra was two-stepping with a masked man wearing a pink bra. Venus touched Tony's knee.

"What's the problem, babe? You look down and out. I know you're worried about Tommy, but he's going to be okay."

"I'm fine, just a little worn out with everything going on, and all."

"Hey, what you need is a full body massage, and I'm just the girl to give it to you. Let's head over to my apartment when we finish our drinks."

Tony glanced at his watch. "It's only ten. Maybe I better go home early tonight."

"Don't be like that. I don't sleep well when you're not in bed with me."

Tony killed his shot of Scotch. "We haven't slept together that many times."

His words made her laugh. "You're right about that. We haven't done much sleeping at all."

Tony's mouth was open and his Scotch-soaked brain searching for a reply to Venus' observation. He didn't readily find one. Seeing his shot glass was drained, Bertram poured him another.

"I have to go to the bathroom," Venus said. "I'll have another Margarita when I get back, Bertram."

"It's right behind you, honey" Bertram said, pointing. "I'll have that Margarita waiting."

"You're a doll," she said, blowing him a kiss.

Tony and Bertram watched her disappear into the crowd. "I heard you'd taken up with a younger woman."

Tony was suddenly all ears. "And where'd you hear that from?"

"Word gets around. This serious?"

"Hell no, it's just a fling."

"Lieutenant, it ain't none of my bidness, but don't you think she's a little young for you? You leading her on?"

"You're right. It ain't none of your business."

Bertram didn't reply, polishing a glass instead as the band cranked up and more patrons began dancing in front of the stage.

"Bertram," Shirley called. "We need three more pitchers of Dixie over here."

When Tony glanced up from his empty glass, Bertram poured him another shot.

"I feel like a total asshole. Venus is infatuated with me, and I don't know how to break it off with her. I don't want to screw my marriage up either. What would you do, Bertram, if you were in my place?"

"You sure you want my advice?"

"I asked you, didn't I?"

"If it was me, I'd tell her right now, not waste another minute."

"I already thought about that."

"And?"

"She's a cop, just like me, and she's packing. Hell, she's likely to pop me, and then shoot the place up."

"You right," Bertram said. "That ain't a good idea at all."

"Now do you see my problem? There ain't no easy answer."

Bertram tipped his trappers hat and rubbed his forehead.

"If I was you, I'd go talk to Mama Mulate. She'd know how to handle the situation."

The return of Venus stemmed Tony's reply as she took a sip from the fresh Margarita and licked her lips

"Come on baby, let's dance."

Grabbing his arm, she dragged him through the throng of people to the crowded dance floor. They'd danced for only a minute when Tony grabbed his knee.

"Oh Tony! I'm sorry. I forgot about your knee."

"It's okay. Let's go back to the bar. One more drink and a couple of aspirins and I'll be good as new."

Venus had another Margarita, and Tony made a dent in the bottle of Dalmor before they'd left the bar. Although midnight, the place was even more crowded than when they'd arrived, showing no signs of slowing down, at least until dawn.

Venus' apartment was nearby, in an upscale

complex near the river. She had to help Tony up the stairs and out of his clothes. He was on his stomach and already asleep when she finally began giving him the full body massage.

Chapter Twenty-Six

Though I didn't feel like getting out of bed the morning following our dinner party, Kisses changed my mind. She licked my face until I'd opened my eyes and stared at the balcony. Rain had fallen during the night, hazy fog rising up from the street below.

"You hungry?" I said.

I didn't have to ask. She bounded off the bed and went straight to her food bowl. I was watching her eat, and tourists passing on the foggy sidewalk below, when Desire awoke and glanced around, looking for me.

"Wyatt, where are you?"

"Out here. Feeding the cat."

Desire didn't bother putting on clothes, much to the delight of a group of college boys passing on the street below. She gave me a sensuous hug then grinned, bowed, and waved when they applauded.

"Oh, Wyatt, I think I'm in love with you. I love your smile, your hair, and even your cat. Come back to bed. I feel like making love all day long."

"King's x," I said. "All I've had to eat in the last twenty four hours is gumbo, and not enough of that. If I'm going to keep up with you, I need protein. Let's get breakfast. After that, I'm at your disposal."

"Do I have to get dressed?"

"You know, Miss Desire, I could look at you naked

all day long."

"But?"

"New Orleans may be the most liberal-minded city on earth, but even the Big Easy's not quite that liberal, at least just yet."

"Spoil sport."

"I know a little riverside café near the Waterfront District that serves the world's greatest breakfast. It's dry outside on the patio. The weather's a little cloudy, but I have an umbrella. We could take the Riverfront Streetcar and reach it in less than an hour. Maybe a plate of bacon and eggs will give me a little strength."

"You're pretty decent even on an empty stomach. I don't know if I can handle you full strength."

"Give it a try."

"I can't. If you're not going to spend the day in bed with me, I have to help Mom with the party tonight. She'll be freaking, right about now."

"I forgot the party."

"It starts at eight. You have to promise you'll be there."

"Your dad would fire me if I missed it. I'm supposed to be working on his case. Remember? I'll be there, though I don't have a clue what costume to wear."

"Do you have a tuxedo?"

"If moths haven't eaten it."

"Wear your tux and a mask. You remind me a little of Errol Flynn. Dauphine and I used to watch his movies in bed with Mom when Dad was out on the town. If anyone asks, tell them you're him."

"Or maybe his reincarnation. He's been dead for quite a few years now."

"Don't be a spoilsport. Everyone's coming as someone else. That's the point of a masquerade ball. You know where we live?"

"I read the Picayune's society page. Your parents' pictures dominate it practically every weekend."

"I could tell you the best place to park, if you had a car, that is."

"This is New Orleans. It's easy enough to get

anywhere I want. I don't need a car."

"Can you even drive?"

"As well as anyone else. I just prefer public transportation."

"I still love you, Wyatt Thomas, even if you are a strange one."

Twenty minutes later we were outside on the sidewalk, something the locals call the banquette, passing college boys wolf whistling every time they spotted Desire's long legs and short skirt. When a taxi pulled up, its brakes screeching, the car behind it stood on its horn, its angry driver shaking his fist as he raced past.

"See, it doesn't pay to get in a hurry in the Quarter," I said, opening the backdoor for her.

She kissed me as if she were walking to the gallows. "I told you this morning I love you. I've never felt this way about anyone else, and I'm not making it up. Do you feel the same way about me?"

"Yes, and it's starting to scare me to death."

Remembering Madeline's dire prediction, I held onto her hand, not wanting the moment to end as she slid into the backseat of the cab.

I wasn't lying about my feelings for Desire and started missing her the moment her cab disappeared down Rue Chartres. I'd convinced myself what I felt for her was no more than old fashioned lust. I was on the clock, her father's clock, and decided not to think too long and hard about my relationship with his daughter.

Gordon Vallee would require a report at the masquerade ball. My subconscious had already drawn a conclusion. It wasn't what he'd want to hear. Though I was fighting hard to cook the books, it wasn't working out very well.

Something about Junie Bug's ghost story kept rattling inside my brain. The question about Gordon being a passeblanc remained unanswered. Claude Sonnier and Mama Marlene kept popping up as possible answers. Though I knew it would hurt

Desire's feelings if she found out I went without her, I decided to pay the old woman another visit.

A parade, coming up St. Charles, was on its way toward Canal, streetcars out of service until it passed. Clouds had disappeared, bright sunlight having burned them away. Since it was such a gorgeous day, I walked, listening to marching bands and crowd sounds as they moved ever closer.

Like the last time I'd called on Mama Marlene, she answered the door on the first knock. Her dark hair, so obvious when I'd met her, had started graying at the roots, and she somehow seemed much older than the first time we'd met. The cigarette between her lips hadn't changed, and she hadn't forgotten my name.

"Why Mr. Thomas, how gracious of you to pay Mama Marlene another visit."

"Wyatt, I said. "Mr. Thomas was my father's name."

When she grinned, I remembered she was toothless and apparently didn't like wearing her false teeth when there was no one around. She quickly remedied the situation after seating me on her old couch.

"What brings you here, Wyatt? I know it's not because you want to spend time with an old lady."

"Not so. I enjoy spending time with you, but there is another reason."

"Tell me," she said.

"Desire and I are seeing each other."

"Oh?"

"I like her very much, and she likes me."

"You're a nice young man. I'm happy for both of you, and you have my blessing, though you didn't need to ask my permission."

I started to protest, say that asking her permission wasn't my intention. Then I thought about it, wondering if maybe it were.

"I'm glad you're okay with it. That's not the only reason I'm here."

"Tell me," she said.

"I was at dinner with Desire, Dauphine, and their mother. Junie Bug told us a story about something that happened to her and Gordon right after they were married. It involved ghosts."

"Oh?"

"She said you know something about it. I thought you might possibly shed some light on the story for me."

"I'm not sure I know what you're talking about. Please refresh my memory."

"Junie Bug and Gordon moved into a house in the Quarter shortly after they married. Claude was still single and lived with them. According to her story, they were visited by five spirits."

"It was so long ago, I really—"

I didn't let her finish. "She said Gordon talked to you about it, and you hired a voodoo woman to look into it for him."

Hearing about Junie Bug's ghost story must have upset the old woman because she placed her burning cigarette in the tray. It had nearly gone out before she remembered to put it back in her mouth. When she did, she stubbed it out in the tray, flicked another from the pack, and then eyed her old Zippo on the coffee table until I'd picked it up and lit the Camel for her.

She drew the smoke deep into her lungs. When she finally expelled it, an acrid cloud wafted like a ghostly fog toward the ceiling. Still clutching the cigarette, she finally began to explain.

"The incident scared Gordon. He was worried about what it all meant. I told him about the voodoo woman, and he gave me money to hire her."

"What did he think it meant?"

"He believed the spirits were trying to reach out to him for his help."

"You told me Gordon has no Creole blood. Why would black spirits be reaching out to him?"

"Because of me."

I stared at her a moment, trying to understand

what she'd just told me. "Pardon me?" I finally said.

"The house on Royal Street was an evil place, owned by a rich lady and her doctor husband. They mistreated their slaves, tortured, and even killed some of them. One night, the cook started a fire on purpose, burning the house in hopes someone would rescue them. One of those slaves was an ancestor of mine."

"How do you know that?"

"My mama told me. Her mama told her."

Mama Marlene nodded when I said, "So the spirits were asking for Gordon's help?"

"Yes," she said.

"Claude said when he lived in the house he stepped out of bed into a layer of thick black sludge that coated everything. That doesn't sound like they were exactly reaching out to him in friendship."

Memory of the black slime brought a smile to the old woman's thin lips.

"No, but he may have done more to free the spirit's souls than Gordon."

"Junie Bug said he talked with a priest."

"Yes, he hired a priest to perform an exorcism."

"An exorcism, for real?"

She nodded. "There was a priest that had come to New Orleans all the way from Italy. He'd helped in some exorcisms there. Claude was given his name. When he contacted him, he was more than happy to help."

"You don't mean Father Alphonso do you, from St. Validius?"

She nodded again. "Yes, that's him."

"What happened?"

"I don't know the result, though I'm sure the exorcism was performed. Claude was scared to death. He moved out of the house. Like Gordon and Junie Bug, he never went back."

"Mama Marlene, do you know anything about a curse on the Vallee family?"

"Where'd you hear such a thing?"

"A fortune teller told me. I thought you might know

something about it."

"Most fortune tellers don't care about past or future as much as the size of your pocketbook," she said.

"You think she was making it up?"

Mama nodded. "There ain't no curse, at least not on Gordon's family. I can tell you that much."

The parade had just reached the intersection of Canal and Basin, the first floats and marching bands already turning back toward the river. One group was playing so loudly the bass instruments vibrated the windows facing N. Rampart.

"Mama, do you remember the name of the voodoo woman?"

"Course I do. Her name was Madam Aja."

"Is she still alive?"

Mama Marlene had me light another cigarette for her, the first puff again launching her into a dry cough before she answered my question. Knowing the way to the kitchen, I got her a glass of water. She drank it all with a hesitant smile and grateful nod.

When she caught her breath, she said, "She was old, even then. I doubt she's still alive."

"I know the incident occurred before the birth of Desire and Dauphine, maybe thirty years ago. Junie Bug was still shaken by the incident. I could hear it in her voice."

She looked up at me and said, "Did she tell you what the spirit told her?"

"No. Can you tell me?

The old woman grinned and shook her head. "That's a question you'll have to ask her."

Chapter Twenty-Seven

Morning sun peeked over the Superdome as Tony left Venus' apartment and hailed a cab. Too late—or too early, whichever your perspective—to go home, he decided to pay Mama Mulate a visit instead. He'd met Mama during a murder investigation. Voodoo had been involved.

Being a voodoo mambo, Mama had provided valuable information that had helped stop the murderer. Along the way, they had become close friends. Right now, he needed a friend, someone to consult with about his ever-encompassing relationship with Venus Hernandez.

The taxi driver dropped him off in front of Mama's old two-story house, purple, gold, and yellow pansies blooming in the flower garden around her front porch. His visit sat a dog to barking across the street. Mama, checking on the commotion, came to the door before he had a chance to knock.

She was tall, not quite six feet although slender enough to pass for it. Her skin was the color of *cafe au lait*, with extra *lait* stirred in. She had dark eyes perfectly highlighted by subtle cheekbones. Her long hair, usually tied up in back to match the persona of the Tulane university professor she was, flowed down her graceful shoulders in curly waves. Morning mist rose up from the lawn as she opened the front door, still wearing her cotton robe.

"Why Lieutenant Nicosia, to what do I owe the pleasure, this early in the day?"

Tony smiled, getting a whiff of the aroma wafting through the open door. "I need your sage advice, but whatever you're cooking has my stomach growling."

"Well come in this house," she said. "First, give me a hug."

After embracing, Tony said, "How you doing, Mama?"

"If I felt any better, I'd start to worry. You've—"

"Gained a little weight?"

It was Mama's turn to smile. "Did you run out of Mama's diet pills and come for more?"

"Awhile back, but that's not why I'm here."

Mama put her arm around his waist and led him down the hallway. "I've got hot Creole coffee on the stove and sticky muffins just coming from the oven. You look as if you could use both."

When Tony started to take a chair at the kitchen table, Mama shook her hand and pointed to the door leading to her back porch.

"Let's go outside. It's so pleasant today we can listen to the birds singing. If crowd noises and marching bands don't drown them out, that is."

"Mardi Gras," Tony said. "I used to love it."

"Uh oh! You must have a problem. Grab a chair. I'll get the coffee and muffins, and join you."

Mama's covered porch wrapped around the back and sides of her house, overlooking her yard that featured raised vegetable gardens, flowerbeds with lots of multicolored flowers, gargoyle fountains, and koi ponds. Ferns and flowering baskets hung from the porch ceiling as sounds of a distant Mardi Gras parade failed to drown out songs of robins, redbirds, and blue jays in the backyard.

When Mama appeared with coffee and muffins, her old robe was gone, replaced by jeans, and a form-fitting gold and purple tee shirt that highlighted her busty body. When Tony whistled Mama grinned, as if expecting nothing less.

"If it wasn't for Lil and my new girlfriend, I'd have to make a play for you, Mama."

"Girlfriend?" she said, placing muffins and carafe on the table. "Maybe I should lace your coffee with Jack Daniel's, so I can get the whole story here."

Mama filled Tony's cup with strong, chicory-laced, Creole coffee. He took a drink before replying to her comment.

"I got a problem, and I don't need whiskey to help me tell you about it."

"Then tell Mama," she said, resting her chin in her palms and leaning toward him.

"I met this girl—"

"Girl?" Mama said, interrupting him.

"Someone young enough to be my daughter. Worse yet, she's the daughter of one of my oldest friends."

"Does Lil know?"

"I'm sure she suspects something. I don't think she knows the whole story. At least as yet."

"Do you want her to know?"

Tony frowned, sat the coffee cup on Mama's white tablecloth, and slowly tilted his head. A dauber buzzed overhead. Tony watched until it landed on its red clay nest in a corner of the ceiling.

"I don't know what I want. Venus is giving me the best sex I've ever had. That's not the main reason I'm attracted to her."

"Then what is?"

"She treats me special, like a hero, and not some chump, beat cop."

"You are special, Tony," Mama said, clutching his hand. "You know that."

"I've served on the force long enough to retire, and Lil's nagging me to do it."

"How do you feel about retirement?" she asked.

"Except for a summer of minor league baseball, police work is all I've ever done. I think I'd rather ride horse patrol in the Iberville Project."

"Tell me about Venus."

"She's young, gorgeous, and smart, though not quite as smart as you are, Mama."

"Flattery will get you everywhere. Meantime, we're talking about Venus."

"I met her while my new partner and me were investigating a murder at the Golden Bough Casino. She's the daughter of my old friend, Mo Hernandez. He and I broke out in the force together, and he later moved to Baton Rouge. Venus is the director of security on the Golden Bough. She carries a gun and has a degree in criminal justice from U.N.O."

"Did you instigate the affair?"

Tony grinned and sipped his coffee. "Let's just say I didn't resist very strongly. Marlon says some women like older men."

"Marlon?"

"Marlon Bando, my new partner. I don't know if you heard. Tommy took a knife in the gut while we were staking out a Carnival parade."

"Oh my God! I didn't know. Is he okay?"

"I hope so. Meantime, I got this pasty-faced, college educated nerd-ball that's about to drive me crazy."

"Lil's a smart woman. Are you sure she doesn't know about your little fling?"

"What I'm sure of is she suspects something's going on. I don't think she's figured it all out quite yet."

Mama topped up their cups from the metal pot and pushed a muffin toward Tony. "Do you want a divorce?"

"Why hell no! Lil and I've been together so long I don't know what I'd do without her, not to mention our girls would kill me."

The steady bass of a distant tuba echoed off the walls, momentarily silencing songbirds in Mama's yard.

"So you want to break it off with Venus, but don't know exactly how?"

Tony smiled and nodded, took a quick bite of one of the muffins and followed it with a sip of coffee.

"Something like that. Now tell me how to do it

without breaking the poor girl's heart and I'll be forever in your debt."

A hummingbird hovered near a feeder filled with red nectar. Mama glanced at it and then back at Tony.

"I can help you, Lieutenant, but I'll need a favor in return."

"Lieutenant? What happened to Tony?"

Mama laughed, put her arms around his neck and hugged him. "Because when you hear what I want you to do, you may tell me to go to hell."

Tony felt like hell, his stomach churning, and the pounding in his temples threatening to turn into an all-out migraine. When Mama slowed for an intersection, glanced at him and saw his eyes closing, she pulled her fully restored 1964, British racing green, Bugeye Sprite to the side of the road.

"You didn't tell me how much you drank last night. I have something that will help."

Reaching for her purse, she retrieved an ornate, metal container filled with brownish powder. After dumping some into her palm, she bent over the stick shift and blew it up his nose. The hit caused his eyes to open widely. When he took a deep breath and popped his neck, she handed him two aspirins and a silver flask. After downing the aspirins, he took a deep swig from the flask.

"Old Billy Goat," she said when his eyes crossed.

Mama continued watching him until a smile appeared on his face.

"I swear, Mama, you got the best hangover remedies in New Orleans."

"In the world," she said with a grin. "Are you going to make it now?"

"Hell, I feel so good all of a sudden maybe I should take a cab back to Venus' and go another round."

"You're already in enough trouble as it is. Even Mama's going to have a difficult time extricating you from this little problem."

Mama had the top down on the Sprite, glimmers of

bright sunlight warming their necks. Despite the sun, it was chilly as they tooled toward City Park, Mama detouring through the recreational area on her way to Pontchartrain's Lakeshore Drive.

"Wow!" Tony said. "The place looks beautiful."

"Hard to imagine it was underwater for weeks following Katrina."

The large park teemed with visitors enjoying gardens, lakes, and oak trees draped with Spanish moss. A flock of snowy egrets rose up from a lagoon, their wings driving them skyward as the Sprite tooled past.

"Maybe you need to tell me exactly what we're about to do," Tony said.

"A close friend of mine has a problem."

"Such as?"

"She's a bird hoarder."

Tony gave her a sharp look. "A what?"

"Valerie is a veterinarian specializing in rare and exotic birds. The rich often buy expensive parrots and cockatoos, realizing once the novelty wears off they don't like the hassle and noise the birds create. Some only see what a mistake they've made when they try to return them to the pet store where they bought them, or attempt to give them away. Valerie started taking in these avian rejects years ago. Now she has hundreds of birds."

"Hundreds?"

"I'm not exaggerating. They're all over her house, not to mention numerous cats and dogs their owners took to her clinic to have her put down."

"Oh my God! I think I'm getting sick again."

As Mama turned on Lakeshore Drive, the scenic route that followed the banks of Lake Pontchartrain, she reached over and touched his wrist.

"You have to help me, Tony. Valerie is eccentric as hell, but she has the proverbial heart of gold."

"What can I do?"

"I've thought this all through, and I have a plan. I want you to pretend to arrest her."

Tony grimaced as he stroked the morning stubble on his cheek and gazed at a sailboat wafting in the breeze, far out on the lake.

"Sounds to me like a job for animal control."

"That would kill her. You have to promise you won't take her in."

"You just said you want me to arrest her."

Mama's bouffant hair whipped in the breeze when she shook her head. "That isn't what I said. I only want you to pretend to arrest her."

"Okay, tell me what you want me to do, and I'll do the best I can."

When Mama reached Lakeshore Drive, she headed east to the entrance of an exclusive subdivision. Like City Park, Katrina had flooded many of the ultra-expensive homes. Because of their desirable location, most, but not all, had been restored. Others remained as empty shells, even years after the killer hurricane. Valerie lived in the biggest house on the block, surrounded by empty houses. Mama parked on the street.

"Won't seeing your car make her suspicious?"

Mama laughed. "Though Valerie's one of the smartest people I've ever met, she doesn't have a lick of common sense. She'll never put any of this together."

"And you have somewhere to go with the birds and animals?"

"They're all placed, either with the zoo, bird sanctuaries, or bird and animal lovers. They'll all be well cared for. My psychiatrist friend and I will keep Valerie sedated until we convince her this is all for the best."

"She's not gonna commit suicide, or something I'm going to feel guilty about for the rest of my life, is she?"

"Trust me, Tony."

Mama smiled when he said, "Last time I did I became the star performer in a voodoo sex extravaganza."

"Not this time," she said.

"Okay, what else?"

"You have handcuffs?"

"No."

"Then take these," she said, handing him a pair.

"I'm not even gonna ask where you got these."

Mama grinned. "You don't need to know. Just cuff her and bring her out. I'll take care of the rest."

"That's it?"

"Not exactly. I want you to scare her."

Tony shook his head, got out of the car and headed for the front door, knocking instead of using the doorbell. A young woman answered on the third knock, her dark eyes looking at him suspiciously as she peeked through a gap in the door.

"Who is it?" she asked.

"Water department. I need to check your pipes," he said

"There's nothing wrong with my pipes," she said.

"Look, ma'am, I'm here on official business, and I don't have time to argue with you. Now let me in."

When she opened the door for him, the jarring din of birds, many birds, accosted his ears. The large room he entered was empty except for several long perches that hung from the ceiling. The room resonated with chirps, squawks and screeches. A large cockatoo landed on his shoulder.

"I think he likes me."

Valerie didn't reply, grabbing the bird and scolding it severely before lofting it back to the perch from where it came.

"That's Brutus," she said, talking loudly, so he could hear her above the dissonance. "He's a mean one. You could have lost an ear."

Tony's hand went to his ear in an involuntary response.

"He's a mean one!" the parrots began repeating.

Valerie shook her head. "Don't say anything around here you don't want repeated."

As Tony listened, he started hearing everything from Polly want a cracker, to the most vulgar profanity.

"Are they always like this?" he asked, almost in a

shout.

She nodded. "Sometimes much worse."

Birds were flying around the room. Macaws and parrots, seemingly every color of the rainbow; cockatoos and other rare birds Tony didn't recognize; parakeets, canaries, and exotics.

"Why do you have so many?"

"I'm a vet. I specialize in rare birds. You'd be surprised how often their owners simply abandon them."

Tony turned away briefly, so she wouldn't see his smile.

"No I wouldn't."

"I know I have too many birds. You're not going to report me, are you?"

Tony saw his opening. Pulling out his badge, he showed it to her. "I'm afraid I'm going to do more than that. I'm placing you under arrest. Stick out your hands."

Valerie was a tiny woman, barely five feet tall with short, brown hair. When she extended her hands, Tony cuffed her. Her wrists and hands were so small she could have slipped out of them if she'd tried. She didn't.

"I can't go to jail. Who'll care for my birds?"

"You need to worry about yourself, not the birds," he said, pointing her toward the door.

"What'll happen to me?"

"You're going to do hard time, believe me. Maybe even Angola. This is as double-dog rotten as anything I've ever seen. The city can't let you get away with it."

"But I'm not hurting anyone."

"That's not for me to decide."

Mama and another woman dressed in a pin-striped, business dress waited outside the door, giving Tony dirty looks when he pushed Valerie to hurry her up. Several cars and vans had lined up on the street behind the Bugeye Sprite. Mama grabbed the little woman and hugged her.

"Oh Val, are you all right?"

Valerie began to cry.

"I've been arrested. What'll I do?"

"I called your dad and Chloe's here to help. We'll do whatever we can for you."

The woman named Chloe, apparently Mama and Valerie's psychiatrist friend, grabbed Valerie's arm. After quickly administering a sedative, she gave Tony another dirty look and then hustled Valerie to an awaiting Mercedes limousine. When they reached the curb, a chauffeur opened the back door for them, returned to the driver's seat and then hurried away, tires squealing.

More vans began arriving. As Mama and Tony watched, they immediately dispatched people dressed in work clothing and carrying nets to retrieve the birds and animals. As they passed on the sidewalk, Mama continued glaring at Tony.

"What?" he finally asked.

"You didn't have to be so cruel to her. Couldn't you see how frightened she was?"

Tony didn't answer. Just shaking his head, he walked toward the Bugeye. After buckling her seatbelt, Mama patted his knee before driving away.

"I'm sorry, Tony. I didn't mean to snap at you. You did a fantastic job. I'm just upset because this is all so stressful."

"Hey, don't worry about it. If that was the worst shit I had to step in every day, then I'd be in heaven. What's going to happen to Valerie?"

"That was her dad in the limo. He's extremely well-heeled, and they have an estate on the lake not far from here. We'll soon have her convinced all her birds are in excellent homes, and this is for the best. Bird hoarding isn't incurable. Chloe will work with her until she's better."

Mama laughed when Tony said, "It was scary in there, and I'll probably have bird nightmares the rest of my life."

"Maybe Chloe can work with you too," she said.

"I think I'd rather work out my own problems than

deal with Chloe, thank you. She looked as if she could wrestle professionally."

"Now that's not very nice," Mama said with a grin.

"Don't be mad at me, Mama. I still need your help with Venus."

"I've been thinking about this," she said. "She's apparently attached to you. We need to break the attachment and then present her with someone else to tie herself to."

"And how do you propose to do that?"

Mama pulled the Bugeye to the side of the road, retrieved a pair of scissors from her large purse and proceeded to snip a lock from Tony's hair.

"What the hell!"

"Now, you need to bring me a lock of Venus' hair, and a lock from someone you think might replace you when you're gone. I'll take care of the rest, though you're going to have to deal with Lil on your own."

Chapter Twenty-Eight

Jacque had grown up near the river. He knew its smells and sounds. Like a faulty though necessary aorta of the city's heart, it had failed more than once. So far, it had never failed him.

He hadn't visited New Orleans since before Hurricane Katrina. Tales of death and destruction he'd heard while in prison had been hard to fathom. Now, permanent scars from the disaster were visible everywhere.

It didn't seem to matter much to the citizens because they appeared more vital to him than ever before. As he walked along a sidewalk free of streetlights, he hoped what he'd seen wasn't just a shadowy illusion.

Jacque had found a temporary hidey-hole, Velvet waiting for him there as he prowled the dark backstreets along the riverfront. He sought a man, hoping to find him in one of the old multistoried warehouses overlooking the river.

Finding the scarred and abandoned structure, he gazed up at its windows, their broken panes reflecting scattered light from passing boats on the river. A tug's foghorn echoed against old masonry, and then died away in the shadows.

The gloom didn't matter to Jacque. He'd spent many hours in this warehouse hiding from the authorities when he was younger. Little had changed he realized as he picked his way through its musty confines, as much a creature of the night as the rats scurrying across the floor in front of him.

Stairway steps, groaning and creaking like old bones, sang to him as he climbed to the building's second floor. Wind whistled through a broken window, along with the screech of bats, flying out into the night. Though he couldn't see in the dark, his eyesight had atoned to dimness and shadows, guiding him on a path through boxes and broken crates. He soon found what he'd come for.

Jacque glanced at a man sleeping on the floor beneath an unfolded newspaper, an empty bottle of Tokay beneath his arm. When he prodded him with the toe of his shoe, the man, though still asleep, began mumbling. Jacque prodded him again, harder this time.

"What the hell! Leave me the fuck alone. Can't you see I'm sleeping?"

Recognizing the voice, Jacque kicked the man, rolling him across the rough concrete floor. The startled person, grabbing his side in pain, stared up in disbelief, flickering lights from the river highlighting his anger.

"Maybe it's time you woke up," Jacque said.

"Who the hell are you?"

"You know me. It's Jake, your stepson."

The man rubbed his eyes as he stared up at the shadowy persona towering over him.

"You ain't Jake. You're way too big."

A bat flying through an open window punctuated Jacque's silence before answering.

"I grew."

"Jake's dead. I heard he died in prison."

"You heard wrong."

"Well what the hell you want from me? Someone to bugger your little ass like I used to?"

"I'd almost forgotten about that. I didn't forget what you did to Mama. Now I'm going to kill you."

"Kill me? At least I kept you fed. You wanna kill someone then go after your real papa. He hurt that whore of a mama of yours way more than I ever thought about doing."

Suddenly curious, Jacque let the comment about his mother pass.

"And who is my real papa?"

"Why hell, I can't believe you don't know. Everyone else in town does."

"Maybe you better tell me."

"Then will you leave me the hell alone?"

"Try me," Jacque said.

"It's Father Alphonso over at St. Validius. You know the priest I'm talking about. He's the one that knocked your mama up and then had her drummed out of the Order. He's the pathetic prick you need to kill, if you have to kill someone."

"I thought I'd find you here," Jacque said. "What do you call yourself these days?"

"You know who I am, you little shit. I'm Russ LePinto, your daddy, and don't you ever forget it. Now why don't you get your dumb ass outta here and let me get back to sleep?"

Jacque had something in his hand. "You know what this is, don't you?" Russ LePinto didn't answer. "You broke some of my bones with a baseball bat like this. When you cracked Mama's skull and smashed her face with one, and put her in the hospital, I was too small and too scared of you to do anything about it. Well guess what?"

"I'm telling you Jake, you better get the hell outa here right now."

"Or what?"

"You can't beat up a defenseless man."

"I'm going to do more than beat you up, I'm going to make you suffer, just like you made me and Mama suffer. If you remember how to pray, you better start now."

On the sidewalk outside the empty warehouse, a feral tomcat hissed and backed into the shadows of a commercial dumpster as cries of sheer terror began emanating from within.

❧

After my second visit to Mama Marlene's, I spent the better part of the day napping in my room, still tired from the night out with Desire. When Bertram knocked on my door I was already awake, Kisses licking my face with her warm, raspy tongue.

"You gonna sleep all day in there?"

"It would have been nice, if my favorite Cajun bartender hadn't banged on the door until my teeth rattled. What's up that's so urgent?" I said as I opened the door.

"Don't be handing me your sassy mouth! You told me to wake you up at three. There ain't nobody in the bar right now. Come on down and tell me what's happening with you and that pretty new girlfriend of yours."

"You're just like a little old lady. What if I want to keep our relationship private?"

"You can tell ol' Bertram."

"And I suppose you'll never breathe a word of it to anyone."

"Whatever you say is safe with me. Just like between a lawyer and his clients."

"Right," I said. "I'll probably be reading about it in the grocery store check-out line. You don't have a hidden camera, do you?"

"My lips are sealed, I promise. Cross my heart and hope to die."

"You'd better watch it, Bertram. God's going to get you for lying one of these days."

"Hey, I'm Cajun. Not even God expects absolute truth from these lips."

I grinned and said, "Good, because he's never going to get it."

"What's going on so important you wanted me to get you up at three?"

"Big party in the Garden District. I need to stop by Mama Mulate's on the way there."

"I got a pot of gumbo on the stove. You better hurry and get a bowl before tourists eat it all up."

"Thanks, Bertram," I said. "I'm starving. I'll hurry fast as I can."

Still dripping from my shower, and with a towel wrapped around my waist, I found my vintage tuxedo in the closet. It was a classic, and I knew it would meet my needs for Gordon Vallee's party. As I walked down the stairs, Bertram's eyes got larger. I joined him at the bar, trying to seem indifferent about how I was dressed. He just grinned and scratched his chin.

"I know you got a fancy new girl and all, but don't you think you're going a little overboard?"

"Get used to it, Bertram. It's the new me. Besides, I'm going to a costume ball. This is the best I could do for a costume."

"I was gonna give you some gumbo, but I don't want you to get any on that pretty suit of yours."

He smiled when I said, "I'll take my chances.

Bertram brought me a bowl of gumbo, side of rice, glass of lemonade, and a large bib with a red crawfish on it. A horse drawn carriage passed on the street outside, its noisy passengers getting an early start on the nightly festivities. Bertram glanced across the bar, looking for something.

"Where's your mask? You can't go to a fancy Mardi Gras ball without a mask."

Before I could answer, he reached under the counter and produced one of the most elaborate masks I'd ever seen.

"Take this one. I know you don't believe me, but it was worn by a former King of Rex."

"Where'd you get it? Those jewels look real."

"You wouldn't expect King Rex to wear a mask with fake jewels, now would you? The King and Queen wandered in here years ago. They didn't have any money with them so they give me this mask, instead."

"Uh huh," I said. "This isn't going to get me put in jail, is it?"

When I reached for the mask, Bertram yanked it back. "You aren't gonna forget where this come from, are you?"

"You know it's safe with me."

He handed me the mask. "Now tell me how you got invited to this fancy party."

"It's part of my investigation for Gordon Vallee. Check out his party guests to see if someone other than Claude Sonnier has a reason to spread a rumor that he's a passeblanc."

"Where were you today before you passed out in your room?"

I told him Junie Bug's ghost story. "You think there's any truth to it?"

"Hell, you've lived here long as I have. They's more ghosts in this town than probably any place on earth. Don't know why it wouldn't be true."

"Then why haven't I ever seen any?"

"You know, sometimes you like a cold fish, gazing up with lost eyes, dead as a mackerel."

"Hey, I like you too."

"Your Lieutenant buddy Tony was in here last night."

"I saw him when Desire and I were heading up to the room."

"Did you get a look at the young squeeze he had with him? She couldn't be more than twenty-five. She's pretty as a picture, too.

"Who is she?"

"He said she's the daughter of an old friend."

"And?"

"Word on the street is he's having an affair with her."

"Hell, Bertram, I have troubles of my own. I don't have time for Tony's. Besides, he's a grown man. What's your problem?"

"Ain't me that's got a problem. He's about to get his little pecker whacked that's what."

"We've all been there. Let him make his own mistakes. He can handle it. Hey, this is the best gumbo

I've ever tasted."

"Yeah, when was the last time you eat?"

"Last night."

"Maybe you should try three squares for a change. When are you seeing Desire again?"

"I told you, at the party tonight."

"Well, then maybe you need a dozen oysters and some of my special sauce."

Before I could respond, Bertram went into the kitchen, returning with a platter of oysters.

"They do look good," I said.

"Too bad you don't drink beer no more. These baby's go perfect with cold Dixie."

"Lemonade is all I need, thank you very much."

As if on cue, Bertram began topping up my lemonade. "What did Mama Marlene tell you?"

"Junie Bug said that Gordon consulted Mama Marlene after they'd seen the ghosts at the house in the Quarter."

"And?"

"According to Mama Marlene, Father Alphonso performed an exorcism twenty or thirty years ago. You hear anything about it?"

Bertram just shook his head. "Sorry, bro. Can't help you on that one."

Chapter Twenty-Nine

Bertram's spicy gumbo lingered on my lips as I caught the streetcar on Canal. I was the only person on board as the rumbling vehicle turned right on St. Charles. The Garden District lay further up the avenue, past the statue at Lee Circle. I had a stop and a walk to take before I got there.

As most everyone knows, New Orleans is eclectic, neighborhoods with million-dollar houses bordering areas that are little more than slums. While Mama Mulate's old house wasn't far from the Garden District, it resided in an area dominated by overgrown lawns, big dogs, and junk cars up on blocks.

A horn blasting from a passing car set off the neighbor's dog, howling as I tapped on Mama's front door. When Mama opened it, she smiled, grabbed my arm and pulled me inside.

"I was praying some handsome man would knock on my door this evening. Come in this house."

Mama's long hair, usually tied up in back, flowed down her graceful shoulders in curly waves. In addition to her tenured professorship in English literature, she was also a practicing voodoo mambo, probably knowing as much about spells and hexes as any person in New Orleans. Local practitioners considered Mama a powerful mambo. I'd witnessed her powers and knew they were real.

Mama was no shrinking violet. Though she always dressed professionally when teaching, usually in tailored skirts, starched blouses, and stylish, high heels, she dressed just as appropriately when practicing voodoo. Simply put, she had the body of a college athlete and didn't mind showing it. Moreover, she liked showing it. Tonight was no different

Mama was wearing a lime green peek-a-boo gown that draped to the hardwood floor of the old house, its low-cut décolletage making it almost impossible for me to keep my eyes off her nipples. Over the years, I'd finally quit trying to cover up my wandering eyes.

"Quit staring at my tits, or else rip off my clothes and haul me up to the bedroom," she finally said.

She grinned wickedly when I replied, "One of these days I'm going to give you the surprise of your life and do just that."

"By then I'll probably be too old to enjoy myself."

Mama and I had a professional relationship that had proved quite successful. Rich clients seeking to connect with the city's darker side often consulted us to help them experience it. For a price, we never disappointed. Because of our work together, we'd kept our personal feelings separate. Good for business; bad for the libido.

"I know you're a clothes horse, Wyatt, but I've never seen you so decked out. What's the occasion?"

"Masquerade ball in the Garden District. I'm on a job, and mixing business with pleasure."

"You look so good, maybe it wouldn't hurt to mix a little business and pleasure ourselves."

"If I even thought about pinching your gorgeous ass, you'd knock me into the middle of next week."

"Try it sometime and find out."

"If I did, you'd probably cast a spell on me and cause a certain body part to shrivel up and drop off."

Mama grinned. "I might do something to that particular body part of yours. It wouldn't involve casting a spell on it. At least an evil spell."

"Keep talking, and you're either going to take me to

your bedroom, or let me spend five minutes in your bathroom before I go to the party."

Mama gave me a playful slap, then kissed me, her body heat further exciting my already elevated sexual feelings.

"I think we both need to take a deep breath. Let's have a strong cup of Mama's coffee."

"Lead the way, pretty woman. With a derriere as well turned as yours, someone needs to ogle it."

Mama gave her ass an extra twitch as she led me to the kitchen, motioning me to take a seat at her chipped enamel table. After pouring each of us a cup of coffee, she exited the kitchen, returning in a floor-length, terrycloth robe.

"Cold feet?" I asked.

"You get me to thinking a little too much sometimes, Wyatt Thomas. Tonight, you're here for something other than a booty call. Tell Mama your problem."

After a sip of coffee, I said, "My ex-wife Mimsy just died. I went to her wake a few days ago."

Mama leaned closer and clutched my hand. "Oh Wyatt, I heard. I'm so sorry."

"Her wake was like a kick in the gut. Father Alphonso told me forces are wrestling for my soul."

"What a strange thing to say."

"He also made some uncomplimentary remarks about Mimsy's husband, Rafael. He accused him of being a gypsy, his mother a witch."

"I can imagine what he says about me. What does a mother's occupation have to do with her son?"

"I'm baffled. I've known the padre all my life and don't recall the venom I heard coming from his mouth during the wake."

"Maybe he has his reasons."

"Maybe. I have other questions. Rafael's mother Madeline told my friend's fortune."

Mama Mulate sat her cup on the table and looked at me. "Friend?"

"Desire Vallee, daughter of my new client, Gordon

Vallee."

"Desire the supermodel? Now I am jealous. What did Madeline tell her?"

"She said there's a curse on her family, and she will reach a crossroads, the direction she takes ultimately determining her future. I'm not so sure I believe what I saw and heard. What do you think?"

Mama held her cup with both hands and sipped her coffee before replying to Madeline's prediction.

"There are those with the ability to see into the future, and the past. I've heard of Madeline and her powers. I'd believe it if I were you."

"What did she mean?"

"The crossroads is a fundamental concept in the Vodoun religion. The direction we take when we reach a crossroads is often the only time we can ever alter our destiny."

"If it's true, is there anything we can do about the curse?"

"Curses can be broken. There are ways. Still, I'd have to know more about it to continue."

"Have you ever heard of a voodoo mambo named Madam Aja?"

"She's a legend in this city. Some say she apprenticed under Marie Laveau herself. Why do you ask?"

I told her Junie Bug's ghost story and related my ensuing conversation with Mama Marlene.

"Madam Aja is very old. She's still alive."

"You know her?"

"Yes."

"Then can you take me to see her?"

"What happened to you and me going up to the bedroom?"

"You're still kidding. I'm not."

❦

We were soon on our way in Mama's vintage Sprite to the Faubourg Marigny district to see Mama Aja, stopping at a liquor store along the way to buy a couple bottles of bourbon. Mardi Gras festivities had spread

221

out of the Quarter, spilling into adjacent neighborhoods. We found a parking space, but had to walk several blocks to reach Madam Aja's old French cottage off of Esplanade. A youthful-looking woman, except for her shoulder-length, gray hair, answered the door on our first knock.

"Mama Mulate, come in. To what do I owe this honor?"

When the two women broke away from their hug, Mama Mulate said, "Senora, this is my business partner, Wyatt Thomas."

Senora was fifty-something, clad in a floor-length African print dress with a yellow shawl draped around her shoulders. We entered a room that was as eclectic as Madeline's shop, cabinets filled with jars and bottles of herbs, secret potions, and voodoo paraphernalia.

"You came to buy some of my potions, Mama Mulate?"

"I'll restock my larders while I'm here, but that's not the primary reason for our visit."

"Oh?"

"We'd like to speak with Madam Aja."

Senora hesitated a moment before answering. "Madam Aja isn't well. I don't think she has long for this world."

"We brought something for you, and for Madam Aja."

Senora grinned when Mama held up a bottle of Old Crow.

"Madam Aja's favorite."

"And something for you," Mama said, showing her a bottle of Weller's.

Senora grinned again. "You have a well appreciated memory, Mama Mulate. Follow me. Just try not to get Madam Aja too excited. At her age, she tends to become agitated."

She led us to a small room in back of the house. The room was dark. It took a moment for my eyes to adjust to dim light, only a single candle burning on the nightstand beside the bed. An old woman opened her eyes and glanced up at us.

"Madam Aja, it is Mama Mulate. Do you remember me?"

"I'm old, but not that old. Of course, I remember you. How are you child?"

"I'm doing well. Madam Aja, this is Wyatt Thomas. He and I work together. I hope you don't mind I brought him along."

Madam Aja extended her hand, so cold I had the feeling I was shaking hands with a corpse. She must have read my mind and grinned. Like Mama Marlene, she didn't have a tooth in her head. Facial skin was stretched so tightly over her skull it almost seemed as if it were a rubber mask.

"I ain't dead yet," she said. "You okay?"

I couldn't help but smile, and I squeezed her hand tighter. "You have cold hands."

"And a warm heart. You're a Traveler."

"What exactly does that mean?"

"I think you already know. We are all ephemeral beings. Our lives are fleeting when compared to the age of the universe. A Traveler comes and goes. You've been here before. You'll be here again. That's why you know things, and people seek you out for advice."

I wasn't prepared for Madame Aja's explanation.

"If I'm a Traveler, then why don't I know all the answers myself?"

"Travelers know where and how to find answers. You know, don't you?"

"Then you're a Traveler too?"

Madam Aja's head nodded ever so slightly. "We've met before, many times, though you don't remember. Now, what is it that you seek from Madam Aja?"

"Answers," I said.

"I got the answers," she said. "Give me the questions."

"Maybe you should have a drink first," Mama Mulate said.

Screwing the lid off the bottle of Old Crow, she held it to Madam Aja's mouth, letting a few drops slide between her lips.

"That's good, baby. Life ain't worth much without a little whiskey every now and then."

"Got that right," Mama Mulate said.

The candle flickered and died, leaving us in a dark room. Only flashing neon reflecting through the lone window provided any illumination.

"Damn spirits," Madam Aja said. "They like darkness and keep putting my candle out. Senora," she called.

Senora must have been used to relighting the candle because she smiled at us when she entered the room and relit it.

"You believe in spirits?" I said.

"They are real, don't ever doubt it. That is why you're here, to ask about spirits, isn't it?"

"You're very wise."

"I got a little too little, and a lot too much," she said, chiming the words from an Irma Thomas song. "I don't have much time left on this earth. Don't matter because I can still tell you about Claude and Gordon's spirits."

"Then you already know the answer to what I came to ask you."

"Both men came in contact with the spirits at the Royal Street mansion."

"Is Gordon a descendent of the slaves that were mistreated and died there?"

"Yes."

"And Claude?"

"Oh he's a descendent of someone from the house, all right, but not the slaves."

"The couple that owned the house, then? Do you know about the curse?"

"A curse placed by Madam Laveau herself, the most powerful mambo ever."

"Then you knew about it when Mama Marlene called you?"

"Yes, a curse bought and paid for by the blood of the tortured slaves at the Royal Street house."

"Madam Marie placed the curse?" Mama said.

"Yes. You know what that means don't you child?"

"It's all but unbreakable." Mama said.

Madam Aja nodded.

"And Gordon Vallee descended from those slaves, Claude Sonnier from their owners?" I asked.

"Yes, and now, so many years later, the curse is about to come full circle."

"Both Gordon and Claude know about the curse. Is it the reason they've feuded all these years?"

"One of the reasons."

"What is the other?" I asked.

"Someone else will tell you this very night. You will also learn the hard way some questions should go unasked."

I stared at Madam Aja a moment, trying to decipher her cryptic reply.

"Gordon hired a priest to perform an exorcism at the mansion."

"Yes, the padre wouldn't let me help him." She chuckled when she said, "He called me a witch."

"Was the exorcism successful?"

"God only works through innocents."

"What do you mean by that?"

"You're a Traveler. You don't know the answer just yet. You soon will."

❧❦

Mama purchased a grocery bag filled with potions, herbs and home remedies from Senora before we left her home in Faubourg Marigny.

"Senora doesn't look old enough to be Madam Aja's daughter," I said when we were back in Mama's Sprite.

"She's not."

"Granddaughter? You mean she's Madam Aja's great-granddaughter. That would make Madam Aja—"

"At least a hundred and ten, probably lots older."

"Wow! Well she looks every year of it, even though her mind's still strong."

"Did she give you the answer you sought?"

"Vallee hired me to prove he's not a passeblanc.

225

Now I know he is though there's no way to prove it. It's not what he expected me to learn."

"Maybe that's why he hired you."

"Maybe. He never thought I'd come up with the correct answer. He took me for a fool."

"Looks like the joke is on him."

"Maybe not. I don't want to give his money back for proving what he hired me to refute. What'll I do?"

"You're the Traveler, not me. You figure it out. Where to?"

"Let me off at the next corner. I have a masquerade ball to attend."

Chapter Thirty

I hoped the packet of information I had for Vallee would satisfy him, and he wouldn't demand his money back. Mama left me with a thought before I waved goodbye and walked the few blocks to the streetcar station on St. Charles.

"Marie Laveau's reputation was well deserved, her powers beyond compare. I doubt I can counteract her curse. I'll think about it. Maybe I can figure something out."

I was waiting at the streetcar stop when a street vendor walked up the sidewalk and approached me.

"Wanna buy a rose, mister?"

The young man's baseball hat was pulled down over his eyes and his L.S.U. sweatshirt stained red with wine and marinara sauce. He was holding three fake roses in his hand. They flashed like mini-neon in the dim light of the streetcar stop.

"I don't think so," I said.

"Help me out, man. I've been at this all day, and I'm about to drop."

"How much?"

"Five bucks apiece, but I'll sell you all three for ten dollars."

"All right," I said, handing him a ten spot. "Go home and get some rest."

The young man handed me the three electric roses,

flashing like fireflies, and then shot me the finger. The streetcar was almost empty when it rumbled to a halt to pick me up. The ancient machine was slow, but covered the distance to my stop faster than If I'd walked. I saluted the driver as I stepped out on the sleepy, tree-lined promenade that was St. Charles Avenue.

The Garden District, mostly spared by Hurricane Katrina, had only gained in luster and value. The two largest and most elegant homes were adjacent to each other, owned by Gordon Vallee and Claude Sonnier. A block from St. Charles, I began seeing the commotion of arriving Range Rovers and departing limos.

Gordon's magnificent house sat on a fenced quadruple lot. A security team was checking I.D.s on the sidewalk. A strapping young man in a dark jacket with no tie held up his hand when I approached.

"Sorry, sir. I need to see some I.D.," he said.

When I showed him my identification, he made a call on his cell phone.

"You're good to go, Mr. Thomas. Sorry for the delay."

A butler in white jacket and black pants met me at the front door. From the grand entry foyer, I could see the crowd of partiers, amid a beautiful staircase and polished hardwood floors. I also saw someone I knew—Eddie Toledo, the Assistant Federal District Attorney.

"Wyatt, my man. How you doing?" Eddie asked in an affected New Orleans accent.

"Swell, Eddie. How about yourself?"

Eddie was all wavy hair, brown eyes and Pepsodent smile, looking resplendent in a Union officer's dress uniform, complete with gold braids and red sash around his waist. The Scotch and soda in his hand was almost empty and probably not his first of the evening.

"I'm good. Nice tux," he said.

"Nice uniform," I said, "Some people around here still aren't happy with the outcome of the war."

Eddie grinned. "Let them get used to it. Running a little late, aren't you?"

"I had some things I needed to do first."

"What's that you're carrying?"

"Fake roses. Don't ask."

Eddie didn't, just shaking his head. "You caused quite a problem down at the shop yesterday."

"How's that?"

"The person you I.D.ed.

"How is that a problem?"

"Maybe you fingered the wrong person."

"You know me, Eddie. I never forget a face."

"Yeah, well this is one you'd better forget. It's already gotten your buddy, Lieutenant Nicosia in a number nine bind."

I decided to let the comment pass. An actress from Hollywood dressed in white gown and angel wings, smiled at us on her way to embrace a local real estate mogul, huddled with a large entourage.

"If they dropped a bomb on this house, there wouldn't be an important person left in New Orleans," I said.

"Or L.A. Did you see that Hollywood babe? She has to be the best looking woman in Louisiana."

"She's gorgeous, but she isn't even the best looking woman at this party."

"Then you must be describing a goddess."

"See for yourself. She's coming down the stairs."

We both watched, along with the hundred or so other party people, as Desire began her sensuous strut down the circular staircase, looking like a runway model that well understood her effect on a crowded room. Eddie's eyes grew wide as he watched her descend.

Desire's hair was rolled in tight cornrows and oiled into a lustrous shine. Some talented stylist must have spent hours doing her makeup because she looked like the silent screen vamp Theda Bara in the movie *Cleopatra*. Her indigo-colored skirt was cut to her waist and made of sheer silk that wrapped around her shiny bikini bottoms. Her coiled metal bra barely covered her nipples.

From the twinkle in Desire's eyes as she walked down the stairs, she was lost somewhere in exhibitionism heaven. Seeing Eddie and me through the crowd, she joined us, giving me a passionate hug and long kiss that caused Eddie to finish most of his drink in a single swallow.

"What's that you have?" she asked.

"Electric roses. A red one for you and pink ones for Dauphine and your mom."

"I love it," she said. "It's so Mardi Gras. You're the most thoughtful person in the world."

"I wouldn't say that."

Desire didn't spend much time worrying about the roses, turning her attention to Eddie, instead.

"Who's this gorgeous man?" she asked.

"Desire, meet the incomparable Eddie Toledo. But watch yourself, he's a barracuda."

"I love barracudas," she said.

"How do you know this reprobate?" Eddie asked, his arm encircling Desire's waist.

"You mean Wyatt? He's working for my dad."

"That's a relief," he said. "For a minute, I thought you two were a couple. If he's just working for your dad, then maybe I have a chance with you."

"How do you know I'm not married?" Desire asked.

"I don't see a ring," Eddie said.

I had little time to experience even a pang of jealousy as someone grabbed my arm, directing my attention away from Eddie and Desire. I gazed into the brown eyes of a stunning woman dressed as a Storyville prostitute. She raised her sequined mask, revealing the facial features of a beautiful Creole courtesan. Her costume, or lack of it, was a frilly white corset over striped stockings that stopped at her thighs. Sexy red garters held the stockings in place. Her costume was slightly more demure than Desire's, but not much.

"I'm Cayenne. Mr. Vallee would like you to join him.

Please, come with me."

Seeing the look on my face, Desire had to put her hand over her mouth to keep from laughing out loud.

"Eddie will keep me company," she said.

"That's what I'm afraid of," I said.

Eddie grinned and waved as I followed Cayenne to an elevator that took us to the third floor of the large house. She led me into a darkened room, lighted only by the glow of many flat-screen monitors. When someone spoke, I immediately recognized Gordon Vallee's gravelly voice.

"My war room. From here, I can see who's screwin' who, and who's just trying too. Sit here," he said, patting the chair beside him.

I handed him the packet of information I'd copied for him. "You're going to need this."

"What is it?"

"All the proof you'll need to show you're not a passeblanc."

Cayenne disappeared for a moment into another room, returning with an icy glass of lemonade for me. As I watched, she draped her arms around Gordon's shoulders, massaging his chest with her long fingers. He barely reacted to her touch as he placed the package on the table beside him.

"How do you know Eddie Toledo?"

"Eddie and I go way back."

"I'm impressed. Who else at the party do you know?"

Before answering, I scanned the flat-screened, high resolution monitors.

"The man dressed like the King of Persia is Judge Henri Montegut, even more powerful than those two U.S. Senators he's talking with."

"Go on."

I saw someone I recognized, though had never met. The man was dressed like Rhett Butler and looked like him, right down to the haircut and signature Gable moustache.

"Rance Parker," I said. "Up for best actor this year,

I believe."

"They make lots of movies here in Louisiana. Parker even had the nerve to make me an offer on this house. Pretty generous one, too. Those ladies he's with are my wife Junie Bug, and daughter Dauphine."

He cast a frowning glance at me when I said, "I met them at dinner the other night at Rue Bourbon Café, in the Quarter."

Dressed in pink period dress and pillbox hat, Junie Bug looked remarkably like Jackie O. Dauphine's costume seemed to channel Marie Antoinette, complete with hoop skirt, plunging neckline, and powdered wig. They were all laughing and having fun when a young man dressed as a riverboat gambler joined them.

"That's my son-in-law Sonny, Claude's son."

Sonny glanced up in our direction, smiled, and winked. After shaking Rance Parker's hand, he left the group and made his way through the swarm of noisy guests. Dauphine, his pretty wife, didn't seem to notice.

"He was at Rue Bourbon with your wife and daughters, though he didn't stay long," I said. "I didn't get the impression he cares much for his father."

"Sonny's my right hand man. He'd kick his daddy's ass before he'd cross me. He don't think any higher of his old man than me. Who the hell else you meet? That snake Sonnier?"

"He was there."

Gordon caught me by surprise with his next question. "Was he and that wife of mine screwin' on the table in front of everybody?"

"No."

"I'll bet they had their hands all over each other."

"Is that one of the reasons you two have feuded all these years?"

Gordon wheeled around in his chair. "That ain't none of your damn business, and not what I hired you for anyway. Understand?"

"Yes sir. I just thought it might be why Mr. Sonnier

is spreading rumors about you."

"I'm sure Claude's spreading the rumor, Sherlock, and he don't need no reason. What I hired you to do is prove I ain't no passeblanc. You got any answers?"

"I've done a thorough background check. There's not a shred of evidence your family is anything other than lily white."

He stared at me a moment before replying. "I don't need no background check. What I want is proof I'm not a passeblanc."

"I made a copy of your birth certificate and family tree. I don't know what other evidence you need. This seems unarguable to me."

"Maybe so, but it don't stop Sonnier from running his mouth. You can bet on that."

"Look, Mr. Vallee, the way I see it is you two have been in this pissing match so long, everyone expects you to say terrible things about each other. Who's going to believe him, no matter what he says about you?"

"Maybe, but what if they do?"

"Head it off at the pass. Call a meeting of your club. Show them the genealogy information I provided you in the packet of documents. After that, it's just your word against his, and no one will believe him."

"What if he's got something else?"

Sonny Sonnier entered the room without knocking before I could answer.

"Sonny boy, this is Wyatt Thomas, the person I hired to check out my situation. I think you two already met the other night at Rue Bourbon."

Sonny flashed me a smile and pumped my hand. "Good seeing you again, Mr. Thomas. Like I told you the other night, Gordon and me already know who's behind all this."

Suddenly losing interest in our conversation, Gordon returned to watching the monitors. When he did, Sonny wrapped an arm around Cayenne, a playful hand taking liberties with one of her breasts beneath her low cut blouse. He didn't seem to care that I was watching, and neither did the smiling Cayenne as she winked at me.

"You need anything else from me?" I asked.

"I ain't fired you yet, Mr. Thomas. You're not done till I say you're done."

"I have no problem with that. Who do you want me to kill?"

Gordon glanced at me and snickered. "That would solve my problem, now wouldn't it? Go on back downstairs. Mingle with the crowd and make sure you talk with Sonnier.

You the hotshot detective. Maybe you'll figure out what he has in mind, and then neither of us will have to kill him."

Chapter Thirty-One

The crowd had grown larger during my absence. A five piece combo had fired up a hot jazz number, and many of the masqueraders were rocking out to the music. I found Eddie and Desire talking with Junie Bug and Dauphine.

Even more than the first time, Junie Bug seemed gorgeous as her two daughters. She'd kept her figure and her looks and could have easily passed as their older sister.

Junie Bug and Dauphine held on to their pink electric roses, Desire her red one. I was considering the sister's physical differences when a harried waiter arrived with a drink tray, revealing a side of Dauphine I hadn't seen during our last meeting.

"Louis, you got to be the laziest black man in Nawlins."

"Sorry, Miss Dauphine."

"Well you ought to be. My martini's been empty for ten minutes," she said, the slur in her words cluing me she'd had a few already.

Taking two martinis from the tray, she held one in each hand as Louis hurried away through the crowd.

"Pardon my daughter. Sometimes I think she's a bigger racist than her daddy," Junie Bug said, slurring her own words.

"If that were even possible," Desire said.

Apparently not caring we were talking about her Dauphine smiled and waved to an older man dressed as a dapper vampire. Despite the costume, I recognized him as Gordon's nemesis Claude. Grabbing Junie Bug, he moved closer to her. Eddie also noticed, giving me a smile and a wink. When Claude bit her mother's neck, Dauphine frowned, handed Desire her rose, and then hurried away through the crowd without so much as an adieu.

"Stop that, you devil!" Junie Bug said, pushing him away, though without resolve. "You know Gordon's watching us from his command post."

"Screw him and the horse he rode in on," Claude said.

Ignoring his outburst, Junie Bug handed the two roses to Desire.

"Baby Doll, will you take these weird things?" she asked.

Eddie looked surprised when Desire handed them to him and said, "Will you hold these for me?"

She just shook her head when he said, "Anything you ask, my dear."

Claude quickly forgot about Gordon and said, "Do I know you two gentlemen?"

"Sir, I'm Eddie Toledo," he said, shaking Claude's hand.

"Of course, now I recognize you. You're the Federal D.A. And who are you?" he said, looking at me.

I pulled off my fancy mask to show him who I was. "I'm Wyatt Thomas, local dog catcher. We met the other night at Rue Bourbon."

Claude grinned. "Now I get it. You aren't here chasing mongrels. You're the man Gordo hired to prove he ain't a passeblanc."

"Guilty as charged."

"Well?" he asked, not letting go of my hand.

"Don't know yet. You think he is?"

"Mama Marlene does. Now wouldn't that be a kick in the head?

Claude wrapped his arm around Junie Bug's waist

again, his comment seeming to displease her, though not enough for her to pull away from his grasp.

"Please, Claude, you said you wouldn't bring any of this up at the ball."

Desire either hadn't noticed their antics, or else had other things on her mind.

"Wyatt, would you and Mister Toledo like to see the garden?"

"Don't know about my old buddy here, but I'd be delighted," Eddie said.

"Join you in a minute. I have a quick question for your mom."

Desire gave me a perplexed look before kissing Junie Bug, and then stepped into the crowd, Eddie in tow. With both daughters gone, Junie Bug allowed Claude to hug her even tighter.

"What question is so important to ask that you let that dashing gentleman leave with my daughter?"

"The story you related the other night at Rue Bourbon."

"The ghost story?"

"Yes, Mama Marlene told me one of the spirits spoke to you, but she wouldn't tell me what they said. Will you tell me?"

"I'm not sure what you mean."

Claude must have known what I meant because he became suddenly animated.

"That was so many years ago. Junie Bug doesn't remember anymore."

Ignoring Claude's comment, I directed the question to Junie Bug. "Please, what did the spirit tell you and Gordon?"

Though my question was provocative, I didn't expect the response I got from Claude. Letting go of Junie Bug, he got in my face.

"Did Gordon put you up to this?" he demanded.

"It's an honest question. I meant no harm."

"Can't you see it's upset Junie Bug? Why don't you go play somewhere else and leave us alone?"

Hearing the anger in his voice, I decided to take his

advice. Backing away into the crowd, I began looking for the exit to the garden as the trumpet player in the combo hit a sour note. I quickly learned Desire and Eddie hadn't made it to the garden yet. They were behind me, the electric roses looking out of place as they glowed in Eddie's hand.

"Desire thought better of leaving you with her mother. We were returning for you."

"What were you and Uncle Claude arguing about?" she asked.

"Just a misunderstanding. I'll apologize to him when he cools down a little."

Apparently satisfied by my explanation, Desire linked her arms through ours and led us to a manicured garden surrounded by high walls covered with creeping vines. Somewhere in the distance, yet another parade was passing, old mortar dampening the blare of a brass band. Eddie was enthralled.

"This is spectacular."

"Dauphy and I used to play hide and seek in the mazes, when we weren't in the pool."

"Your sister's quite stunning, though you're not identical, are you?"

"You're a smart man, Eddie. We're fraternal twins. Dauphine's an hour older, slightly taller and never lets me forget it."

"She's also—"

"A closet Ku Klux Klanner?"

Eddie smiled. "I'm from New Jersey. This is the old south. I'm certainly not passing judgment on anyone."

"We're different in many ways, though closer than any two humans on earth."

The moon and several gaslights illuminated the garden without the need of electricity. We followed Desire as she led us down a cobblestone path winding through manicured shrubs. Squealing tires, over on St. Charles Avenue, momentarily disturbed my thoughts.

"Dauphine's married. You're not," Eddie said.

"Sonny swept her off her feet. I'll find my own true love someday," she said, giving my hand a gentle squeeze.

"Your mother seems like a wonderful woman," Eddie said.

"She loved having twins and used to dress us exactly the same. So did Daddy. When we got old enough to drive, he bought us identical cars."

"Sounds as if you've had wonderful childhoods."

"We were inseparable as two sisters could be. Dauphy always used to say they built the twin, Crescent City Connection Bridges just for us; one for her and one for me. We have a pact."

"Oh?" Eddie said.

"A promise we made to each other. If anything ever happens to make our lives less than perfect, we've vowed to hold hands and jump off the bridge together."

"Oh my! Then I'm glad your lives are perfect. My world wouldn't be the same, now that I've met you, if something ever happened to either of you."

Desire smiled. "Why Eddie, you're so sweet."

"Watch him," I said.

"You're just jealous," she said.

Someone had opened the French doors connecting the back porch with the ballroom, letting the steady wail of a sax meld with the garden's chirping crickets.

"Your mom seems friendly with Mr. Sonnier," Eddie said.

"You noticed."

"It must make your dad furious."

"You saw Cayenne when she came for Wyatt. She is his passion, and I'm not sure he even has feelings for Mom anymore."

"I see," Eddie said.

Desire turned her attention to me. "Were you able to learn anything tonight about Dad's little problem?"

"Nothing much."

"Then maybe you weren't talking to the right person," she said.

"Please tell me."

"He's not here at the party, but if you want to know more about Dad, ask Vincent, Mama Marlene's son."

"Thanks for the tip. I'll do that."

"You never told us what you and Uncle Claude were arguing about."

"It wasn't an argument. I asked your mom a question, and he took offense to it."

"What did you ask her?"

"I told you I was going to talk with Mama Marlene about your mom's ghost story."

"No you didn't. You visited Mama Marlene without taking me along? You knew I wanted to go with you."

"You were helping your mom."

Desire let go of my hand, crossing her arms as if there were a sudden chill in the air.

"What did she tell you?"

"She told me a spirit spoke to your mom and dad. She seemed to think it was vital. She wouldn't tell me what was said and told me to ask your mom."

"So you asked her and the question upset her?"

"She was okay with it, but Claude took offense."

"Did she answer your question?"

"She said she couldn't remember."

"Is that why Uncle Claude got so upset, because you kept badgering Mom to get an answer?"

"That's not it at all," I said.

"I know you're working for my dad—"

I could see where the conversation was going. I tried to diffuse it before it went any further. Holding up my hand, I interrupted her in midsentence.

"Desire, I'm sorry. I didn't realize my question was going to cause so much trouble."

"Because you already know the answer, don't you?"

"I—"

Her voice grew louder, rising above the sax, crickets, and distant parade.

"What did you expect her to tell you?"

Before I could defend myself, Junie Bug's voice from behind me answered her angry daughter's question. By now, from the sound of her slurred words, she was quite soused.

"I'll tell you what they told us. The spirit said they were ancestors of your father. They begged him for justice, and to help free their wretched souls from the house on Royal."

Desire stared first at her mother and then with accusing eyes, at me. "So Uncle Claude is right. Dad does have black ancestors. You knew it all along and just pretended to like me, so you could squeeze him for more money."

Uncle Claude, himself feeling no pain, had accompanied Junie Bug into the garden. "That's right, baby. Your new beau is little more than a blood-sucking vampire."

"Desire, you have it all wrong. Please—"

"Save your breath you lying sack of shit," Claude said. "Why don't you get the hell out of here before your vile stench sickens the real guests?"

When I reached for Desire's hand, she slapped me hard across the face. Grabbing the roses out of Eddie's hand, she tossed them at me. I could do nothing except stand there in silence, the three electric roses at my feet, like my face, flickering crimson. Clutching her mother, she began to cry as Dauphine suddenly appeared, frowning at me as if I were an axe murderer.

"What did you do to Mom and Sis?" she demanded.

I picked up the roses and began backing away, everyone including Eddie glaring at me.

"I'm sorry," I said. "Desire, I'll call you."

"Don't bother," she shouted as I slunk away toward the raucous party behind me.

Chapter Thirty-Two

The party was just getting cranked up as I hurried out the front door, the feel of Desire's slap still burning on my face and the three electric roses still in my hand. Gordon's wasn't the only party in town. Music, shouts, and laughter resonated through the old neighborhood.

It was late, cars still jamming both sides of the road as harried valets parked and retrieved vehicles for going and coming guests. As I crossed the street, a tan Ford sedan drove up behind me, blasting its horn. Eddie Toledo was grinning when he pulled to the curb and rolled down the window.

"Need a ride, loser?"

"After the scene back there, what I need is a double shot of Jack Daniels."

"You have enough problems as it is. You better stick to lemonade."

"You didn't have to leave just because I did."

"When Desire ran to her room crying after your rude exit, I lost my party mood. Nice roses."

The electric roses continued flashing in my hand. I had no idea why I was still carrying them, except maybe as a grim reminder of what had just happened.

"Sorry you had to be part of all that. Things got ugly pretty quickly."

"No problem, Cowboy. It was fun watching you squirm. Get in and I'll give you a ride. I'd forgotten you don't own a car."

"Thanks, Eddie," I said. "I wasn't looking forward to waiting an hour for the streetcar."

"No problem. Eddie's taxi company is always ready to serve."

Eddie continued sitting, letting the motor idle long after I'd joined him in the car.

"What?" I finally said.

"You like Desire a lot, don't you?"

"I didn't know how badly it showed."

"You two were giving off a glow you could have seen all the way to Laplace."

"Well I think I may have stepped in it with her. She didn't seem happy."

"She'll forgive you. If I'd pulled half the stunts you have with women, I'd be castrated, dead, or both by now," Eddie said.

"Desire is different. I never thought it could get this serious, this fast. Now I have the worst hangover I've ever had that didn't come from a bottle of Everclear."

"Oh hell, now you are bringing up old memories. I drank so many purple passions at a frat party one night I was puking for a week."

"Don't remind me," I said. "We had a frat party down by the river when I was at L.S.U. When I woke up the next morning, I found out someone had buried me up to my neck in sand. I'm lucky a dune buggy didn't run over me."

"Like I said, Desire will forgive you."

"Maybe and maybe not, but thanks for saying so anyway. You're a pal, Eddie."

"Don't mention it," he said. "I heard your ex passed. You're okay with it, aren't you?"

"It's always difficult when someone close to you dies. I'm okay."

"Good. That was quite a show you put on back at the party. I can't recall ever seeing anyone back out of a place as fast as you did."

"I thought you were trying to cheer me up."

"Just having a little fun," he said. "It was quite

amusing watching Claude Sonnier come unglued. Everyone seemed to know what was going on except me. Mind filling me in?"

"Gordon Vallee, Desire's father, hired me to prove he's not a passeblanc."

"What the hell's a passeblanc?"

"A person of mixed blood with skin fair enough to pass as white."

"You kidding me? Who gives a shit?"

"Apparently you don't know as much about New Orleans as you let on. The people Vallee deals with would crucify him, both socially and financially, if they thought he was even part black."

"Is he?"

"There's absolutely no proof, unless you take the hearsay testimony of a group of French Quarter ghosts."

"Ghosts, huh?"

"It's a long story."

"I have all night, though it doesn't sound like anything that would stand up in court to me. And hell, like you said, I'm not from New Orleans."

"Don't get your panties in a wad. I didn't mean anything by it."

"No problemo! I can see you're on a roll and trying to piss off everyone tonight, including your old bud."

He grinned when I said, "Sorry I hurt your delicate feelings."

"So why did Vallee hire you instead of just looking up the stuff himself?" he asked.

"Probably because he knew I'd find no proof, material or otherwise, and then he could use me to validate his whiteness with his colleagues. Claude Sonnier apparently realized as much and took offense."

"That's a fact," he said. "What's this feud you and Desire were talking about?"

"Claude and Gordon are the same age. They grew up together the best of pals. Claude told me they often had shared girlfriends, of which there were apparently many."

"You think Junie Bug was part of their harem?"

"Seems reasonable to me. The three of them were living together in a house on Royal Street shortly after Junie Bug, and Gordon married."

"And they never quit sharing," Eddie said.

"That's right, until Gordon started taking offense."

"Why would he suddenly take offense at something they'd all agreed on?"

"I think he was probably already thinking about the situation when something else pushed him over the edge."

"Like what?"

"Like finding out he wasn't as lily white and as blessed as he'd always thought. The house on Royal is supposedly haunted."

"I've heard the story. The Countess who owned the house had to flee to France."

"Yes and Claude Sonnier it seems is a direct descendant of the Countess. Madam Aja, an old voodoo mambo, told me so."

"I heard you were into voodoo."

"My business partner Mama Mulate took me to see Madam Aja. She avowed that Claude is a descendant of the Countess, her tortured slaves the ancestors of Gordon. Both Claude and Gordon and their families she said, are affected by a curse placed on the Countess."

"How does she know?"

"Gordon paid her to check out the ghosts about the same time Claude arranged for a Catholic priest to perform an exorcism on the house."

Eddie released the wheel and threw his hands in the air. "I don't believe I'm listening to all this. How can you possibly believe such bullshit?

"You're the one carping for me to tell it to you."

"Well there's one little flaw in your story, compadre," Eddie said.

"What flaw?"

"You said there's documentary evidence that

Gordon is as white as Claude. Now you're saying he isn't. How do you get around that little discrepancy?"

"I'm still working on that part of the explanation, Mr. D.A. Any further cross-examination?"

Eddie grinned and shook his head. "You believe Gordon descended from the slaves and Claude from their white owners because a voodoo queen named Madam Aja told you so?"

"Hey, I said it wouldn't stand up in court, didn't I?"

"Do you believe it's true?"

"Apparently Junie Bug, Claude, and Gordon do. So does Mama Marlene, the Vallee's former housekeeper. At least it explains the conflict."

"That, along with Claude and Junie Bug's ongoing affair."

"Hey, you're pretty sharp for a Yankee general."

"That's why they pay me the big bucks. What are you going to do now?"

"Gordon said I wasn't finished with the job until he says I'm finished. I'm not sure what to do about it. He's taking me for a fool, and I can't let that stand."

A fireworks display had begun, rockets exploding over the river, filling the night with exploding color and smoke melding with an already cloudy sky.

"All right, I'm back to playing taxi driver. Where to?"

Before I could answer, someone I recognized walked out the front door of the party. It was Sonny Sonnier, grabbing the keys to a black Jaguar.

"Can you follow that car?"

Eddie was on it in an instant. "Maybe, if you don't mind telling me who we're tailing."

"Dauphine's husband, Sonny Sonnier. I have a hunch he's not headed home."

"Where is he going?"

"Don't know, but I think we're about to find out."

Eddie followed the black Jag up St. Charles Avenue. Traffic was sparse, and he stayed far enough away so as not to cause suspicion. He needn't have worried as Sonny apparently had other things on his mind.

"Good job," I said. "Who taught you how to tail a car?"

"I used to be with the F.B.I."

"Hey, thanks for telling me. I'll consider what I say before blurting it out when I'm around you from now on."

"Don't bother," he said, grinning. "I don't waste time on petty criminals."

The night's parties had all moved toward the French Quarter. Eddie had no trouble keeping Sonny in sight. He led us on a circuitous path along the riverfront to a group of exclusive riverside condos that must have sold for millions each.

"F.B.I., huh? You sure you weren't on the other side of the law?"

"Hell, the F.B.I. is the other side of the law," he said.

Sonny exited his Jag and bounded toward one of the upstairs condos. We parked far enough away, so he wouldn't notice us, though close enough to see what was going on. Eddie pulled out a pair of binoculars and handed them to me as Sonny knocked on a door.

"Night vision," he said. "Never know when you might need them."

"Hell, Eddie, it sounds as if you're angling to take over my job."

"I may need something to keep me occupied when I quit the Service."

As I adjusted the binoculars, Cayenne, dressed in a wispy negligee, came into view. Clutching Sonny in a passionate embrace, she kissed him and then pulled him into the condo.

"I don't need a star scope to see she isn't Dauphine," Eddie said. "What's going on?"

"You remember Cayenne from the party?"

"How could I forget? That babe was dressed hotter than a Vegas hooker."

He grinned again when I said, "I didn't know you cared about such things. She works for Gordon and is the main squeeze Desire was talking about. She's his mistress, and it looks as if Sonny is sampling his father in law's girlfriend's charms."

"Sweet," he said. "Seen enough?"

"As much as we're going to see," I said. "I doubt they're coming back outside. Let's visit Bertram. I'll buy you a drink, unless you need your beauty rest."

"That's a 10–4 on the drink, good buddy," Eddie said in his best contrived southern drawl. "I wasn't planning on sleeping tonight anyway."

Eddie eased the Ford out of the parking lot, and then onto River Road where we followed winding blacktop past running lights of oilers anchored just off shore. Big Easy neon danced on the horizon, like Mardi Gras revelers on Bourbon Street.

"Say Wyatt, not to change the subject, but did you notice anything unusual about the man you I.D.ed for Nicosia?"

"You mean other than he was almost seven feet tall?"

"Scars, limps, bandages, you know?"

"There was something strange about him. Something I'll never forget."

"Like what?"

"His eyes. I've only known two other people with eyes that color."

Chapter Thirty-Three

Crime tape cordoned the sidewalk, and entrance to a mostly empty warehouse. Technicians were scouring the area where a murder had occurred. Tony and Marlon watched as a body was bagged, and then carted off to an awaiting vehicle.

"Jesus! No one deserves to die like that. Jimmy, you got an I.D. yet?" Tony asked.

The forensic investigator named Jimmy dropped a specimen into a plastic bag, and then glanced up at Tony.

"Russ LePinto, street derelict."

Marlon smiled as he studied the computer print-out in his hand.

"Got something?" Tony asked.

"Jake LePinto. Six-eight, two-ten when he played football at Brother Taylor's High School. He was expelled for an act of violence."

"Does it give his home address?"

"We're not far from it. Over in the Irish Channel."

Tony grinned. "My old neighborhood."

The Irish Channel wasn't far from the Mississippi River. Irish immigrants originally populated the district, though it later became a melting pot for many ethnicities. Well after dark, Marlon pulled their patrol car to a stop in front of an old shotgun house, pit bulls in a neighbor's pen raising a ruckus as he and Tony walked to the front porch and knocked. A woman with gray hair, sack dress and beer in her hand, answered the door quickly, as if she'd been watching from the window.

"A little late for a visit," she said in an instantly recognizable Irish Channel accent.

Tony flashed his badge. "Sorry about that. Lieutenant Anthony Nicosia, N.O.P.D. Mind if we ask a few questions, Mrs—"

"Banowski. What's this about?"

Tony didn't bother answering her question.

"How long you lived around here, Mrs. Banowski?

"Forty years, give or take a year or two."

"Then you probably remember the LePintos."

"Russ LePinto was a real piece of work. Would have screwed his own mother. Even tried to hit on me once with my old man in the backyard."

"What can you tell me about him?"

The woman finished her beer and tossed the can into a box on the front porch before answering.

"A welder out in the Gulf. Always drunk or stoned when he was in town. Don't know how Ruth put up with him."

"Ruth was his wife?"

"Lafitte was her maiden name. She fell in with him after she got kicked out of the Order."

"Order?"

"A nun, over at St. Validius Catholic School. One of the priests knocked her up, then got her booted."

"A priest was the father of her child?"

"Little Jake. His real dad, according to Ruth, was Father Alphonso. I suppose it's true because the two of them had the same gray eyes. Jake was friends with my son Jeffry."

"I see," Tony said. "You and Ruth still keep in touch?"

"She's dead. Russ got drunk one night and beat the hell out of her. Once too often because she shot him when he passed out on the couch."

"Don't tell me she killed him."

"Too bad she didn't. The bastard had her convicted and sent to prison. She died there."

"What about Father Alphonso? Did Jake know the priest was his real old man?"

"Hold on," she said, disappearing inside the door. She returned with three Dixies, handing one to Tony, the other to Marlon. Popping the cap on her own, she gulped a drink before answering. "I'm sure the boy never knew who his real father was. Ruth didn't want to tell him until he was grown."

Tony opened the beer and took a drink. "What happened to the boy?"

"Welfare people took him. He kept running away; living out on the streets."

"It's cold and wet out there. How did he survive?"

"Jeffry saw him from time to time. He said Jake lived in the abandoned warehouse down by the river. Stole money and panhandled; whatever he needed to do to survive."

"You mean the old brewery warehouse?"

"That's the one."

Tony killed the Dixie and tossed it into the box on the porch.

"Thanks, Mrs. Banowski. You been a big help."

"Is Jake in trouble?"

"You could say that," he said. "Thanks for the Dixie."

Marlon followed him to the car, handing him his unopened beer. After Marlon had driven them away from the unnerving interview, Tony popped the cap on the beer, staring out the window.

"It's late. You ready to go home?" Marlon finally asked.

Tony continued gazing out the window, not looking at anything in particular.

"I'm thinking."

"And?"

"There's something we need to do."

"Like what?"

"Check out the old brewery warehouse. Leguerre's

there, I'm sure of it."

"Should I call for back up?"

"Hell no! You heard what Toledo said. He'll have our heads on a pole if he thinks we're interfering with the Feds. Besides, we're Marshals ourselves now. If we called for backup, it would have to be from the Feds."

"If they want it that way, why not let them do the heavy lifting?"

Tony's stare burned a hole in Marlon's forehead. "If Tommy was here, he'd be with me on this instead of looking for excuses. If you're too chicken shit to come with me, I'll go alone."

Disgusted, he turned toward the passenger door his arms tightly crossed when his cell phone rang. He held the receiver close to his ear, so Marlon couldn't overhear the words of Venus Hernandez.

"Tony, where you at?" she said. "I been thinking about you all day."

"On the riverfront, not far from the Golden Bough. Where are you?"

"Just getting off work. I thought you might want to join me for a drink."

"Be there in five minutes," he said, flipping the phone shut. "Drop me off at the casino. Venus and me are going for drinks. She'll take me home."

"What about Leguerre?"

"He ain't going no place. We'll take care of him tomorrow," Tony said.

Marlon dropped him at the entrance to the Golden Bough, drove around the block and parked in the shadows, across the street. Venus and Tony soon exited the Casino and hurried down the gangplank. When her car pulled out of the garage, Marlon followed them.

It wasn't far to the abandoned waterfront warehouse, and Venus and Tony drove right to it. When Tony got out of the car, Venus opened the window.

"Tony, let me go with you."

"I'm doing this alone."

He began looking for a way into the weather-beaten building. Finding an open window accessible by a rusty fire escape, he drew his service revolver and stepped through the opening.

The warehouse was dark, lighted only by filtered reflections from moon, stars, and distant neon. Halfway up the rickety staircase, he faltered, grabbing his sore knee. Allowing himself a brief rub, he grasped the metal rail for support and continued upward to an empty room.

The metallic whine of a rusty old fan, driven by a musty breeze, filled the darkness with grating sound. Lowering his revolver, he bent forward and rubbed his knee again as a mouse scurried across the floor. Momentarily distracted, he didn't hear someone coming up behind him.

In an instant, someone lifted Tony off the ground, slamming him into a brick wall. His pistol slid across the floor as he landed on dusty cement with a sickening thud. Jacque Leguerre piled on top of him, grasping handfuls of hair and banging his head against cement.

Tony fought back, kneeing Jacque in the groin and throwing largely ineffective punches. Battered and bloody, his consciousness began dissolving into a muddled stupor as the back of his head was repeatedly bashed against the unforgiving floor.

When Marlon reached the top of the stairs, Tony had already stopped fighting, his body limp and eyes closed. Launching himself at the flailing giant, Marlon began pounding him with his revolver. The surprise attack did little more than anger Jacque, although it did end his assault on Tony.

Tony regained consciousness in time to see the giant of a man beating the life out of his hapless partner. Pain shot up his leg when he tried to stand. Biting his lip, he got to his feet and dove into the fight, surprising Jacque and dislodging him from Marlon.

Though not nearly as large as Jacque, Tony had grown up fighting. He knew how to punch, bite, scratch, and gouge eyes. It didn't matter. Jacque also knew all the dirty tricks. Tony was getting the worst of the fight when a single gunshot rang out.

It was Venus, putting a bullet into the surprised Jacque Leguerre. When he released Tony, she fired again, this shot errant. Shoving Tony to the floor, he started for the stairway, but stopped before he got there. Though Venus was pointing her pistol straight at him, she didn't fire as he walked toward her, gazing at her with mesmerizing eyes.

Ripping the pistol from her hand, he said, "Please, take care of my dog."

When he tossed the pistol across the floor, Venus dived for it, retrieving it when it hit the wall and rebounded into her hands. She opened fire as Jacque tumbled down the stairs. Landing on his feet, he dove through a window, disappearing into riverfront darkness. A stray cat screeched in the alleyway below as Venus rushed to Tony, cradling his head in her arms.

"Tony, Tony!"

Blood streamed down his forehead as he opened his eyes and said, "Get help!"

As Venus dialed her cell phone, Tony struggled to rise, and then stumbled to the badly beaten Marlon, lying unconscious in a pool of blood. Kneeling beside him, he crossed himself, said a silent prayer, and then buried his face in his hands.

Jacque crashed through the window, spraying glass across the sidewalk and disturbing the stray cat that lived behind the dumpster. Bleeding from the wound in his shoulder and cuts from broken glass, he ignored the pain, stumbling toward the river.

He could already hear the wail of distant sirens, and knew where they were headed. The area would soon be teeming with cops, and he needed to get as far away as possible before they arrived.

His clothes were bloody and tattered, and because of his size he stood out in a crowd. Six years had passed since he'd lived in New Orleans. With his mother gone, he had no relatives. Because of the job he'd had with the local crime syndicate, he'd purposely made no friends. Probably a smart thing, he thought. No place for the police to look for him.

He worried about Greta. Velvet would be okay. The young woman in the warehouse could have killed him if she'd wanted to. Her eyes told him everything he needed to know about her. She would care for the dog. Of that, he had no doubt.

He had one more job to finish before leaving New Orleans and he needed to hole up for a few hours, off the streets and hidden from police. He knew of a flophouse motel a few miles away. For twenty bucks in cash, the owner didn't care what you did, or who you did it with.

Jacque knew if he could make it there he could wash his wounds and grab a few hours of sleep, hungry mice and aggressive cockroaches the only nuisances he'd have to contend with.

Chapter Thirty-Four

It was almost dawn when Eddie and I finally made it to Bertram's. The place wasn't empty, and someone was there I didn't expect to see.

Mama Mulate was sitting at the bar sipping a Margarita through a red straw. Eddie saw her before I did and was immediately entranced by the stunning woman in black. Mama wasn't alone, Rafael Romanov sitting next to her.

"A bit early to be out drinking," I said.

"Depends on your point of view," she said. "It's Mardi Gras. How do you know I've been to bed?"

"Have you?"

"I got to thinking about the family curse, and I couldn't sleep."

"I see you've met Rafael already."

"Bertram introduced us."

Eddie apparently wasn't thinking about Rafael. "Hey, pal, aren't you going to introduce me to this gorgeous woman?"

"Mama Mulate, this is the esteemed Eddie Toledo."

Seeing the Yankee general's attire Eddie still wore, Mama eyed him with a sly grin. "I'm honored. A brave Yankee general here to protect little ol' me from the dirty old Confederacy."

Mama's response failed to unsettle fearless Eddie Toledo. "I thought I'd met the most beautiful woman in

N.O. earlier tonight. I stand corrected."

Eddie didn't stop at the blatant compliment, bowing and kissing Mama's hand. Mama just nodded and grinned.

"When I saw Wyatt in his tux several hours ago, I thought he was the best looking man in N.O. I'm the one that stands corrected. Of course, that was also before I met Rafael."

"Hi Rafael, I'm Eddie Toledo. Sorry I didn't notice you before now. The beautiful woman beside you had my attention totally locked."

"Perfectly understandable," Rafael said. "I've been staring at her legs for quite a while myself."

"Keep it up, boys," Mama said. "I love every minute of it."

Bertram cleared his throat. "When you four stop kissing each other's asses, I'd like to mix some drinks here. In case you didn't notice, bidness is kinda slow right about now."

"How are you, Bertram?" Eddie said with a smile. "I'll have a—"

"Chivas and soda. I never forget a good customer's drink."

I was sitting at the bar, still holding the three roses when Bertram poured me a glass of lemonade.

"You look like someone just stole your favorite puppy. What's the problem, Cowboy?"

"Lover's spat," Eddie answered for me.

"You and that pretty little girl are already squabbling? What happened?"

"She busted his nuts at the party."

"Okay, Eddie, I can answer for myself, thank you," I said.

"I don't know if you know it, Eddie, but Wyatt and Rafael are both recent widowers," Mama said. "I just learned they were married to the same woman. Bertram, pour everyone a shot of tequila, on me."

"Sorry to hear it," Eddie said as Bertram began pouring shots.

"Technically, Rafael is the only widower. Mimsy

and I were divorced when she died. Still, I'll admit it was quite a shock."

Mama held up her shot glass and said, "*Salud.*"

"Bring us another, Bertram," Eddie said. When Bertram, grinning like a possum, had poured the second round of shots, Eddie held up his glass and said, "This one's for Mimsy."

"Hear, hear," we all chanted.

"What do you do, Rafael?" Eddie asked.

"I'm a rent-a-priest for a cruise line that sails out of New Orleans."

"A what?" Mama asked.

"I'm defrocked, but once a priest always a priest. The cruise line doesn't care that I'm defrocked, and I do marriages, services, etcetera."

"They pay you to go on cruises?" Mama said.

"Yes, and very well, thank you."

"I love cruises. I wonder if they need a rent-a-mambo."

"You're a voodoo mambo?" Rafael asked.

"The best in town," I said. "With the possible exception of Madam Aja."

"I thought that stuff was just for tourists," Eddie said.

"Watch it, or Mama might put a spell on you," I said.

"She already has," he said.

"Bertram, another shot. This time on me," Rafael said. "And one for you, too."

I grinned because Bertram, during every shot so far, had already poured one for himself.

"Here's to my favorite voodoo mambo," Rafael said.

"Hear, hear," we all chanted again.

"You're next, Cowboy," Bertram said.

"Do it then," I said.

After the next toast, Eddie said, "You have more will power than I do, Wyatt. If I were on the wagon, I couldn't sit with my friends while they got smashed."

"I work on my sobriety every day. Bertram keeps a bottle of Jack Daniel's under the counter for me in case

I ever need it. So far, I've resisted the temptation."

"Is the curse the real reason you're out so early this morning?" Rafael asked.

"I have questions only your mother can answer," Mama said.

"Then maybe we should visit Madeline."

"I'd love to meet her, but it's barely dawn outside."

"I'm not sure she ever sleeps," Rafael said. "We have coffee and tea around this time every morning when I'm in town."

"You don't think she'd mind?"

"*Au contraire.* I'm sure she'd love to meet you."

"Is there something I'm missing here?" Eddie asked. "Who is Madeline?"

"The purveyor of Madeline's Magic Potions," Rafael said. "Some people say she's a witch. She's my mother."

"I also have a question for Madeline," I said.

"You're not leaving me behind," Eddie said, throwing a credit card on the counter. "Put it all on this, Bertram. I still have my party clothes on and don't have to be at work for a few more hours."

We strolled the short distance to Madeline's Magic Potions, morning mist rising up from the streets as shouts emanated from the ongoing party up on Bourbon Street. Wrapped in a shawl, Madeline appeared at the door when Eddie rang the bell.

"I'm closed," she said.

"It's Rafael. I brought some friends. Can we come in?"

Madeline opened the door, jostling the bell as she did, motioning us to enter.

"What an unexpected pleasure. I know Wyatt. Who are your other two friends?"

"This beautiful woman is Mama Mulate, voodoo queen. The Union soldier is General Eddie Toledo."

"Your reputation precedes you, Mama Mulate," Madeline said, shaking her hand, and then Eddie's.

Eddie was all eyes as she led us through the shop,

eerily lighted by morning reflections through imperfections in antique glass. We followed her to the courtyard. Madeline turned toward her small kitchen, just inside the doorway.

"I raised my son badly. He prefers strong New Orleans' coffee instead of gypsy tea. Both beverages are available."

"Thank you, ma'am," Eddie said. "Coffee is just what I need, the stronger the better. Some of us still have to work today."

"You won't get any sympathy from us," I said. "It isn't our fault the Feds don't celebrate Mardi Gras."

"I'll have hot tea," Mama said. She looked at Rafael, as if seeing something for the first time. "You have the most intriguing and mysterious eyes I've ever seen."

"Hey, what about me?" Eddie said.

"You also have nice eyes," Mama said.

Madeline returned from the kitchen with a tray of cups, coffee, and tea. "When Rafael is in port, we always have morning coffee and tea."

"Wyatt told me about the Vallee family curse," Mama said. "Perhaps I can help if I know more about it."

"Vodoun is a powerful religion, and you a potent practitioner. Perhaps you can."

"Then you weren't jesting," Rafael said.

"I never jest about spirits," Mama said.

"Mama also has a PH.D. in English lit, and teaches at Tulane," I said.

"Now I am impressed."

Eddie sipped his coffee, and then joined Mama on the settee, unmindful that the quaint piece of patio furniture had barely enough room for two, much less three. Neither Mama nor Rafael seemed to care.

"It's not fair," he said. "Gorgeous women should be dumb and blonde."

"Why not?" she said. "That's how I like my men."

"Enough," Madeline said, smiling and shaking her head. "You have questions about the Vallee family curse. As do I. Rafael told me Desire has a twin sister."

"Dauphine."

Eddie and I glanced at each other when Madeline said, "But they're not identical."

"How did you know?"

"I didn't, I just suspected as much. I'm sorry for the confusion. If I'd known Desire had a twin sister, I might have interpreted differently what the crystal ball told me."

"So, maybe there's not a curse? Is that what you're getting at?" I asked.

"I didn't say that. I'd like to use the crystal ball again, but I need Desire and her sister to be here, or at least have something personal of theirs."

I handed her the three electric roses. "The red one is Desire's, the two pink ones Dauphine and her mother's."

The roses had no on-off switches, and they'd continued flashing since I'd bought them at the streetcar station. Madeline led us back into her shop, to the room with the round table where she'd told Desire's fortune. After lighting the black candle in the center of the table, she motioned us to sit.

"This is my crystal," she said as she removed it from its case. "The case has a meaning, though the secret of its carvings is lost with time, even to me."

"The crystal ball is beautiful," Mama said. "I can feel its power."

"It's very much alive," Madeline said.

"I've never seen a gazing ball with more fire," Mama said."

"Not everyone can see into the future. Those that have the gift must be prepared for the consequences of what they scry," Madeline said.

She placed the gazing ball on its base, the room dark, except for flickering, candle light, the three roses, and the fire smoldering inside the crystal. She gazed intently at the crystal ball until a deep-throated hum began emanating from her lips.

The gazing ball began looking like a close-up of the sun's surface, flaming and exploding, and obviously not deriving all of its light from the flickering candle and pulsating roses. Madeline finally turned away, her eyes closed as she rubbed her forehead.

"Rafael, will you put the gazing ball away for me?"

Rafael wrapped it in its silken covering, and then returned it to the mysterious case.

"It's done, Mother," he said.

The room continued resonating with strobe-like emanations of light, even after the crystal ball was in its case. Mama was the first to speak.

"I recognize your pain, Madeline. Was what you saw that terrifying?"

"Knowledge of the future is always enlightening, but also upsetting. I was mistaken. There is a curse all right, but it isn't on the Vallee family. Desire, however, will soon be profoundly affected by it."

"Is there anything we can do?" I asked.

Madeline glanced at the ceiling and then shook her head. "The curse is near its crescendo. It will continue to its conclusion, and there's nothing anyone can do to prevent the final result."

As the prophecy died on her lips, the candle flickered once more, and then went out. As one, the three electric candles stopped pulsating. For a long moment, we sat in total darkness.

Chapter Thirty-Five

Early morning sun shined through the emergency room window as Venus clutched Leguerre's dog in her arms. Wires, tubes, and blinking instruments were the only signs of life for Marlon. He hadn't moved a muscle since Tony and Venus had arrived.

Tony's struggle with Leguerre had left him bruised and bleeding, and he had the worst headache he could ever remember. The E.R. staff had cleaned him up and doctored his wounds. Finding no broken bones, they'd wanted him to stay overnight anyway, and so did Venus. He would have none of it.

Marlon was also in the same E.R. Tony and Venus soon found him. He gazed at his partner until Venus finally broke the silence.

"This isn't your fault."

Tony leaned his head back and closed his eyes. "He's my partner. I let him down."

"You didn't. Leguerre's a professional killer. He got the jump on you."

"I'm a professional cop, and I shouldn't have let him. Marlon was right. I should have called for backup. I was stupid and bullheaded. Now I've got two downed partners on my conscience."

"You were just being human," Venus said, touching his arm.

"If it hadn't been for you, Marlon and me would

both be dead. What are you going to do with the dog?"

"Oh, Tony, I don't know."

"Don't worry about it. I know somebody that would love to have her."

"There's something I have to tell you. I could have killed Leguerre, and I didn't"

"Don't be silly."

"I put a bullet in his shoulder, and then missed with my second shot. He was heading for the stairway when something made him stop. He turned around, stood straight up and walked toward me. I wanted to shoot, but he was staring at me with those strange gray eyes. I couldn't pull the trigger. He walked right up to me and yanked the pistol out of my hand."

"Shit, you're lucky to be alive," Tony said.

"He just stared, pleading for me to take care of his dog. When he tossed the pistol across the floor, it bounced off the wall. I grabbed it off the floor and emptied it as he dove down the stairs. I don't think I hit him again."

Tony patted her cheek, and then hugged her. "You saved our lives, baby. If you hadn't come up those stairs, he'd have killed me and Marlon. That's a fact, and the only thing that counts right now."

"You sure?"

"I'm more than sure, I'm positive."

The dog licked her nose and wagged its tail when she said, "Thanks for believing in me."

When they heard a moan, they both turned. As Marlon opened his eyes for just a moment, Tony clutched his shoulders and leaned closer.

"Can you hear me?" Marlon nodded. "You a real partner. You saved my life. Why didn't you just blow the bastard's brains out when you had a chance?"

Marlon smiled ever so weakly, his words a whisper. "I couldn't do it. I'm sorry."

Tony opened his mouth to say something but thought better of it. Instead, he said, "You're a cop. Cops have to kill people sometimes. Don't matter. You're not only a good cop you're a real hero."

Marlon smiled. "Then Mom was right. Maybe I coulda been a contender."

As his head sank, his blood pressure dropped, setting off an alarm. Nurses and doctors rushed into the room, not bothering to usher Tony and Venus to the door. They watched as the trauma team worked on him, pounding on his chest. When Marlon's vitals stabilized, the trauma team moved toward the door.

"Close call," a young doctor said as he walked past.

"They must not be giving him much of a chance. They didn't even ask us to leave," Tony said.

"Don't think that way," Venus said. "He's going to make it. I know he will."

One of the nurses had left a pair of surgical scissors by the bed. Marlon was just lying there, comatose, when Tony used them to snip a lock of his hair, and then put it into an evidence bag. He backed away after patting Marlon's head.

"What are you doing?" Venus asked.

"I'm Catholic. We collect locks of people's hair to remember them by. Now I want one of yours."

Before she could protest, he snipped a locket of her hair, stowing it in the same evidence bag as Marlon's. Venus took the scissors away from him, grabbed his arm and led him into the hallway.

"Tony, you all right?"

He turned away from her, shaking his head. "I'm never gonna be all right."

"Tony—" she said.

When he kissed her forehead like a father, not a lover, she started to cry.

"Mo would be proud of you, any father would be proud. You're one hell of a woman. Don't ever let anyone tell you different."

"Why are you acting like this?"

"Because this is it for us. I know it, and so do you."

"No, Tony. I won't let you end it like this."

"You're quite a woman, and you don't need a busted down cop, and I don't need a failed marriage. There's someone else out there for you. You know it, and so do I."

Taking the dog from her, he kissed his fingers and touched them to her lips.

"Tony, where you going?"

"Something I gotta do, and it can't wait," he said as he punched the down button on the elevator.

The morning had turned chilly in the hazy courtyard. Leaving the group for a moment, Madeline returned with a shawl wrapped around her shoulders as Eddie, Rafael, Mama, and Wyatt drank tea and coffee. Wyatt sat his cup on a bench when Madeline rejoined them.

"There's something I have to ask. You might want Rafael to leave before I do."

Rafael glanced at Wyatt and then at his mother. "I'm not going anywhere," he said.

"Madeline?"

Madeline closed her eyes and bowed her head. "I already know what you are going to ask. The answer is yes. Father Alphonso is Rafael's father. How could you see those beautiful eyes of his and not know that it is so?"

"Thanks," I said.

Madeline glanced quickly at Rafael, and then back at me, "I was right about you. You are a Traveler."

When her words sank in, Rafael stared at his mother in disbelief.

"Why didn't you tell me?"

"I'm sorry. I've always meant to. I could never find the right time to do it."

"But why?"

Madeline raised a hand. "I was a young nun, mesmerized by a handsome priest with an Italian accent. He had the most hypnotic eyes. Your eyes."

I could almost see the cogs in Eddie's mind turning. Fishing his cell phone out of his Union uniform, he got up from the bench.

"Gotta run. Mama, can I call you?"

"Do, please. I've always had a soft spot in my heart

for Yankee generals."

"I also have to go," Rafael said as he followed Eddie to the sidewalk in front of Madeline's shop.

"Guess the party's over," I said. "There's one more thing I need to do, and I also have to go. Mama, will you be okay?"

"Tulane's on Mardi Gras break, and I'm a big girl. I'm enjoying my conversation with Madeline. We'll finish our tea, and I'll be fine."

I had one last question for Mama Marlene as I hurried up the street, past the Louis Armstrong Cultural Center to the Iberville Project. This time, I didn't bother stopping for flowers. A burly man answered the door on the first knock.

"I'm Wyatt Thomas. Can I speak with Mama Marlene?"

"Mama's sick," he said. "I'm Vincent, her son. Please, come in."

I followed him into Mama Marlene's apartment, unable to take my eyes off the handsome man with brown hair, pale eyes, and skin white as a Nordic prince. Not stopping in the living room, he led me to Mama Marlene's bedroom, the old woman lying in bed, wheezing as she lay propped against a pillow.

Her hair had turned totally gray since the last time I'd seen her. She took my hand, squeezing it in a gnarly vice without opening her eyes. When she finally spoke, her voice was low, barely discernible.

"Son, I knew you'd come. The good Lord about to take Mama Marlene, and there's something you just got to hear before he does."

When I glanced at Vincent, his pleading gaze prevented me from replying to the old woman's words.

"She thinks you're Gordon," he said, his words a murmur.

It didn't matter because Mama Marlene either didn't hear or else didn't care.

"Light Mama a smoke," she said.

I lit the cigarette perched in her thin lips. The first

long drag set her coughing. Opening her bony fingers, she dropped the aromatic Camel to the floor.

"Damn things don't taste good no more. Come closer, Gordon. Gots something I need to tell you."

I squeezed her hand, realizing she thought I was Gordon Vallee. Drawing closer, I listened intently to her words that were becoming ever softer and harder to understand.

"Tell me, Mama," I said.

"Your real name is Gordon Gigoux. You're my true son, not Vincent. Sorry I angered you when I told you. You was so white and pretty when you was born it almost made me cry. You two was both born the same week, and I switched you right after that."

"Why, Mama?"

Mama Marlene's voice got a catch in it as tears welled in her eyes.

"I knew the Vallee's would give you all the best, and it was me that raised you anyway. I know'd they was so busy with their powerful friends, country club and all that they would never notice. I had you all to myself, and you had the best of everything."

I tried giving her the cigarette, but she opened her hand, dropping it. Retrieving the Camel from the floor I eased it to her lips relighting it and holding it until she inhaled a lungful of strong smoke. When she turned away from the cigarette, I stubbed it out in the ashtray.

"Only problem is Vincent," she said. "Now I love him much as I love you." She broke into tears and said, "Oh God, please forgive me."

When her sobbing finally ceased, she grasped Vincent's hand, along with mine, her words a dying whisper.

"Sons, both my sons, can you ever forgive an old woman?"

By now, tears were streaming from Vincent's eyes. Squeezing her hand against his heart, he said, "Mama, you know we both love you, no matter what."

It was all she needed to hear. With a smile on her face, she slumped back in bed. Vincent sprawled across her sunken chest and began to sob. There was little I could do. I just sat there until he finally regained his composure.

"Mr. Sonnier was here last night, and Mama told him the same story," he said.

"What was his reaction?"

"He rushed out of here like a man possessed. There's an article in this morning's Picayune. He's demanding D.N.A. testing to verify his story."

"Do you have a phone?" I asked.

Vincent shook his head. "Mama doesn't have one, and my cell phone is in my truck."

I didn't wait for Vincent to offer to go for his phone. Instead, I bolted for the door, sprinting down the sidewalk to the Canal Street streetcar stop.

The streetcar never seemed so slow but finally rumbled to a halt. Rushing to the pay phone in a convenient five and dime, I dialed Gordon Vallee's number. I wasn't surprised when Junie Bug answered.

"Oh my God! Gordon read something in the paper and went running out of here with his pistol."

"Call the police," I said. "I'm on my way."

I rushed out the door, only to see the streetcar disappear around the corner. With no other option, I chased after it up the street, through masked Mardi Gras revelers, heading toward the French Quarter without a worry in the world. I wasn't as lucky.

Chapter Thirty-Six

Jacque was about to drop when he made it to the fleabag motel on the outskirts of the Warehouse District. Blood soaked his shirt from the wound made by the round from the woman's gun.

The bullet had passed through his shoulder without hitting either bone or artery. Though it hurt like hell and continued to ooze blood, he knew it wasn't fatal. He also knew it opened him up to infection, so prevalent in the steamy city crawling with mice and roaches.

The night clerk didn't even look at him when he checked in, paying for one night's lodging in cash. Before passing out on the bed, he tore a pillow case in strips and bandaged his shoulder wound, awakening the next morning with sheets soaked in blood. Wobbly on his feet, he went to the bathroom, dousing his face with cold water from the tap. Cracking the window blind, he peered out at the parking lot.

It was several miles to St. Validius. Someone would notice and report him to the police even if he were capable of walking the distance. He saw what he needed in the parking lot. A painter, dressed in a long smock, was removing ladder and cans from the back of a van.

He left the room through the back, exiting into the parking lot as traffic sounds from the nearby Interstate accosted his ears. He tapped the man on the back of the neck, just enough to render him unconscious. Dragging him into the van, he removed his smock and white painter's cap, and then tied him securely and gagged him. He found the keys to the van in the ignition.

More than a year had passed since he'd driven a vehicle of any kind, much less a large work van. He began with caution, knowing that New Orleans' drivers are among the worst in the United States, possibly the world. Seeing three wrecks before he'd gone two miles only reinforced his belief. Despite rush hour traffic, angry drivers, and a few near misses, he made it to the parking lot of St. Validius unscathed.

Before locking the van, he took a brush and can of paint to complement his smock and cap. The disguise was effective as no one gave him a second look, even when he asked directions to Father Alphonso's apartment from a passing priest. If he didn't find Father Alphonso there, he planned to jimmy the lock and remain in his room for him. If he were there, a similar fate as the one his stepfather had suffered was in store for him. When he reached Father Alphonso's room, he found the door ajar.

♣◯⁊⌒ↄ₰

Jacque wasn't the only battered and bloodied man that morning. Tony left the hospital, the small dog under his arm, without looking back as Venus called to him. The cabbie did a double take when he got a close look at the person that had flagged him down.

"Sorry, pal. Catch the next one," he said as he hit the gas.

Tony didn't allow the next driver an opportunity to peel out and drive away, pointing his service revolver at him and looking angry enough to pull the trigger.

"I'm N.O.P.D," he said, showing his badge.

"Oh yeah, then where's your squad car?"

"I wrecked it, asshole, now take me to Prytania and turn right. I'll tell you where to go from there."

"You got it, buddy. Just put that gun away, will

you?"

Tony holstered the pistol as the cabbie pulled from the curb in a screech of rubber, driving Tony to Mama Mulate's house.

"Wait here. I'll be right back," Tony said when he got out of the car.

"Like hell, I will," the cabdriver said, spinning tires in loose gravel as he raced away down the street.

"Sorry prick," Tony said as he walked up the sidewalk to Mama's house, the dog under his arm.

He banged on the front door, hoping Mama was somehow in, even though her car wasn't in the driveway. The door was unlocked. He opened it, went into the kitchen and found an empty pan for the dog, filling it with water from the tap.

"I know you're probably hungry," he said as the dog lapped up the water. "I'll bet Mama will fix you something when she gets back."

He gave the pooch a pat on the head and then backed out of the front door, shutting it behind him. He fumbled in his jacket for the evidence bag, notepad and pen.

"Mama," he wrote. "Here are the hair samples we talked about the other day. Please perform your magic and see that these two people get hooked up. As usual, I'm counting on you. Thanks, Tony. P.S. I hope you don't mind that I left the dog with you for a bit. I'll be back for her."

After placing the evidence bag and note in Mama's mailbox, he started up the street on foot. There was a streetcar stop at the next intersection. Though it was slow, it would take him where he needed to go.

Tony didn't have all the answers, but had a policeman's intuition that Jacque Leguerre was either on his way to St. Validius, or already there. He also knew when everyone found out what he intended to do there would be hell to pay, assuming he survived. After seeing Marlon comatose in the hospital bed, he didn't care anymore.

Deep in thought, Father Alphonso gazed out the window of his second-story, St. Validius apartment. When his door opened, he turned to face a giant of a man with eyes he vaguely recognized.

"You must have the wrong room. I didn't request a painter," he said.

"I'm not a painter," Jacque said, tossing the cap to the floor and letting the smock fall off his shoulders.

Seeing Jacque's blood-stained shirt, bruised face and gashed left eye rendered Father Alphonso immediately apprehensive.

"I have no money," he said in his discernible, though understated Italian accent. "Take anything else you want, and then leave."

Jacque glared at the man that was only an inch or so shorter than he.

"Retribution is the only thing I want, and I'm not leaving until I get it," he said.

"Retribution? What am I guilty of, and who are you anyway?"

"Don't you recognize me? I'm your son, Jacque."

"I have no son."

"Then maybe you remember my mother. Her name was Ruth Lafitte. She was a nun here at St. Validius about thirty years ago."

"There have been many nuns here in the last quarter century. I don't remember all of them, and I certainly don't remember anyone named Ruth Lafitte."

"You got her pregnant, and then tossed out of the Order, and the Church. You saw to it she was excommunicated. Because of you, she died in prison."

"That's absurd," Father Alphonso said.

"No, it's the truth. I didn't know you were my real father until yesterday, though I knew someone was responsible for ruining my mother's life. Before I killed my stepfather, he told me about you. Now I'm going to kill you, but not before making you beg me to end your pitiful existence."

"You're crazy. You have the wrong man."

"You're the only person I've ever seen who has eyes

the same color as mine."

Jacque had left the door ajar, and Rafael entered.

"Then maybe you should look at mine," he said.

Jacque turned to see Rafael, taller than Father Alphonso though not quite as tall as he. He stared into gray eyes he recognized as his own, and Father Alphonso's.

"Who are you?"

"Apparently I'm your brother because Father Alphonso is also my father. Like your mother, mine was also a nun he got pregnant. I also have plenty of reason to hate him. I don't because hate is a destructive emotion that destroys everyone that indulges in it. Please, reconsider your actions."

"Save your sermons for someone who cares. Our father is about to die," Jacque said. "I hope you're here to help me. If not, then don't get in my way."

Rafael wound around him, grasping his rosary and holding it to his heart.

"You mustn't do this. You can't correct a sin by committing another. Your soul is in danger. I won't let you do this."

"Sorry, Brother, there's nothing you can do about it."

Jacque pounced like a cat, yanking the rosary out of Rafael's hand and tossing it against the wall. Grabbing his neck, he lifted him bodily off the floor, Rafael's eyes bulging. Jacque tossed him against the wall and then stared at Father Alphonso, cowering in the corner.

"Spare me, please," Father Alphonso said.

"Don't beg me," Jacque said. "I'm not listening, and it won't help you to beg. If God doesn't see fit to save you, then you're doomed.

When the streetcar rumbled to a stop a block away from St. Validius, Tony hurried across the street, his knee buckling beneath him. Sinking to the pavement, he popped his last two pain killers into his mouth. He rose to his feet as a car screeched to a halt in front of him. The driver stood on the horn, shaking his fist until Tony pulled his pistol and stuck it in his face. He didn't wait for the man's response, hurrying around the car to the other side of the street.

St. Validius was more than a church. It was also a school where young priests attended classes to learn about their religion. Tony stopped two men on their way to class.

"Where do the priests live?"

One of the men, startled by Tony's battered appearance, pointed.

"That first red building is the presbytery."

Tony didn't bother thanking them as he hurried as fast as his aching legs would allow him.

"Do you know where Father Alphonso lives?" he asked a priest, tending flowers in the bed outside the two-storied, brick building.

"You're the second person to ask in the last few minutes," the man said. "Upstairs. The first apartment on the right."

With adrenaline pumping through his veins, Tony bounded up the short flight of stairs. He found Father Alphonso's door ajar. Leguerre had his back to him, glaring at a cowering priest. Another man he didn't recognize was propped against the wall, his eyes closed as he rubbed his forehead. Tony grabbed his service revolver.

Nailing Jacque in the back of the head with the barrel of the pistol, Tony piled on top of him. Jacque somehow managed to snatch the pistol from his hand, and it slid across the floor. It didn't matter. Tony was short, though stout as a bull. Grabbing Jacque's neck, he began to squeeze, and nothing on earth was going to cause him to loosen his grip. When Jacque's lips turned blue, and his eyes bulged, Tony retrieved his pistol. Fumbling with it briefly before straddling the man's back, he put the weapon to his head.

"Die you sorry mother fucker!"

"Tony, no!" a man yelled as he rushed into the room. "Don't kill him!"

Eddie Toledo, James Landry, Landry's beefy partner Matt Rivera, and many Feds, all with weapons drawn, burst into the room. Rivera didn't hesitate, hitting Tony with a running tackle and rolling him across the floor. He banged Tony's head against the wall, grabbed his wrist and cuffed it. Whipping him around, he cuffed the other wrist.

The scene was more than Father Alphonso could take. Clutching his heart, he sank to the floor as Rafael struggled to his feet.

"I am dying," he said. "Please, Father, administer the rites."

Though he raised his hands, words didn't issue from Rafael's lips. Turning, he watched as agents cuffed and restrained Jacque. Father Alphonso clutched his wrist.

"Don't let me die without the words."

"Do it, padre," Eddie said, joining them. "You're more Catholic than he ever thought about being."

Chapter Thirty-Seven

When Tony opened his eyes, the first thing he saw was Marshal Landry talking on his cell phone. Trying to stand, he realized his hands were cuffed.

"We got Leguerre," Landry said. "The boys are bringing him in right now."

The Marshals were taking no chances with Jacque. His hands were also cuffed behind his back, a belly chain around his waist, and leg irons on his ankles. Seeing Father Alphonso dead on the floor, he wasn't trying to resist. Rafael joined them.

"I'm his brother. I'm going with him."

Landry nodded his approval as they herded Jacque to the door. Jacque forced the guards to stop pushing him when he saw Tony. As they made eye contact, a smile appeared on his bruised face.

"I have to talk to him," he said.

"You don't need to talk to anybody," Eddie said. "Get him out of here."

Jacque held his ground as the Marshals tried to turn him toward the door.

"I'm not going anywhere until I talk to him."

"Want me to tase him?" one of the men asked.

"Why hell no," Landry said. "Let them talk."

Eddie started to protest, but after seeing the look in Landry's eyes, he thought better of it. A Marshal pushed Tony toward them.

"What I have to say is for his ears only," Jacque said.

Landry held up a hand when one of the Marshals protested."

"All right but don't push your luck. You can talk alone in the corner. That's as far away as we're going," Landry said.

Tony followed Jacque to the corner of the room, about ten feet from everyone else. Both had hands cuffed behind their backs.

"You're a brave man," Jacque said in a whisper. "And so are your two partners. I never wanted to kill you."

"Tell that to my partner in the emergency room. If he don't make it, I'm never gonna stop till I see you join him."

"I'd expect nothing less from you. Now I have a favor to ask."

"You got the nerve to ask me for a favor? You gotta be kidding me."

"Please, take the dog to Greta Gjertsen for me. We won't meet again but tell her I'll never forget our time together. One more thing."

Bending close to Tony's ear, he whispered something into it. Then he nodded and turned for the door. As Tony watched them leave through the crowd of priests, nuns, and gawkers that had gathered outside, Eddie rushed over to him.

"You're going down, Lieutenant. I hope you're happy."

Tony didn't answer, kneeing him in the groin instead. As Eddie sank to the floor in pain, Marshals Landry and Rivera led him out the door and down the stairs. When they reached their car, Landry held up his hand again.

"Uncuff him." Without questioning the order, Rivera removed the cuffs from Tony's wrists.

"Get in," Landry said.

Tony slid into the front seat, quickly surrounded by the two burly U.S. Marshals.

"You taking me to jail?" he asked.

Landry didn't answer his question. "You know, Lieutenant, you're one tough son-of-a-bitch. You'd have made one hell of a Marshal."

"I don't feel so tough right about now."

"What's the matter with your knee?"

"Tore it up playing baseball. With everything that's gone on today, I think I finally blew it out altogether."

"Baseball, huh? You look more like a tackle to me. I played alongside a few men like you in college. Quit worrying about the knee. I'll give you the name of my doctor. He'll fix you up good as new."

"I doubt they'll fix it for me in prison."

"You're not going to prison."

"You heard what Toledo said. He's the D.A."

"Just the assistant D.A. The real District Attorney was my roommate in college. Who do you think he's going to believe? Besides, I've wanted to put a knee in that mouthy prick's groin for longer than I can tell you. What about you, Matt?"

Rivera smiled but didn't answer.

"You'd do that for me?" Tony asked.

"You're a good cop. There are never enough good cops on the street. We're not taking you off. Where do you want to go?"

"Prytania and turn right. I got a dog to pick up."

When the black sedan pulled up in Mama Mulate's driveway, Tony opened the front door and whistled. Velvet came running, her tail doing a dance.

"Come on, baby. I'm taking you to Greta."

Tony, James Landry, and Matt Rivera walked into the Monteleone Hotel, Tony carrying the little dog under his arm. When the man at the counter, the same one that didn't like Tony, saw them, he called out.

"Hey, you can't take that dog in there. I don't care if you are N.O.P.D."

Landry and Rivera turned to face the man. "Go ahead. We'll take care of this."

Tony opened the door to the Carousel Lounge,

glancing around before he entered. Matt Rivera grabbed the man's shirt and yanked him over the counter. He cuffed him, leaned him against the wall and spread-eagled him. Tony didn't wait to see what else was about to happen.

Just as the last time he'd visited the Carousel Bar, Greta Gjertsen and her father were sitting there, talking with Marvin the bartender. Greta recognized the dog, got up from the stool, ran to Tony and took it from him. With tears in her eyes, she clutched it to her breast. Seeing Tony, Greta's father just turned away and kept drinking.

"Oh Velvet, where did they find you?"

"Jacque asked me to bring her to you. From the way she's wagging her tail, I'd say it was a smart decision."

"Is Jacque—"

"Alive and in custody."

"What will happen to him?"

"He's set to testify against his former bosses, some of the kingpins that control crime here in the city. The clock is ticking."

"And then?"

"The Feds have promised to release him into Witness Protection."

"Will they?"

Tony smirked. "Hell, if it was me, I wouldn't trust them. Who knows though? Jacque seems to have led a charmed life, at least to this point."

"Did he say anything else?"

Tony nodded. "He said he'd never see you again, but he'd never forget you. He said for you to take care of Velvet, and your child when it's born. One last thing. If you have a boy, he'd be honored if you'd name him Jacque."

Tears streamed from Greta's eyes. "Is there a chance they might send him to Norway?"

"Never know," Tony said.

Still holding the dog, Greta put an arm around Tony's neck and hugged him.

"And you. You look as if you've been—"

"Wrestling alligators? Don't worry about it. These torn and bloody clothes are the least of my worries right now. I've got two partners in the hospital, and an angry wife at home that wants to rip my head off."

Greta touched his split lip. "What will you do?"

"Next time I see her, I'm gonna lie like a dog. If she doesn't believe me, I'll go down on my hands and knees and beg her to forgive me." Tony started for the door. Stopping before he exited, he pulled a jar of pills from his jacket. "And, I've got my ace in the hole, provided by my favorite New Orleans voodoo mambo."

"What is it?" Greta asked, still hugging Velvet.

"A little New Orleans' specialty called Love Potion Number Nine."

When Tony exited the bar, a group of people were watching as Matt Rivera read the counter clerk his rights. Seeing Tony come out of the lounge, Landry tapped his shoulder and stopped him.

"I talked with headquarters. This isn't our man. Let him go."

Rivera removed the cuffs from the hapless clerk, giving him one last push into the counter as he did.

"Hey," he said, starting to complain.

Landry stopped him, putting his finger to his lips and shaking his head. "You know, you could get in a lot of trouble real fast trying to undermine a search for a dangerous Federal criminal. You want to do some jail time? If so, I'll see to it."

The clerk Don didn't say another word as the three men walked out of the charming, old French Quarter hotel.

"Where to now?" Landry asked when they were back in the car.

"I have two partners in the hospital I need to see. After that, I'm going to Carlucci's and get rip-roaring drunk. You two game? I'm buying."

"We're game," Landry said. "But your money's no good with us. Uncle Sam's picking up the tab tonight."

Chapter Thirty-Eight

In tears, Junie Bug sat on the side of her antique, four-poster bed when her daughter Dauphine came rushing into the room.

"Mama, Mama, Daddy killed Uncle Claude!"

Junie Bug grabbed Dauphine, hugging her to her chest and not commenting as Gordon followed in behind her, still carrying a smoking pistol.

"Daddy, how could you?"

Gordon's insane expression frightened Dauphine, and she shrank back into her mother's arms.

"I ain't your daddy," he said. "Maybe you ought to ask that whore of a mama who your real daddy is."

When Dauphine glanced at Junie Bug for answers, all she saw was an expression of resolve.

"What's he talking about?"

"Tell her, God Damn it!" he shouted, slapping Junie Bug hard across the face. Though her head snapped back, she glared at her husband, stoically refusing to talk to him. Instead, she caressed Dauphine's forehead, speaking softly to her.

"Gordon just killed your real father."

"Yes, I killed the bastard. I hope you're happy now, after all these years.

Dauphine's hand went to her mouth. "Oh my God! Then Sonny is—"

"Don't matter none," Gordon said. "He don't love

you, and never did. He only married you because of me. You been living a lie, girl."

In tears, Dauphine clutched her mother again. "Is it true, Mama? Is my whole life just a lie?"

"No, baby," Junie Bug said. "It's Gordon's life that's a lie. He isn't worth a swift kick in the head."

Still waving the gun like a crazed maniac, Gordon said, "Shut your damn mouth, woman! You don't have a clue what I'm about."

"You're full of shit. I know more about you than anyone on earth. You're a pathetic coward and a mother fucker. Your whole life is a lie. You profess to hate blacks and yet you're the real son of Mama Marlene. I know it; Claude knew it, and now everyone knows it."

"I'm as white as you are, you bitch."

"Your skin, maybe, but your soul's as black as the ace of spades," Junie Bug said, fairly spitting the words.

It was more than Gordon could take. "I told you to shut your damn mouth," he said.

He banged Junie Bug across the face with the pistol. As her head snapped back and blood dribbled from the side of her mouth, he pointed it at her forehead. Before he could pull the trigger, gunshots rang out. When Gordon clutched his heart and sank to the floor, Dauphine hugged her mother, and then fled the room, brushing past the policeman that had just shot her father. Wyatt and Desire had come in behind the policeman. In hysterics, Dauphine kept running, down the stairs.

⁙

Desire and I checked on Junie Bug as the policeman prodded Gordon with the toe of his shoe. Satisfied her mother was okay Desire knelt beside her dead father. Then, as if a light had suddenly come on in her brain, she rushed out the door, not stopping when I called to her.

I followed her down the stairs, watching from the sidewalk as Dauphine raced away in a gold Ferrari

283

convertible. Distant sirens were blaring, drowning out the sounds of a nearby Carnival parade. Before I could ask questions, Desire got into her own Ferrari, identical to Dauphine's, except purple.

"Wait for me!" I yelled, diving into the car as she powered away from the curb.

Desire stood on the gas and raced up the street, barely avoiding a streetcar, vehicle traffic, and several pedestrians as she slid the car around the corner of St. Charles Avenue.

"Slow down! You're going to kill somebody!"

"I've got to catch her," she said.

"Where is she going?"

Intent on avoiding a collision, she swerved in and out of traffic, the throaty roar of the Ferrari my only response. With few other options, none of them good, I held my breath as we raced toward the Crescent City Connection Bridge that crosses the Mississippi River.

We soon saw Dauphine powering into the nearly empty H.O.V. lane sliding her car to a halt when she reached the highest point of the bridge. Desire accelerated even faster, losing control when she hit the concrete rail dividing the H.O.V. lane from the rest of the traffic. The car spun, almost flipped and then crashed into the railing.

My ears were ringing when I opened my eyes, blood trickling from Desire's forehead as she lay against the dash. My elbow was bleeding where I'd banged into the window. When I reached across the console and touched her arm, she opened her eyes.

"You okay?"

Realizing what had happened, she was instantly alert and concerned.

"Dauphine, you have to stop her."

I turned to see Dauphine standing on the edge of the bridge, staring at the river below. No time for anything else, I leaped out of the wrecked car and began sprinting toward her, almost reaching her before she jumped. Almost.

She glanced my way when I yelled at her.

"Dauphine, no! Don't jump!"

Reaching for her, I touched her hand as I watched her slow descent into the river.

By now, a crowd was gathering. Desire struggled up behind me, sobbing uncontrollably. When she attempted to follow Dauphine into the swirling Mississippi, I wrapped my arms around her, holding on and refusing to let go.

The hour was late as Tony sat between Lillian and Tommy in the waiting room outside of Intensive Care. As Marlon began his second hour in the O.R., Lillian squeezed her husband's arm.

"He's so young. I can't imagine he's been in the operating room so long."

"First Tommy and now Marlon. He's gonna die, I can feel it, and it's all because of me."

Dressed in a hospital gown, his arm in a sling, Tommy leaned closer to Tony, glared at him and spoke in a whispered voice.

"Yeah, well that's what partners have to do sometimes."

Lillian and Tommy each grabbed an arm as orderlies wheeled Marlon out of the operating room. Breaking free, Tony chased them down the hall.

"Is he—"

A nurse, half Tony's size, dropped her operating mask and blocked his way with a raised palm.

"He's in pretty bad shape. We did what we could for him."

Lillian clutched Tony's arm, leading him back to the couch.

"Oh no! God, no!" Tony wailed.

Tommy made a face and banged Tony's shoulder with the heel of his hand.

"Will you shut the fuck up? This ain't Hollywood, Tony, it's the Big Easy. Now get a grip."

Fat Tuesday found Rafael, Madeline, Mama, and Eddie sitting in Madeline's garden. Eddie and Mama held hands as sounds of celebrating revelers resonated in the background. Eddie finally spoke.

"I'm glad Wyatt tipped me about the Father Alphonso, Jacque Leguerre connection. If he hadn't, Tony would have killed our star witness."

"I'm sure Wyatt was happy to help," Rafael said. "I was overjoyed to meet my brother, even though he's not exactly a stellar citizen."

Eddie smiled and glanced at Mama Mulate. "I wish Wyatt was here right now, so I could thank him personally for introducing me to you."

"He's pretty low, and I'm worried about him," she said.

"He'll work it out. He always has," Eddie said.

"This time's different, coming on the heels of Mimsy's death."

"Tell me about it," Rafael said. "Within a matter of days, I lost my wife, learned who my father is, and also that I have a brother."

"And no telling how many more," Eddie said.

"Enough," Madeline said. "Except for a little haze, it's a beautiful Fat Tuesday, and we're all alive and well."

"Except for poor Dauphine," Mama said.

"And so tragic," Rafael said. "I still don't understand how two twins can have different fathers."

"Fraternal twins," Eddie said. "It's possible for two eggs to drop during a single ovulation period. If it happens, and the woman has two different lovers, each could fertilize an egg. The result would be fraternal twins conceived by two different fathers. In Dauphine and Desire's case, this is what happened, Claude and Gordon their respective fathers."

"And did Dauphine know?" Mama asked.

Eddie nodded. "Vallee blurted it out during their confrontation. At least that's what her mom, Junie Bug told police."

"My God!" Rafael said.

"Vallee was Desire's father, Sonnier Dauphine's," Eddie said. "Dauphine was married to her own half-brother. Gordon, the man she idolized as her father, wasn't even related to her."

"So ironic," Mama said. "The twin sister she adored is half-black, her entire life a lie."

"Not only that," Eddie said. "The man she thought was her father and her husband, were both having an affair with the same black woman."

"Desire was a Vallee," Rafael said. "The curse came from the Sonniers."

Madeline raised her palm and shook her head. "Seers aren't perfect. In truth, the curse affected both families, both inexplicably intertwined. Who cast it, maybe we'll never know."

"What do you think, Mama?" Rafael asked.

"There's only one person that could have cast that spell. The most powerful voodoo mambo in the history of New Orleans, Marie Laveau herself."

Madeline glanced at the large raven watching over the gathering. "Voodoo, witchcraft or black magic; what does it matter in the City of Spirits?"

"Then Dauphine's suicide was the crossroads you prophesied for Desire," Rafael said.

"After they took her away in the ambulance, her family refused to let Wyatt see her," Mama said. "They never had a chance to say goodbye, and it's breaking him into little pieces."

"And since she's given up her worldly existence for the lonely life of a cloistered nun, he'll never see her again," Rafael said."

Eddie glanced at the hazy sky. "It doesn't seem fair."

Madeline also glanced upwards. "Life is often cruel, and sometimes no more than a beautiful lie. Either way, it's never fair."

Epilog

Almost three in the morning, Wyatt stumbled along the sidewalk in front of a two-storied, brick building. The apartment he was looking for was on the second floor, up a steep flight of stairs. Halfway up, he tripped and fell, tearing his pants and skinning his shin. A half-empty bottle of Jack Daniel's tumbled from his grasp, shattering on cement steps.

"Damn it," he said, avoiding broken glass as he pulled himself up by the railing and rubbed his shin.

He'd almost forgotten how difficult it was to walk when he was almost too drunk to stand. Holding on to the railing tightly, he made it to the top without falling again, though his clothes were wet and stank of bourbon. When he found the familiar door, he knocked and waited. A woman's voice with a Scottish accent spoke from just inside the door.

"Who is it?"

"It's me, Wyatt."

He continued standing there until someone cracked open the door. It was Chrissie, the bartender at Brannigan's, the Irish pub where he'd first met Desire. Moonlight reflected from red hair draping her shoulders. She opened the door. Not inviting him in, she just stood there, staring at him as tears formed in her blue eyes.

"You bastard," she said.

Not trying to defend himself, he said, "Chrissie, I need you."

❦

Amid sounds of Carnival echoing from Bourbon Street, a mist settled over Madeline's courtyard, cloaking the introspective people sitting there. Calpurnia began flapping her wings, and then slowly spiraled upwards, voicing one last word before she disappeared into the haze.

The single word, "Nevermore," echoed in the courtyard as she vanished into cold mist, away from Mardi Gras madness and the raging silence of the City of Spirits.

End

About the Author

ERIC WILDER is the author of *Big Easy*, as well as *A Gathering of Diamonds, Murder Etouffee, and Prairie Sunset – of Love and Magic*, among other books and novels.

He lives in Oklahoma with his wife Marilyn.